"Plenty of cheese lore enriches a mystery that's puzzling in more ways than one." —*Kirkus Reviews*

"A series that readers will be eager to revisit."
—*First Clue*

"Readers will love the cheese shop employees, Mrs. Schultz and Archie, as well as Willa's neighbor, Baz."
—*Kings River Life*

"A highly likable character and a good sleuth."
—*Fresh Fiction*

"Riveting." —*Military Press*

"Deliciously addictive." —Bree Baker

"Winning." —Maddie Day

"A fabulous heroine." —Cate Conte

"Willa charmed me to the core." —Linda Reilly

St. Martin's Paperbacks titles
by Korina Moss

CHEDDAR OFF DEAD
GONE FOR GOUDA
CURDS OF PREY
CASE OF THE BLEUS
FONDUE OR DIE
BAIT AND SWISS

BAIT AND SWISS

A Cheese Shop Mystery

BY

KORINA MOSS

St. Martin's Paperbacks

This is a work of fiction. All of the characters, organizations, and events portrayed in this novel are either products of the author's imagination or are used fictitiously.

First published in the United States by St. Martin's Paperbacks, an imprint of St. Martin's Publishing Group.

BAIT AND SWISS

For information, address St. Martin's Publishing Group, 120 Broadway, New York, NY 10271.

www.stmartins.com

ISBN: 978-1-250-89394-9

Our books may be purchased in bulk for promotional, educational, or business use. Please contact your local bookseller or the Macmillan Corporate and Premium Sales Department at 1-800-221-7945, ext. 5442, or by email at MacmillanSpecialMarkets@macmillan.com.

Printed in the United States of America

St. Martin's Paperbacks edition / May 2025

10 9 8 7 6 5 4 3 2 1

For you, the readers

ACKNOWLEDGMENTS

I must always start by thanking the people who've made this series possible—my incredible editor Madeline Houpt and the rest of my extraordinary team at St. Martin's, including copy editor John Simko; executive managing editor John Rounds; Alan Ayers and Danielle Christopher, who are responsible for my gorgeous covers; and the best cheerleaders a girl could ask for, publicist Sara LaCotti and marketer Allison Zeigler. I'm very proud to be a St. Martin's author.

I'm forever thankful to my fantastic agent, Jill Marsal.

To those people who are first in my heart—my son, my family, and my friends, who aren't reserved in their show of support and pride—I appreciate you.

To my niece, Jennifer "Mama Jen" Brunetti-Irizarry, the best baker I know, who was kind enough to share her recipe for No-Bake Chocolate Cheesecake Jars. I love you, Jen!

I've dedicated this book to you—the readers. My sincere appreciation goes to all of you, and especially those in the cozy mystery community, including the bloggers, booktubers, and bookstagrammers, who share their excitement about my series with their followers and with me. You've made this cozy mystery writing experience everything I hoped it would be. #TeamCheese!

When friends aren't available, there's always cheese.

—Willa Bauer

CHAPTER 1

❧

"Raclette. It's an Alpine cow's milk cheese that's been popular since the Middle Ages. Salty, nutty, slightly pungent—more so the longer it sits on the wheel—and it melts beautifully. The name *raclette* comes from the French word *racler,* meaning 'to scrape,' which as you know, is how it's served from its wheel after being warmed." I described the Swiss cheese to Archie and Mrs. Schultz, my indispensable cheese shop employees who had been with me since Curds & Whey's inception two years earlier and had since become good friends. "And now you know why I was so excited to see this particular delivery today." The three of us stood behind our checkout counter as I knifed open the cardboard box the delivery woman had just dropped off. From beneath layers of bubble wrap, I pulled out the raclette warmer I'd ordered. "Thank the cheese gods, it came today! It's been backordered forever. We'll use this for our party tomorrow."

Archie, my twenty-one-year-old cheesemonger in training, rubbed his palms together in anticipation, simultaneously bouncing slightly on the balls of his Chucks-clad feet. His easy smile was as ever present as his freckles and the quarter-sized port-wine stain birthmark across his left cheek. "I've been watching videos on how to do it. That's going to be a big hit," he said. He could always be counted on to add his Tigger-like enthusiasm to every Curds & Whey event, but we were all feeling excited about this one.

My cheese shop's second birthday was the following day, and we were having a big bash to celebrate. It hardly seemed possible that only two years ago I hadn't known a single person in Yarrow Glen when I decided to open a shop here. I was raised in Oregon and spent over eight years working in cheese shops and cream-eries around the country. Passing through this small town in northern California's Sonoma Valley changed everything. It was the first place I wanted to put down roots. Maybe I was just finally ready to stop being afraid of life. Or maybe there was something in me that knew the people in this town would lift my grieving spirit over the death of my brother and a broken engagement, and help me to create a life that I only ever dreamed of having.

Mrs. Schultz—who was "smack dab" in her sixties, as she liked to say—started separating the decorations she'd ordered for the birthday bash. "The shop is going to look very festive, Willa. I know we want to keep the cheese shop classy, so I didn't go as bold as I might've otherwise," she said.

Mrs. Schultz knew bold. A retired high school drama teacher, she had a flair for the dramatic, which was dem-onstrated by her vibrant dresses, cinched at the waist and most often paired with a complementary scarf and bright lipstick. Her personality was no different—I'd seen it bloom even more over the past two years that I'd known her, to what I imagined it had been before her husband's passing several years prior.

Archie turned to the three customers, female friends in their forties, who were taking one final browse before leaving the shop. They'd been enjoying our In Bloom cheeseboard in our kitchenette area, which was now our Cheeseboard Café, where my new employee, June, had been taking care of them.

"Did you like the cheeseboard?" Archie asked them.

"It was fantastic. All the cheeses went so perfectly with everything on the board," one of them answered. "I had no idea chocolate and cheese taste good together."

Although I had personal reasons for having an aversion to chocolate, I still appreciated the pairing with certain cheeses.

"And the wine! Well, we all know how good that tastes with cheese," another said.

This brought laughter and agreement among the others.

Our In Bloom cheeseboard consisted of aged Gouda, the creamy yet piquant Cambozola, which was the reason for the dark-chocolate pairing, a marinated CHEEVO goat cheese, and the buttery Carmody from Bellwether Farms. Paired also with rice crackers, prosciutto, olives, almonds, and three kinds of plump berries, it was a bright and flavorful board.

"Who knew the ambiance of a cheese shop could be so nice? I feel like we're in France," the third woman said.

That was music to my ears. My shop's aesthetic was inspired by my brief time working at a fromagerie outside of Lyon where my passion for cheese blossomed. I wanted to bring the color, warmth, and romance of France into my shop. Raised panel wainscoting the color of light butterscotch wrapped around the lower portion of the textured walls, offset by one full antique oak-paneled wall behind the checkout and sampling counters. Yarrow Glen's dairy roots were also represented with a gold-framed bovine oil painting.

"We're so glad you enjoyed yourselves," I said to the group.

"We sure did. Thank you, June!" one of the women called.

June, in her early twenties with dark brown eyes, a wide nose, and cherub cheeks, gave them a wave and a smile as she approached the front of the shop with the rest of us. Her long brown hair she wore loosely pulled back with a clip, rendering the burn scars on her neck she'd suffered from a childhood fire barely noticeable.

We were lucky enough to meet June last fall at the Dairy Days festival, where she'd impressed me with her knowledge of cheese, and we thought she'd make a great fit to our team when our Cheeseboard Café opened. She'd been reluctant to take a job in customer service where she'd be meeting new people every day, but we finally convinced her to join the crew. I loved seeing her become more comfortable in her own skin throughout the months she'd been with us.

"Enjoy the rest of your day," she said to the customers.

"We will! We're going to the new bakery's grand opening. Cheese and wine, now dessert. I think we should make this a regular thing, don't you?" The ladies laughed and merrily left the shop through the front door that my homemade mascot, Guernsey—a cow scarecrow—perpetually held open year-round. Since it was spring, Guernsey wore a necklace of flowers that matched the ones in the flower boxes under the large windows flanking the door.

"Is it that time already? We'd better get down

there," Archie said, taking off his wheat-colored apron. Underneath he wore a Curds & Whey T-shirt and cargo shorts. I knew he wanted to support his friend and former girlfriend, Hope, who owned the bakery.

"I hope it's a success. I have to admit, I'm concerned for her. She's taking a very successful business and changing it completely," Mrs. Schultz said.

"I give her credit for following her passion," I replied, although I had the same concerns. Rise and Shine was a bread bakery and a staple in Yarrow Glen for over twenty years. It had been a bumpy two years learning the ropes of running a business since Hope took it over, especially because she had her own ideas of what she wanted it to be—namely a cakery that would sell cakes and cupcakes, not breads. "How is she handling her new pursuit, Archie?"

"I know she's excited about it. She said they painted the inside, and she had to do some renovations to the kitchen, but honestly, she hasn't said much about what she's doing."

"I noticed she even papered over the windows," Mrs. Schultz commented with an arched eyebrow of disapproval.

"So you weren't able to peek in then, huh?" I asked her with a wink.

She put a hand to her chest and opened her mouth wide as if she was shocked by my mild accusation. Then she looked off in innocence, fluffing her short curly hair. "She was very thorough," she replied, breaking into a barely there mischievous grin.

I chuckled. "She *is* being very secretive. Has she let you see it?" I asked Archie.

"No. I've barely talked to her in weeks, but I just figured she was super busy with it."

"She probably wants everyone to be surprised and impressed with the finished product, especially you," Mrs. Schultz said to him.

Archie shrugged, apparently uncertain about his status with Hope. Even though Archie had been hurt by their breakup, they'd remained friends.

"I'm sure we'll all be impressed," June said.

"I'm sure we will be. I'm more concerned about pulling off *our* event tomorrow. I hope I didn't go overboard with all the activities," I said, beginning to feel overwhelmed as the date grew closer.

"Don't worry, Willa. We can handle it. Besides, we've got June," Archie said, unfazed.

June smiled timidly.

"We'd better go so we don't miss it," Archie said, already at the door.

"I can stay back and watch the shop," June offered. She was from Lockwood, the next town over, so she didn't know Hope very well and wasn't as invested in the grand opening as the rest of us.

"Come with us. We can close the shop for a bit," I said, as we took off our aprons. I knew we wouldn't miss any customers in the fifteen minutes we'd be gone—everyone in town would be in front of Hope's shop.

I hung the Be Back Shortly sign on the front of the teal door before locking it. As soon as we stepped onto the brick-lined sidewalk, the fragrance of the crepe myrtle trees, their pink blooms awakening for spring, was unmistakable. We passed Carl's Hardware, the shop that shared a building with mine, and crossed the alley to Lou's Market, which had a cute green awning that shaded today's fresh stock of beets, carrots,

and avocados. Lou, whose white hair and grumpy demeanor made him appear older than his mid-fifties,
kept the sidewalk in front of his market meticulously
clean and thus was shooing the excess people away with
his broom.

When he saw Mrs. Schultz, his bushy eyebrows
relaxed, and he greeted us with a smile. Well, he greeted
Mrs. Schultz.

"Mrs. Schultz. Beautiful day!" he said as we approached.

"It certainly is. Are you going to Hope's grand opening?" she asked.

"I'm sure I'll be able to see what's going on from
here. I have a market to run," he reminded us unneces-
sarily.

"Well, I'll let Hope know you're sending your support from across the street," Mrs. Schultz replied with
her toothy grin.

He cleared his throat. "Of course. Yes. Please do,"
he mumbled, nodding.

We continued to make our way down to the bakery,
which meant passing Read More Bookstore & Café
and crossing the street. Already a crowd had formed,
spilling onto the diagonal parking spaces on the street
abutting the bakery's sidewalk.

Pleasant Avenue was a hodgepodge of mostly older
flat-roofed buildings, which had been renovated into
shops and cafés with second-story offices or cozy apartments, such as mine. The shops were uniformly connected in pairs with alleys in between the buildings
separating them from the next pair of shops. Hope's
bakery was the exception. It was located in a single-
story cottage with faded clapboards. The new bright

pink awning shaded the door as well as the two over-sized six-over-six-paned windows to the right of the entrance.

Today, brown butcher paper covered the windows to keep us from peeking inside, as Mrs. Schultz had tested, and a long piece of fabric covered the sign above the front door that used to read Rise and Shine Bakery. We'd all put up flyers in our own shop windows to announce her grand opening, so I was glad to see she was getting a good turnout.

I recognized most of our shop neighbors, except for a guy in his twenties wearing sunglasses and overly gelled hair slicked forward who weaved through the crowd toward the bakery. In one hand, he held a camera; in the other, he held up a name tag from a lanyard around his neck.

"Move aside, please. I'm from the press," he announced as he pushed his way through.

The only press around here was our free newspaper, the *Glen Gazette*, but I knew the reporter who covered most of the town's events and she certainly never behaved like that.

Finally, the door to the bakery cracked open, and Hope squeezed through it to get outside, revealing as little as possible of the inside. Archie's eyes lit up upon seeing her. She closed the door behind her. She looked possibly nervous but excited, repeatedly running her pink polished nails through her blonde pixie-styled hair with its matching pink streak. Finally, she shoved her hands into her pink overalls and spoke to the crowd.

"Hi, everyone! Thank you so much for coming!" She waited for the chatter of the crowd to ease then raised her voice. "I'm so excited to unveil my new shop, starting with the new name. Are you ready?"

We all applauded, Archie perhaps the loudest.

Hope grabbed the cord to the fabric covering the sign and pulled, causing it to slip off, revealing Hope's Cakery in fat pink lettering with a rosette tacked to the end of the *y*. More applause resounded. I wasn't sure if Hope was blushing from the praise or if it was the reflection of all the pink, but I was happy to see her looking so proud.

When the applause died down, she continued: "That's not all. Inside, you'll see the new look of Hope's Cakery, but there's also one more surprise you'll find. I've paired up with another shop to offer you the *sweetest* deals. Ready?" Hope knocked on the window, and from inside, the paper on the glass was torn away, revealing another new sign hanging in the window: Chocolate Bliss.

It was a name and logo I recognized. My stomach lurched. "No way," I said under my breath, not believing what might be happening.

My ears started to buzz as Hope announced, "Ready to replicate the success of their Oregon shops in our town, meet Yarrow Glen's newest chocolatiers!" The door behind her swung open and a man and woman emerged, hand in hand, smiling and waving like the president and first lady.

I didn't have to meet them. I already knew who they were: my ex-fiancé and my ex-best friend had secretly set up shop right here in Yarrow Glen.

CHAPTER 2

❧

"Willa, are you okay?" Mrs. Schultz asked me. I couldn't even try to hide my feelings.

"No, I'm not," I answered.

I stared at my ex-fiancé and my ex–best friend, my mind trying to reconcile what my eyes were seeing. The two people in front of the cakery didn't look much different from the last time I saw them nearly ten years ago. Pearce was fair-haired and much like the Dodge Charger he owned at the time—solid and assertive, with what I thought back then were kind eyes behind dark-rimmed glasses.

Riley was taller than him by a good margin. I remember her in ruffly shirts or loose skirts with dark tights and boots. Today she was in a loose skirt that fell to her ankles, matching blue Crocs, and a Chocolate Bliss T-shirt. She pulled her abundance of curly hair back with two clips.

She looked uncomfortable standing to the side of Pearce, her nervous habit of gnawing on her lower lip prevalent. She'd practically chewed it off when Pearce finally told me that the three of us wouldn't be opening a cheese shop together as we'd been planning—they'd fallen in love and our engagement was off. I threw the engagement ring at him, which I later discovered helped to initially fund the new chocolate shop they opened shortly afterward in our hometown in Oregon. And here they were now, trying to encroach on the life I'd built in Yarrow Glen.

Mrs. Schultz put an arm around my waist. She had no idea what was wrong. "Are you not feeling well? Do you need to sit down? Should we go back to the shop?"

"No, I'm okay," I assured her, even though I wasn't. "I want to hear this." I was like a rubbernecker passing a car wreck—it made me ill to watch, but I couldn't look away.

My ex-fiancé, Pearce, stepped forward to speak. He didn't have any trouble being heard over the crowd. "Hello, Yarrow Glen! I'm Pearce Brenner and this is my partner in chocolate and in life, Riley Stephens."

I felt the knot that had twisted in my stomach about thirty seconds ago tighten.

Pearce continued: "I would like to thank Hope for this introduction to your great town and the opportunity to be a part of it. With the incredible success of our flagship store in Eugene, Oregon, and more recently, another shop in Ashland, we wanted to test the waters of branching out once more, this time to the great state of California! We want more of you to be able to enjoy our amazing liqueur-filled chocolates made fresh daily. And of course, this is where you can also purchase our own world-class Brenner's Rum, the same rum found in our nationally recognized Brenner Rum Crèmes." He paused and Riley clapped to encourage applause, which worked. "Our success depends on you, so if you'd like Chocolate Bliss to be a permanent fixture in Yarrow Glen, please become a regular patron. To show our appreciation for this amazing welcome, we're offering free samples while they last of our Brenner Rum Crèmes, my own personal creation. Our manager and fellow chocolatier will be handing these out to those of you over twenty-one." He gestured to a clean-cut guy with brown hair, maybe thirty, in jeans and a Chocolate Bliss T-shirt, who was standing next to Hope.

"That's Duncan!" June said, her face lighting up.

I hadn't even noticed he was there and fleetingly wondered how she knew him.

Pearce continued: "Today, there's a special price on *all* our liqueur crèmes and our Brenner's Rum, so take advantage and see what everyone's talking about! Enjoy the chocolate and have a *Bliss*-filled day!"

The crowd around me clapped, which brought me out of my shocked stupor.

Hope could barely be heard as she quickly added, "I've got free samples of my strawberry cake too. Come on in!"

Riley threw open the door and the two women hastened inside before the crowd that surged forward, June among them.

As Pearce stepped aside, our gaze met across the crowd. If he was surprised to see me, he seemed happily so, which ballooned my rage. His attention went back to his potential customers who were streaming in the door, accepting samples of Brenner Rum Crèmes from Duncan.

This was no coincidence—he had to know my shop was here. I could feel my face heating up as I seethed. If I looked the way I felt, I must've currently resembled the Anger emotion from Pixar's *Inside Out,* all red-faced and bug-eyed. "I could kill him."

I hadn't realized I'd said it aloud until some of the

faces of people passing snapped my way in puzzlement before continuing on toward the sweet freebies.

"What's the matter, Willa?" Archie asked.

He and Mrs. Schultz were on either side of me, concern apparent on their faces.

"Willy Wonka over there is my ex-fiancé, and his partner used to be my college best friend."

By their shocked expressions, I was satisfied that I wasn't overreacting. I'd mentioned my broken engagement at some point in our friendship—they knew the origin of my dislike of chocolate—but of course they'd had no idea those two were the cheating chocolatiers from my past.

"What? The Chocolate Bliss people?" Mrs. Schultz asked.

"Pearce and Riley." Their names left a bitter taste in my mouth.

"Why would they be here? Do they know you live here?" Archie asked.

"How could they not? There's no way you'd consider opening a new shop and not do extensive research on the town." I stood and watched as Pearce played big shot, greeting everyone who stood in line to enter like he was a pastor at the church of chocolate. It was just like him to overshadow Hope at her own grand opening.

Would the town make his pop-up shop successful enough for him to stick around permanently? The smiling faces of the crowd and the masses lining up for their free chocolates made me nervous. The only other people besides me and my friends who weren't clamoring for sweets were the married couple who owned Sweet Tooth Vintage Candy. The two men in their forties had their heads together and every muscle in their faces was taut. They had to be worried that fancy chocolate would encroach on their candy business.

"Are you going to say something to him?" Mrs. Schultz asked.

I turned my back to the shop—I couldn't stomach him any longer. "Not right now. I'm too angry and I don't want to ruin Hope's opening."

"Let's go back to the shop," she suggested.

"You guys should go in and congratulate Hope. I need a moment to calm down anyway."

"You sure?" Archie asked.

I nodded. "Give me a minute. I'll be okay."

Archie and Mrs. Schultz did as I asked, with supportive arm and shoulder squeezes before heading to Hope's Cakery.

I moved out of the path of those who intended to go inside. I took a deep breath, but what I really needed was a piece of cheese. Or five. Maybe I *should* go back to my shop. But it wasn't fair of me not to congratulate Hope. Could I be face-to-face with Pearce and Riley and be civil? Even during my short visits back home, I mostly kept to our farm, not wanting to run into them. Okay, I'll admit, I drove past their shop a time or two, but I heeded my parents' advice: *If you go asking for trouble, it's bound to answer.*

"Aren't you coming in?" a voice said over my shoulder.

The hairs on the back of my neck tingled, and not in a good way. I turned, already knowing who it was but still feeling a jolt. Pearce.

CHAPTER 3

"Hey, Willa. How are you?" Pearce said when I didn't answer his first question.

I wasn't in the mood for fake pleasantries. "Long time no see. What are you doing here?" I asked without pretense or a hint of a smile.

His lips contorted into a pout when he saw I wasn't going to play along with his charm routine. "Hey, come on. It's been ten years. Aren't you even going to be cordial?"

"This *is* me being cordial." In fact, I thought I was doing a pretty darn good job of it, considering the shock of it all. "You *meant* to spring this on me. Who keeps a shop opening a secret?"

"I like to open with a bang." He shrugged, his smile returning and his arms open as if that adequately explained it. "If it makes you feel better, it wasn't my idea to open another shop here. But this could be good, right? After all this time, the three musketeers together again? You, me, and Riley?"

His suggestion left me stunned and I could do nothing but blink for a full five seconds. When I found my voice again, I said, "You've got to be kidding."

He doused his smile. "Yeah, I guess that was a

longshot. You're not going to freak out about this, are you?" The question spilled off his lips with a condescending tone.

"Freak out?"

"Well, you're not the most chill person I've ever known."

My back stiffened and my hands flew to my hips. "As if you know me anymore! Why are you here? Why would you open another shop in my town of all places?" I looked off, blown away by his audacity.

Some of my neighbors filtering toward the cakery were now staring at us, having taken notice of my rising voice and my defensive stance, which I'd suddenly become aware of myself. The awkward eye contact made me want to shrivel in embarrassment, and I offered a tight-lipped smile. *Nothing happening here. I'm chill.*

I continued more calmly and quietly. "How did you expect me to react?"

"I don't know. It's just business, Willa. You, of all people, always put business first even before you had one."

"You mean all the hours I put in learning about cheese and how to run a shop so the three of us could go into business together while the two of you spent that same time fooling around behind my back?"

"Yeah, you're freaking out."

"I'M NOT—" I stopped myself, my gaze darting around, now hyperaware that people I knew could be watching. I swallowed my exasperation to say evenly, "I'm not freaking out."

"Good, then. I hope you're chill enough to come inside and take a look at the place. It's nothing compared to our other shops, but the chocolate's just as good."

You want to see chill? I'll show you chill. "Sure. Fine. I have a cake to pick up from Hope anyway."

"Awesome!"

He sauntered toward the cakery and it took all my effort to follow, as if the sidewalk was wet cement and my feet were in eight inches deep.

Once at the door, he said, "Don't mind me, I gotta get to work. Business is booming!" He winked and disappeared inside.

Chill, Willa, chill.

I walked across the Bake Someone Happy mat to cross the threshold. *Whoa.* I felt like I'd stepped inside a blown piece of bubblegum. There was pink virtually everywhere, in possibly every shade pink could be. HOPE'S CAKERY glowed in pink neon on the wall behind the counter.

The area to the left of the counter, where a few café tables used to be, now contained the Chocolate Bliss portion of the shop. The chocolate brown signs reading Chocolate Bliss, stark in contrast not only in color but in elegance, were the only relief from the pink. It was outfitted with a vertical glass display case that showcased their chocolates, and next to it, an even larger display of Brenner's Rum, where Pearce seemed to be doing his sales pitch. I wasn't too sure about the odd pairing of Bubblegum pink and hard liquor, but to each their own.

The clean-shaven manager Pearce had introduced as Duncan held a tray of samples, but his attention was being taken by a woman I recognized immediately— model-thin and taller than him in high-heeled boots, stretch jeans, and a Golden Glen Meadery shirt. Gia. Her hair was pulled back as tight as her clothes. She was cozied up to him, speaking in his ear. Pearce walked by and snapped his fingers at him, and Duncan turned his attention from her to those of us entering the shop. She noticed me then, and her smile turned to a scowl. We didn't have the best history.

She said one last thing in Duncan's ear, then walked toward me with only a glare as a greeting. I forced a smile anyway as she passed me and left the cakery.

It squeezed my heart a little to see Riley, who was boxing chocolates for customers. I looked away from her so as not to make eye contact, relieved that the slew of customers diverted her and Pearce's attention from me. I caught Archie, Mrs. Schultz, and June leaving, as I'd barely moved from the doorway.

"You came!" Archie sounded surprised.

"I want to send Hope my good wishes and pick up the cheesecake," I replied.

"We could've done that for you," Mrs. Schultz said.

"It's no big deal. I'm chill." I put my hand on my hip and tried to affect a nonchalant attitude.

They eyed me skeptically. They knew better.

I gave it up and let my arm fall to my side. "Better to get it over with," I told them quietly. "See you back at the shop."

I got in the register line where Hope's longtime employee, Jasmine, was ringing up the customers' sweets. I waved to Hope, who was practically camouflaged by her pink overalls behind the glass display case of beautiful cakes and cupcakes. She paused handing out free strawberry cake squares and filling customers' requests to say hello. I shouted congratulations over the heads of customers, and she thanked me with a huge grin.

Duncan came by with a tray of tiny paper sample bags with Chocolate Bliss's initials on them. "Brenner's rum chocolate?" he offered.

I managed a smile. "No, thank you."

"Are you sure? At least take a brochure." He pushed a pamphlet of their chocolates into my hand before moving on to the person behind me.

When I got to the front of the line, Jasmine, who was about Hope's age with a nose ring and a sleeve of tattoos, knew about my cheesecake order and went to the kitchen to retrieve it. I stared at the register as if it were a rare museum exhibit so as not to make eye contact with Riley at the chocolate counter nearby. I could only muster up so much chill under the circumstances. I looked up when Jasmine returned through the swinging kitchen door and with relief noticed that Duncan had traded places with Riley and was now weighing chocolates for a customer.

Jasmine set the cheesecake on the counter. Atop it was a long gold box with a ribboned lid, obviously containing chocolates—definitely *not* my order, although a register ticket with my name was attached.

"So *you're* the one getting the special gold box," Jasmine said.

Duncan was now next to Jasmine with his customer's bag of chocolates. He peered over the register. "Wait, that can't be hers," he interjected before I could. He took the box for a closer look.

"He's right. I just have the cheesecake," I told them.

"I'm sorry. They were together in the back, so I assumed they were both going to you," she said.

"How did the gold box get with your cakes? I was looking for it before when that journalist was here. This is supposed to go to the editor of the *Gazette*." Duncan's brows furrowed.

"A. J. Stringer?" I asked. I was well acquainted with the editor of our local newspaper.

"You know him?" Duncan asked. "We're hoping he'll review our chocolates for the *Glen Gazette*. Looks like now I'm going to have to deliver them." He let out a growl-sigh.

"I can bring them to him," I offered.

"Thanks, but that's okay. I'll manage."

"Duncan, you've barely slept in two days, and who knows when this will let up? Give yourself a break. You can trust Willa," Jasmine said, patting him on the back.

"My cheesecake was at fault, after all. I'll put in a word for Chocolate Bliss when I give them to him."

I could see him internally wrestling with his decision, but he seemed relieved, nonetheless. "Okay then. Sure. Thanks. Let him know they're on the house."

I left with my cheesecake and the gold box of chocolates. I'd take them to A. J. and put in a word for Chocolate Bliss, as promised. What kind of word, I purposely hadn't said.

CHAPTER 4

When I returned to Curds & Whey, I was met with a surprised Archie.

"You gave in?" he said, spotting the gold box of chocolates atop the cheesecake container.

I gave him a dubious look that said *Seriously?*

"No. They made these for A. J. I just offered to run them over to him." I stuck the box behind the front counter and put the cheesecake in the back refrigerator. Somehow, I still had the Chocolate Bliss brochure, which I hastily stuck in one of the kitchenette's drawers.

Some of the customers who must've dispersed after the cakery's opening began streaming into the shop. I was glad for the influx of shoppers to take my mind off the Chocolate anything-but-Bliss shop. Just about all the patrons, however, were discussing the new place and some even carried the small white paper bags of chocolates with the shop's initials, C.B., monogrammed on them. I cringed to think this was the way it would always be, and I'd be reminded of Pearce and Riley every day.

Before I knew it, the final hours passed, and the crowds eventually thinned. An hour before our shop closed, our Cheeseboard Café shut down, and June left shortly afterward. Once it neared closing time, Mrs. Schultz and Archie practically pushed me out the door to deliver the chocolates to A. J.

"But we still have to decorate for tomorrow's birthday bash," I said.

"We can handle it. The walk will do you good," Mrs. Schultz insisted.

She was right. And getting rid of these chocolates ASAP would make me feel even better.

I left my shop with the gold box of chocolates, which felt like contraband, walked to Main Street, then took a right. My stomach grumbled at the scent of smokey, charred steak wafting from Apricot Grille on the corner. Farther down, it didn't subside with the savory aromas of the Let's Talk Tacos food truck directly across from the old stucco building that housed the *Gazette*. I well knew the taco flavors accompanying their aromas, and my mouth started to salivate.

Someone calling my name lifted me out of my dreamy street taco haze. Trotting over from the taco truck was Claude Bentley, the manager of Hope's former bread bakery.

"Hi, Claude." I used to pick up our sampling bread from him, but we never communicated beyond that, so I wondered why he was seeking me out.

He adjusted the brim of his cap, which I knew covered a bald head. "I was going to come to your shop after I grabbed a bite. I, uh, wondered if you could use some help. I'm looking for a job." His hand rubbed his shorn goatee. I could tell he wasn't comfortable asking. I imagined when he opened his own bread bakery in his early twenties, he hadn't thought he'd be out of a job entirely twenty years later, but that's the risky life of a small business owner.

"I didn't know you weren't working for Hope anymore."

He let out a humorless chuckle. "It was bad enough working for her when I got to make my breads, but run a cakery? No thanks. Anyway, as soon as that chocolate guy got here, he ran the show. I wasn't about to fight with him, whether his part of the shop was going to be temporary or not." He noticed the box of chocolates in my hand. "Cavorting with the enemy?"

I looked at the box. "It was with my cake order by mistake. They're supposed to go to A. J." I was too embarrassed to tell him the real reason I'd offered to drop them off, even though it put us in the same camp. "So you really left the bakery?"

"Cakery," he corrected with an eye roll. "Bread's my thing, anyway."

I squinted at him. "Umm, I hate to tell you, Claude, but I don't sell bread either."

He chuckled, this time for real, and leaned his back against the building. "I know. I went from owning my own bread bakery to running Hope's, and now I just want a job for a while where I can work regular hours and not have to wake up in the middle of the night worrying if we've run out of rye seeds, ya know?"

This time it was my turn to laugh. I understood that in my own way very well. I'd been nervous to hire new employees, since Archie, Mrs. Schultz, and I worked so well together, but the addition of the Cheeseboard Café had made it a necessity. June was working out and maybe since I felt a bit of a kinship with Claude, he would too.

"You caught me at a good time. Are you available on short notice? We could use an extra hand tomorrow. We're celebrating the cheese shop's second birthday."

"I'm your guy," he answered with a grin.

"Great. After that, we'll see what we can work out."

"Thanks, Willa."

We went over a few details and then we parted. I watched him walk back to the food truck and sighed. My grumbling stomach shushed the argument I started with myself that I'd already given in to the taco truck twice this week. Now that I was firmly entrenched in my thirties, my metabolism wasn't what it used to be, but my cravings didn't care. Reluctantly, I continued into the Gazette building to get rid of the enemy chocolates.

Although it was evening, I wasn't surprised the door was unlocked and the lights were still on. A. J. often worked after hours, especially now that he recorded his podcast here. I was, however, surprised to hear raised voices coming from one of the cubicles. I recognized one of them as Deandra's, the reporter who covered the local interest events. I started toward her desk, not wanting to get in the middle of a spat but willing to defend her if need be.

"So you're really giving up, huh?" a male voice said.

"I've been doing this too long to put up with people like you!" Deandra replied angrily.

I approached them. Deandra, in her fifties, was packing up the items on her desk into a cardboard box, the flowy sleeves of her shirt whipping back and forth across the surface like a kite in the wind. The man she'd been arguing with was loosely gripping a can of soda. He stood casually like he was chatting with a friend, one of his ankles crossed over the other. It took me a moment to place him, but his slicked-forward hair prompted my recollection that he was the guy I'd briefly seen this morning pushing through the crowd toward the new cakery yelling about his press credentials. Without sunglasses on, it was easier to determine his age, late twenties. His flat face and gray eyes registered amusement. I wasn't sure what to make of the scene.

"Deandra, are you okay?" I asked.

Deandra tucked strands of her disheveled hair behind her ear as she continued collecting her items from the desk. "No, I'm not. I'm quitting."

"You're what? Why?"

"She can't handle a little competition," the guy said. He took a swig of his soda.

Deandra turned from her desk to target her furious gaze at him. "We're working for the *Gazette*, Kevin, not the *LA Times*. We're assigned stories or we volunteer for them. We don't compete for them. It's always been a place of community."

"Then you shouldn't get so mad at A. J. for giving me your stories, right?" He gave me a wry smile, as if he and I were on the same side. I hoped my scowl set him straight.

"I was here long before A. J. It's about respect. I have seniority and A. J. shouldn't be giving all my stories to you. I haven't worked here for twenty years to be bullied." Deandra had finished packing up her things. She hefted her oversized bag over her shoulder and lifted the box that held her personal items. "Sorry, Willa. If you're here for A. J., he'll be back later." She turned to Kevin one last time. "And stop leaving your soda cans all over the place!" She blew past me and eventually I heard the heavy front door open, then slam shut.

Kevin looked at me, shrugged *Oh, well*, and tipped the can for one last gulp. "You got a story?" he asked me, sticking the empty can on her desk in a final act of disrespect.

For a moment, I couldn't answer. He'd just made the *Gazette*'s longtime reporter quit and he wasn't ruffled one bit. I didn't know Deandra all that well, but she'd always been very nice to me and my shop, covering all our events with a professional eagerness. I wanted to lay into him on her behalf, but I refrained. I had my own problems. "I'm not here about a story. These are chocolates for A. J."

He gave me a leering grin. "A. J.'s got girls bringing him chocolates? Huh. Good for him." He looked me up and down.

I stared him down, not appreciating the assumption. "Hardly. He's doing a review for Chocolate Bliss."

"Oh yeah, the new place. Hope was smart to get an established business for her relaunch. She's cute too. I did the interviews and took some photos at the reveal. I'll take 'em." He held out his free hand for the chocolates.

I wasn't about to literally hand Deandra's nemesis another story. "I was directed to give them to A. J., so that's what I'm going to do."

He pulled his hand back, palm up. "All righty then. Be my guest. I'm Kevin Wallace, by the way. I'm the new reporter here."

"You seem to be causing a lot of problems for being new."

"It's not my fault if A. J. wants someone who can take the paper to the next level. Deandrea could still have her farmer's markets—I haven't taken *all* her stories. He wants a younger vibe for the paper. Harder-hitting stories. Can you blame him?"

As a matter of fact, I could.

He saw my pursed lips. "Just wait, A. J. and I have big plans for this little hometown paper. You'll be thanking me in a few months."

"Somehow, I doubt that."

I left the cubicle, wishing I hadn't engaged with him

at all. He was a lot like his overly gelled hair—too slick. What was A. J. thinking by hiring him?

I climbed the steps of the back stairwell to get to A. J.'s office, which took up the whole of the second floor. A. J. and I had helped each other look into some local murder cases in the past, and I considered him a loyal person. It wasn't fair of him to treat a *Gazette* veteran like this. With each step I climbed, I got more annoyed with him.

I reached the top of the stairs and opened the heavy door. The loftlike space had a single window on either side looking out to the stucco exterior of the neighboring buildings. In the area closest to the door was a simple table, two chairs, and microphone equipment for his podcast. The other side of the room held the disarray of his office—piled folders and newspapers on an oblong table. A rogue keyboard without a monitor. I noted several mismatched mugs, some used as pencil holders and some with leftover coffee, as I walked farther into the room. Two wheeled office chairs flanked either side of his desk where a computer monitor parted the clutter. I tossed the chocolates onto his desk. They landed on Deandra's resignation letter.

He shouldn't get to eat chocolates in peace after causing Deandra to quit! I stood over his desk, pushing papers aside until I found a small plain white notepad. I scribbled on it, "You're in trouble! W." I folded the note and opened the gold box with the ribbon affixed to its lid. Eight perfect, identical chocolates sat in individual compartments. I placed the note on top of them, closed the box and left it centered on his desk. At least I'd take a little pleasure thinking about him opening those chocolates. If only it were so easy to get back at Pearce.

CHAPTER 5

I once again summoned my willpower to walk past Let's Talk Tacos and returned to Curds & Whey in a hurry to help Archie and Mrs. Schultz with the decorations. When I arrived, they were done with the closing duties and had started decorating for our event tomorrow. With the added help of a helium tank and Mrs. Schultz's knack for directing, it wasn't long before we were through.

Mrs. Schultz stepped back to look at our handiwork. "What do you think?" she asked us.

"I think it's cheesetastic!" Archie exclaimed.

I chuckled. "I agree. The place looks great." I admired the decorations. A flag banner of yellow and spring green triangles hanging across the front windows and counters, colorful balloon bouquets rising from each display table, and a Happy 2nd Birthday! poster propped on the sampling counter gave the shop a celebratory feel. "Thank you two so much for all your extra work this week getting everything ready."

"We wouldn't have wanted it any other way," Mrs. Schultz said.

"I can't imagine Curds and Whey without you. It wouldn't be what it is today," I told them.

"The OG crew," Archie said with a smile, draping one arm over my shoulder and the other around Mrs. Schultz.

"Two years. Time flies," Mrs. Schultz said with a happy sigh.

We spent a quiet moment taking in our two years of friendship and hard work before we finally called it a day. Mrs. Schultz donned her bicycle helmet for the ride home on her retro cherry red Huffy, as she did just about every evening after work. I followed them out the door.

"Do you want a ride home? It's getting dark." I didn't like the idea of Mrs. Schultz riding her bike at night, even though she did it often.

"I like the ride. It's only six blocks." She straddled her bike and clicked on the headlight attached to the handlebars.

"You look like a Christmas tree!" Archie laughed, noting all the reflectors on her bike and helmet.

"The better to see me, my dear! See you tomorrow!" she said as she pushed off.

Archie and I said goodbye before he made the short stroll across the alley to The Kick Stand bicycle shop, above which he shared an apartment.

I went back inside and closed the door, taking in my shop. *Two years.* I inhaled a deep breath, feeling like I was filling my lungs with gratitude. Even more than recognizing that the shop I'd dreamt about for years was prospering, I was feeling deep appreciation for Archie and Mrs. Schultz. I had to include my best friend Baz in that too. As the town's handyman, he never officially worked for me, but he was always quick to offer his help and support.

My phone dinged a text, and I plucked it from my

pocket. Speak of the devil—it was Baz: *Wanna catch some dinner?*

My thumbs flew over the screen as I tapped the keys in reply. *I was hankering for some tacos not too long ago . . .*

Big surprise. Meet you there in five?

You're not upstairs?

Baz lived in the apartment next door to mine, which was above my shop. His reply appeared: *I just finished a job at the inn.*

I tapped the thumbs-up emoji and he replied with tacos. I grabbed my zip sweatshirt, turned off the lights, and headed out the door, locking it behind me. I had fully intended to deny myself the taco truck today, but fate had other plans.

I began to walk up the block for the second time in a little over an hour when blue flashing lights emanating from Main Street caught my eye. Police lights? I picked up the pace until I found myself trotting. The lights were like beacons in the darkening sky, and when I arrived at the intersection, I saw where they were leading—to the Gazette.

CHAPTER 6

I crossed Pleasant Avenue and ran down the sidewalk toward where three police cruisers lined the building. Two officers were busy keeping the quickly forming crowd back on the opposite sidewalk by the taco truck. I spotted A. J. alone, crouched against the stucco newspaper building while two officers stood guard by the Gazette's door farther down. I was relieved to see him.

"A. J., what happened?" He was in his usual attire of worn jeans, T-shirt, and green Salvation Army jacket.

He stood to face me and ran a hand over his curly hair, which looked even more wayward than usual. He was pale.

"Don't tell me something's happened to Deandra," I said, searching his face for a clue. A claw of fear grabbed my stomach.

"Willa." Detective Jay Heath strode toward us from the direction of the door. Seeing the tall, handsome detective made my stomach flutter, even though at the moment he was here as a police detective and not as the guy I'd been dating for the past several months. "I'm sorry, Willa, I have to speak with A. J."

"It's Kevin, my new star reporter. I-I saw him. He's

dead," A. J. said, his voice shaky. He closed his eyes for a moment to get a grip.

"Really? I just saw him," I said, shocked.

Heath's attention returned to me. "You did?"

"Yeah, I was at the Gazette looking for A. J. a little more than an hour ago. He and Deandra were arguing."

"Okay, Willa, can you wait over there, please, until I can question you properly?" He pointed a little farther along the sidewalk.

"Sure." I squeezed A. J.'s arm for reassurance. I'd been in his place—having found a dead body—too many times before. It was a shock, especially when it was someone you knew. He gave me a tight-lipped half smile as thanks, and I left Heath to do his job.

As I took a few steps down the sidewalk, my mind raced thinking of Kevin. He seemed fine health-wise. Being obnoxious never killed anyone as far as I knew. *Shame on you, Willa. The guy's dead.* I closed my eyes and said a little prayer for the deceased and his family.

When I opened them, the white forensics van was pulling up and the chief coroner and her team emerged. She was a striking woman with lips colored deep red that offset the white jumpsuit uniform she wore, and her demeanor was no-nonsense. I recognized her from crime scenes I'd been a witness to. Whether a crime or a natural death occurred, her forensics team was called. She pulled the hood of the jumpsuit over her black hair, which was pulled back in a low ponytail, and went straight over to Heath. He left A. J. and led her and her team inside.

Now left alone, A. J. immediately came over to me.

"What happened?" I asked.

"I found him in his chair like he was passed out.

I got closer to give him a tap to wake him up, but his eyes were still open. He was dead." A. J. looked away, the horrid image likely playing back in his mind's eye.

"What could've happened? He was young, like our age."

"Younger." A. J. shook his head. "I don't know." He patted the multiple pockets of his Salvation Army jacket that hung open almost to his knees, then rooted around in them. He noticed me looking at him quizzically. "Haven't smoked in three years, but I could sure use one now." He gave up on the idea that an old cigarette might be hiding in his coat.

"I'm sorry, A. J." I gave his arm a couple of firm pats, probably the closest we'd come to a hug.

"Thanks, Willa."

I saw the door to the Gazette open and I stepped away from A. J. The circle of police parted, and I recognized the outline of Heath's thick head of hair, broad shoulders, and tailored suit as he strode toward us again.

He put a gentle hand on my back. "A. J., hold tight. I'm going to need to get a full statement from you," he said before leading me away.

"What is it? Do you know how he died?" I asked Heath quietly.

He shook his head and put his hands on his hips, flaring his suit jacket. He towered over me and leaned in to speak quietly. "Not yet, but there are indications it's a suspicious death. I want you to keep that to yourself for now. I'll need to talk to you later about exactly what happened while you were there earlier, but I need to question A. J. For now, was there anybody else in the building when you saw Kevin Wallace?"

"Uh . . ." I could hardly focus on his question, my

mind abuzz with the possibility of murder. "Just Deandra, as far as I know, but she left before I did."

"Okay. No sense in you waiting out here or at the station. I'll reach out later to get your statement."

I nodded, still too shocked to speak, and he squeezed my arm. "You okay?"

"Yeah, just surprised."

"Let me get one of my officers to take you home." He looked out at the growing crowd across the street that his men were endeavoring to keep in place.

"You can't spare an officer right now. Am I in danger?"

"I don't think so. But I want you to be safe."

"I'll be all right. I'll find Baz."

"Good idea. I'll call you later." He tenderly touched my chin, then just as quickly left to question A. J.

I watched him go, then continued down the street. Baz, in a short-sleeved polo shirt that hung over a Dad bod belly to the hips of his baggy jeans, awaited me on the corner away from the commotion. "What happened?" he asked.

"It might be murder."

"What?"

Let's go to my apartment. I've got a ton to catch you up on." I belatedly noticed he was holding a bag of tacos. "You got them, even with everything going on?"

"Don't underestimate me, Wil. Sometimes I literally save your life and sometimes I'm a hero in other ways."

I laughed, a much-needed release from the stress of the day. Baz could always be counted on for that.

We walked back in silence, the seriousness of the situation once again sinking in. What did the police find that led them to think it was murder? What could've happened in the hour since I'd last seen Kevin Wallace?

CHAPTER 7

The next morning, I awoke before my early alarm. It wasn't unusual—my childhood spent doing chores on a dairy farm meant getting up before the sun, and my body had barely adjusted in all the years since. I didn't mind, especially not today with our big second birthday to celebrate.

My thoughts immediately went to Kevin Wallace and his possible murder. Heath had called me last night to tell me he'd be working late, and he would get my statement today. He didn't divulge any further information about why they thought the journalist's death might've been murder. It must've been something the coroner discovered. It didn't give Baz and me anything to go on, so last night I filled him in on the other surprising news, which consisted of my chocolate-fueled anger toward Pearce and Riley and the new Chocolate Bliss.

Before getting out from under the covers of my grandmother's handsewn quilt, I took a slow, deep breath, let it out, then took another. I didn't like what seeing Pearce and Riley had turned me into yesterday. It had somehow thrown me back ten years to all those same emotions, ones that I thought I'd worked through.

I had no feelings for Pearce anymore, it wasn't that. It was the three of us and the future we were going to have together. It wasn't just the betrayal; it was the years I'd spent missing the two of them. All the good times we'd had together in college and beyond made all the memories of the three musketeers bittersweet. Mostly bitter.

On top of that, there were other feelings surrounding that time that pierced my heart, namely, my brother's passing the following year—but of course, Pearce and Riley weren't to blame for those. All the horrible emotions from that period in my life had been as locked away as I could keep them. Grief over my brother was like the air I breathed—a part of my everyday life. Nothing could rid me of it, nor did I want to be rid of it—that grief was my love for him. But being thrown back to the time of his car accident and remembering my parents' faces when they'd told me was something I didn't like to dwell on. Sometimes it felt even harder the more time passed because I missed him so. I let myself cry for Grayson. As I wiped my tears, I wondered if Kevin Wallace was somebody's brother.

I called my parents, but was not surprised they didn't answer. They still worked the farm, now with a few extra farmhands. I left a voicemail and told them I loved them.

One more deep breath. The exhale brought the day ahead into focus. I had a birthday bash to throw.

Three hours later, I opened the shop door to customers. I walked outside to take a look at Curds & Whey at two years old. Seeing my shop—encased in wide cream-colored molding, its name in a sweeping font above the matching teal door—still tickled me with excitement. The large plateglass windows on either side of the door allowed any passersby to get a glimpse of what my shop offered—aged cheeses in differing shapes and sizes, their wheels cut open to reveal their speckled textures in varying white and yellow coloring to entice those who couldn't smell the heady aroma until they stepped inside. On the top tier of wire shelves, brightly painted milk jugs and metal sheep and cow sculptures were displayed beside a stack of cheese-lovers' cookbooks. It was a feast for the eyes.

A. J. sidled up to me on the brick-lined sidewalk with his worn messenger bag slung over his torso crosswise. "Happy cheese shop birthday," he said without much enthusiasm.

"Thanks. What are you doing here? Did you hear any more about Kevin Wallace's death?"

"No. I answered questions last night, and they said they'd call me in sometime today, but they wouldn't tell me anything. I came to interview some of your staff for your birthday bash story."

"Oh, that's right. Deandra won't be covering it." I didn't say more. After what he'd been through, he didn't need a guilt trip from me about his treatment of Deandra.

"I'll talk to her. Maybe now that Kevin's gone, she'll reconsider quitting."

"I think her resignation had more to do with how *you* treated her than how Kevin treated her. If you get another young guy ready to take on the world at the *Gazette*, will she get shoved aside again? She's been there longer than you have, A. J. You've added a lot to the paper since you've been editor, but don't forget its roots in the community. Deandra's a part of that."

To my surprise, A. J. looked contrite. Maybe coming upon Kevin the way he had gave him a new, less cynical perspective. "You're right. I'll talk to her."

His admission left me temporarily stunned. "Good. I take back what I said in the note then."

"What note?"

"With the chocolates."

"What chocolates?"

"You probably never got back to your office after finding Kevin, huh? Just as well. Ignore the note when you do see it."

I walked into Curds & Whey after a customer.

"What note?" A. J. asked again, following me.

I ignored him and attended to the customers in my shop. Archie's and Mrs. Schultz's backgrounds—his as his high school mascot and hers as a drama teacher—kept them eager for any chance to be in costume, so they were already dressed for Italy, the first featured country of the day for our hourly Cheese Around the World.

Our friend, Beatrice, who owned Bea's Hive of Thrifted Finds, did a terrific job of collating the different materials for the costumes. She was also an experienced seamstress, and she and Mrs. Schultz were able to put them together in a a couple of weeks.

Archie's lanky frame looked slightly overwhelmed in his peasant costume—a puffy white shirt, tomato red vest, and baggy pirate pants that fell just below his knees, along with a black, wide-brimmed hat. He stood by the five-tier cheese tower that would serve as our birthday cake display until it was time to serve Hope's cheesecake. He was explaining our game—customers could guess the five types of cheeses we used for the cheese tower and at the end of the day, we'd randomly pick a winner from the correct answers to take a personal-sized wheel of one of those cheeses home.

"You're welcome to have a taste," Archie said to the older woman who was listening intently.

"Is it cheating if I try to find the same cheese in the shop?" she asked.

"Not at all. It's encouraged!" Archie told her.

June was showing Claude the ropes for the Cheeseboard Café, although overhearing their voices, it seemed somehow Claude was doing most of the talking. I wondered if he was having a hard time shedding the manager role he held at Rise and Shine Bakery and hoped that wouldn't present any problems.

As I helped at the front of the shop, I kept an ear trained to A. J., who was asking customers their opinions about the birthday celebration and my shop. To my relief, everything I overheard was positive.

My attention turned toward the door when Lou from the market walked in. *Uh-oh.* Usually when Lou came into my shop during a special event, it was only to complain about my excess customers who were parked in front of his market.

"Lou, how nice of you to stop in! Oh, unless there's a parking problem?" Better to get it out of the way.

"No, no problem," he said, surprising me. He surveyed the shop, and I had an inkling who he was looking for. Since the community Valentine's dance we had last year, I'd gotten the feeling that Lou had been crushing on Mrs. Schultz. Mrs. Schultz, who had just started dipping her toe into the dating pond after being widowed for some years, wasn't picking up the clues of his romantic feelings. However, I'd noticed she'd started doing her shopping at Lou's Market in recent months and Lou had suddenly become a regular Cheeseboard Café customer. I wasn't sure if he was suited for her, but she certainly made him less grumpy. Maybe she would have a lasting positive effect on him.

His eyes widened when he spotted her walking to the

front of the shop, looking somehow natural in a bodice and colorful embroidered skirt she'd embellished herself. Ballet flats and a headscarf completed the traditional costume of an Italian peasant.

"Mrs. Schultz!" Lou exclaimed, his eyes wide with surprise and admiration. His lips kept moving as if to say more, but I think the breath was taken out of him.

"Since I'm letting my actress side come out today, I'll be going by my first name. Everyone can call me Ruth," she declared with flair.

"Ruth," Lou echoed, but again, couldn't seem to say more. He was smitten, and who could blame him? Mrs. Schultz was quite a catch. He continued through the shop in somewhat of a daze.

"Do I have to?" Archie asked her. "That would be like calling Willa Ms. Bauer. It'd be weird for me. I've only known you as Mrs. Schultz."

"Oh, I'm just playing. You can call me anything you want," she assured him.

"What are you comfortable with?" I asked her.

"Either one. Plenty of people call me Ruth, it's just after being a teacher for so long and married for so long . . ." She trailed off, looking melancholy at the mention of her deceased husband. "I like having Mr. Schultz with me in that way," she said quietly.

I put an arm around her. "I'm pretty used to calling you Mrs. Schultz too." I gave her an extra squeeze.

"I think it's time for Archie's big moment," Mrs. Schultz announced, back to her upbeat self.

I looked at the clock. She was right. "Are you ready to crack the wheel, Archie?"

Customers began gathering in anticipation around the large wheel of Parmigiano-Reggiano we'd set up in the middle of the shop. Archie rubbed his palms together, then shook out his arms. He'd been practicing on smaller wheels, but this would be his first of this size and in front of a crowd. I made sure A. J. was positioned to get some good shots as Archie scored a clean line across the center of the top of the wheel.

I spotted Heath standing just inside the doorway. A little fizz of excitement bubbled up inside me upon seeing him and I hurried over to meet him at the door.

"You're just in time for Archie's big moment," I gushed with pride.

"I wish that's what I was here for." He gave me one of his official looks.

Uh-oh. "Late night?" I asked.

"And early morning. I'm sorry, I know this isn't a good time. I thought I might be able to find A. J. here."

A. J.'s journalistic instincts kicked in when he saw Heath. He'd already started over. "Any news?" he asked.

"Can we step outside to talk?" Heath nodded to the door.

He and A. J. walked out. I looked back. Archie was doing fine, and the others were there to assist. I followed Heath and A. J. outside.

"What is it?" A. J. asked him.

Heath turned to me first. "Willa, you said you saw Kevin Wallace when you were at the Gazette earlier yesterday evening?"

Heath was in detective mode. I gave him straight answers. "That's right."

"Was he eating anything?"

I thought back. "No. He was drinking a soda. That's all I saw, anyway. Why?"

"A. J., you didn't mention seeing anything unusual on his desk in your initial statement. Do you recall anything that was on his desk?"

"On his desk? I don't think I got much past the dead eyes. I have no idea what was on his desk. Was this really foul play?" A. J. asked. I could tell he was itching to pull out the voice recorder from his messenger bag but didn't dare.

"Ivy did a preliminary tox report overnight." Ivy was the coroner and head of forensics. "An unusual substance in the victim's system stood out to her right away. It's not something that one would ingest knowingly."

"Do you think it was put in his soda?" I asked.

"We tested all the open soda cans and there are no traces of it except on the rim of one where his lips would've made contact with it. But there *was* an empty box of Chocolate Bliss chocolates on his desk."

"Chocolates?" I repeated. I wasn't expecting that.

"There was a threatening note in the box, as well. We're getting the prints on it."

Oh no. I started to put two and two together. "Did the note say *You're in trouble*?"

Heath arched an eyebrow. "Willa, what do you know about this?"

I grimaced. "It was meant for A. J."

Heath put his palm in front of me. "Don't say any more."

A. J. turned on me, mouth open in surprise. "What do you mean it was meant for me? Were you trying to kill me?"

"A. J.! Of course not!" I cried.

A roar came from inside the shop, and I whipped around to look, panicked that he'd been overheard. Even the applause that followed didn't immediately ease my alarm until it sank in that Archie had successfully cracked the cheese wheel. Luckily, everyone's attention was on the Parmesan.

I turned back to A. J. and Heath. "I didn't know the chocolates were poisoned," I hissed.

My attention went to the patrol car and forensics van in front of Hope's Cakery.

"Are you shutting down Hope's shop?" I asked Heath.

Heath didn't answer, as we both saw Deandra bustling down the sidewalk toward us, her oversized purse banging against her hip with each step. She stopped when she reached us. "Willa, I'm sorry I'm late for your shop's birthday bash. I was telling my husband how bad I felt about not covering it, and he told me to get up and stop sulking. Before I knew it, I was in the car driving here. Unless that hideous Kevin Wallace is here." She threw A. J. a nasty look.

"Deandra, you probably don't want to say any more about Kevin," I warned.

"Why? I'm still quitting, I'm just here because I'd already committed to it. I don't care who knows how much I hate him. *Hate* is a big word, I know, but it's true."

"Deandra, he's dead," I blurted out to stop her from incriminating herself any further.

Her face froze for a moment, then she looked from me to A. J. to Heath, and finally registered Detective Heath's presence might be official. "What do you mean, he's dead?"

Heath took over. "We believe he's been murdered. You three need to come with me to the station."

I hadn't asked for trouble, but it had answered anyway.

CHAPTER 8

A. J. tried to comfort Deandra in his own awkward way, while I pulled Heath aside.

"Can this wait? I've got a shop full of customers on one of the biggest days of the year," I said quietly.

"I'm sorry, Willa. If that's your note we found with the chocolate box, I'll be lucky not to get pulled from the case. I've got to do this by the book." He put a hand on my shoulder and squeezed, the best he could do to comfort me under the public circumstances. He looked into the shop full of customers, who were getting free samples of Parmigiano-Reggiano fresh off the wheel. "I'm really sorry to do this to you."

"Can I at least go in and explain to Archie and Mrs. Schultz?"

"Of course. We'll be waiting in the car."

Heath's unmarked vehicle was double-parked in front of my shop, its strip of lights visible in the back window a giveaway that it was a police car.

"Could you drive it a little way up the street, so my customers don't see me getting into a police car?"

"Sure. I'll park it at The Kick Stand. And I'm going to need anything you bought from Chocolate Bliss or Hope's so forensics can test it."

"Okay. I'll be right out."

I went inside, trying to hide my distress, but Archie and Mrs. Schultz immediately sensed that something was wrong. I nodded to the back of the shop and waited for them through the swinging door where our stockroom and my office were. Within minutes, they came through the door to meet me.

"What's going on?" Mrs. Schultz asked.

I spoke quietly, even though we were behind closed doors. "I'm so sorry, but Heath is making me give a statement at the station. That reporter from the *Gazette* was murdered."

"Oh no!" Mrs. Schultz cried.

"That's not all. They think he was poisoned by the Chocolate Bliss chocolates I brought to A. J. yesterday."

Archie and Mrs. Schultz peppered me with questions in unison. "What? How?"

"I'll explain later. Because I'm sort of involved, they have to interview me, and it has to be now. I'm so sorry to leave you in the lurch."

"Don't worry about us," Mrs. Schultz said, not completely successful at easing the concern for me that was evident on her face.

"June and Claude are working together doing the cheeseboards. Mrs. Schultz and I can handle the rest until you get back. We'll have to tag-team the costume changes, that's all," Archie said, always ready to tackle whatever came his way.

I exhaled in relief. "Thanks. Don't worry about putting on the costumes if you don't have time. I'll be back as soon as I can."

"Good luck," Mrs. Schultz called after me.

I took Hope's cheesecake from the refrigerator and left out the side door from the stockroom that led out to the alley so as not to draw attention. I could've walked the block and a half to the police station, but Heath's car was waiting for me in front of the bicycle shop on the corner like he said. I got in the car with Deandra and A. J. It felt strange being driven in the back seat like a criminal by the guy I was dating.

The police station was on Main Street across from town hall, housed in the modern security complex along with the fire station. Since we were with Heath, we entered through the back door straight into the station. He took the cheesecake, and we were led into separate interview rooms. Mine held nothing more than a rectangular table and three uncomfortable plastic chairs. I was, unfortunately, quite familiar with this room. The bare walls were painted yellow, but it didn't bring any joy to the space. The only light came from two strips of LEDs attached to the ceiling, dispersing an unnaturally bright glow. I pulled out one of the chairs facing the door and sat. It was even harder than I remembered. The only sound was the buzzing of the lights.

I was nervous about what I should say. Should I come right out and admit to the note? I had no choice, really. They'd find my prints on it. It was in my handwriting, albeit angry capital letters. I let out a long breath and closed my eyes, covering them with my hands in hopes that the darkness would somehow rearrange the scene before me once I opened my eyes again.

I heard the door open. *Peekaboo.* Nothing had changed.

The officer who walked in wasn't Heath, which only added to my disappointment. I was sure he wasn't interviewing me for appearance's sake. He might've also had bigger fish to fry—surely everyone from Chocolate

Bliss and Hope's Cakery needed to be interviewed too. Who could've done this? And why?

Officer Shepherd closed the door behind him. He was *Shep* to everyone who knew him, which was just about everyone in Yarrow Glen. He was about my age, mid-thirties, and a friend to everyone, but that didn't keep him from earning the spot of Heath's right-hand man. He didn't have the size to be intimidating—he was tall but lanky—but he was still the officer you'd want to settle a dispute that was getting too heated and also the one you'd want if you needed to receive bad news. Since dating Heath, I'd gotten to know Shep on more of a personal level. Other than Heath, he was the one I was glad came through the door at this particular moment.

Shep sat in the chair across the table from me, a grim closed-mouth smile on his lips in greeting. "Okay, Willa, you know the drill. I'm going to start the recording and that signals the official interview will begin."

I nodded.

"Officer Kyle Shepherd with Ms. Willa Bauer." He stated the date and time.

Swallowing was suddenly difficult. I would have to admit to Shep that I'd written the stupid, now "threatening," note—there was no way around it. But that also meant I had to implicate Deandra. I'd have to tell him everything that had transpired during my visit to the *Gazette*, and it wouldn't make me or Deandra look good.

Forget about wondering who did this; I had to concentrate on getting myself off the suspect list.

CHAPTER 9

When the interview was over, I was led out of the secure space of the police station to the modern atrium of the security complex. Sunlight streamed into the bright, uncluttered lobby through the two-story glass-walled entrance. I waited so I could talk to A. J. My mind was too full of questions and worry to scroll on my phone, so I paced between the two vacant sofas situated across from each other. I ended up scrutinizing a tall, waxy-leaf floor plant that was subbing as decoration. I could never tell if they were real or not.

I heard the buzzing of the department security door open and left my curiosity about the plant to see Pearce walking out of the police station.

"Willa, what are you doing here?" he asked.

"Giving the police a statement."

"They're saying my chocolates were poisoned," he whispered with anguish in his voice.

"I know. I don't think you need to whisper about it. The whole town will know in a matter of hours if they don't already."

His eyes were hollow and scared, and I was suddenly sorry I'd spoken so callously.

"Nobody believes you'd poison your chocolates," I added, trying to soften the blow I'd just landed.

"That hardly matters—nobody pays attention to the details. All that matters is that someone died eating them. We're ruined. Chocolate Bliss is ruined!" His voice cracked.

I tried to think of something comforting to say. If this had happened to my cheese instead of his chocolates, I'd feel hopeless too.

"Detective Heath is excellent at his job. He'll find out who did this."

He continued to spiral. "This'll make its way to Oregon. All because of a stupid little pop-up shop. I should've never listened to Duncan. I just wanted to get him out of my hair." His head drooped—he looked totally defeated.

"I'm sorry, Pearce. I really am." I surprised myself at the truth of this—I really *did* feel bad for him. "Once the person is caught, people will trust you again. It'll blow over." This part, I wasn't being so truthful about. I didn't know what it would take to recover from something like this.

"You've got to help me, Willa." The strength in his voice returned and his plea surprised me.

"I-I don't know how I can."

"I heard you're some kind of amateur detective, aren't you?"

Even more uncomfortable now, I played with my short hair, pressing a strand behind my ear. "Where did you hear that?"

He ignored my question. "You know the people here in Yarrow Glen—you just said yesterday this is your town. Who could've done this to us? Who'd want to sabotage Chocolate Bliss?"

"Is that what you think happened? Sabotage?"

"I don't know. I don't know anybody here except for Hope. But you do." Behind his glasses, his eyes searched mine, hoping I'd say something to make him feel better.

"Pearce, I have to be careful. I'm a person of interest too."

This time, he was the one who stepped back. "You? Why?"

"I brought the chocolates from your shop to A. J."

"You?" His face contorted and he looked at me with disgusted disbelief. "You hate me and Riley that much that you would ruin us?"

I was stunned silent, but only for a moment. "Are you kidding me right now? You think I could do that?" I turned to storm out of the building, but that stupid plant was in the way. I tumbled over it, knocking my shin hard. I let out a cry of pain.

Pearce helped me up, leaving my pride on the floor. He didn't let go of the grip he had on my arms. "I'm sorry. I'm not thinking straight. Willa, put yourself in my shoes."

I didn't want to allow him to play on my sympathies, but if I were in his shoes, I'd take whatever help I could get. Maybe even from him.

"First, let go of me," I said calmly.

He looked at his hands still gripping my arms, then released me. "Sorry. Willa, will you help me?"

I crossed my arms, trying to ward off my growing sympathetic feelings. He stared into my eyes, and I looked away, but not before seeing the desperation in them.

"I'm not making any promises," I told him.

He let out a breath. "Thank you. We've worked so

hard for Chocolate Bliss. We can't lose our business this way."

"You won't," I heard myself tell him.

Didn't I just say I wasn't making any promises?

The door buzzed again, and this time it was Riley.

Pearce met her with a hug. "You okay?"

She nodded, but it was obvious she was shook. "Have you seen Duncan?" she asked.

"No. He must still be in there." Pearce led Riley over to me, and she stared at me tentatively. "Ri, Willa's going to help us," he said.

"How?" she asked. The fingers of one hand immediately began fidgeting with a lock of her curls.

"I'm not sure yet," I admitted. "But I need to know more about Chocolate Bliss."

"Like what?" she asked.

"How does Duncan fit into this shop?"

Riley spoke. "He's been with us almost from the start."

"He came with you from Oregon to open the pop-up?"

Pearce nodded. "He started working for us about a year after we opened. He was willing to learn the business of being a chocolatier and we promoted him to manager pretty quickly."

"He's really good," Riley said, taking one of the clips out of her hair to push her curls back, then reinserting the clip.

"Then what was your problem with him?" I asked.

"There's no problem," Riley stated immediately.

"Pearce said he wanted to get him out of his hair. That sounds like there might be a problem."

"I was just frustrated," he said, plopping on the couch.

Riley sat next to him and slipped her hand into his. I

joined them on the couch, my capri khakis inching up my bruised shin, awakening a sting of pain.

Pearce continued, "Duncan's the one who wanted to open a Chocolate Bliss here because he's from around here—Lockwood—and he heard through the grapevine that Hope was looking for someone to share the expenses on her bakery space. We opened the Ashland shop not too long ago, so Riley and I weren't ready for another, but he wouldn't stop bugging us about it. So, we compromised. I said we could do a pop-up and if it took off, it could become our third Chocolate Bliss." He glanced at Riley as if to confirm. She nodded.

"Can you think of any reason he might try to sabotage the shop?" I asked.

"Duncan? No!" Riley replied without missing a beat.

Pearce took a few moments longer. "Not off the top of my head. I know he wanted to spread his wings, but we gave in and agreed to let him manage the pop-up. Maybe that wasn't enough for him."

"How would ruining the reputation of the shop he's been working at help him? It's not Duncan," Riley insisted.

Pearce didn't push it further.

If it wasn't an inside job, I had to start looking at who else might've wanted to take them down.

"I'm tired. I just want to go back to the inn," Riley said.

"You've been staying at the inn? How did I not see you?" I asked.

The Inn at Yarrow Glen was just past Main Street and the library. I went to the inn's pub, The Cellar, a few times a week, usually with Baz or Heath, so it was odd to me that they were able to keep themselves so hidden in the days or weeks leading up to yesterday's opening.

"We stayed with Hope until last night. It was convenient, but a little too close for comfort. We booked the inn for the next week until we go back to Oregon," Pearce explained.

"I was going to stay home to run our flagship store, and Pearce would come back here for short stints. I guess we don't have to worry about that now," Riley said. Her body drooped forward. Pearce squeezed her hand.

My heart tugged at seeing Riley so dejected. I didn't want to walk away from this conversation with nothing to show for it. "Is there anyone else who had access to the chocolates who could've done this?"

"Only Hope and Jasmine, but this hurts Hope almost as much as it's hurt us," Pearce said. He shook his head, out of answers. He and Riley rose from the couch, and I did the same.

"Jasmine doesn't really have a stake in it, and she doesn't seem to like us much. Maybe it was her," Riley suggested.

"Oh, I don't think it would be Jasmine," I said. I only knew her from the bakery, but I'd never gotten anything but a positive vibe from her.

Pearce ran a hand over his forehead and adjusted his glasses. "If you're not willing to believe that it could be someone from your town, there's no way you can help us," he said, barely hiding his frustration.

I sighed, crossing my arms. Unfortunately, he was right. "Okay then, why do you think she doesn't like you?"

Riley shrugged. "I don't think she liked having us

there. She was probably used to the way things ran with Hope and that other manager."

"Claude," Pearce provided, drawing out the name to sound like *clod*. His expression indicated he wasn't a fan. Recalling what Claude had said to me, the feeling was mutual.

Riley gave me a half smile and her eyes softened. "Thanks so much for helping us, Willa. You might not believe me, but it's good to see you."

I didn't know what to say to that. My mixed emotions kept me from reciprocating the sentiment.

Pearce tugged on her hand, and they started toward the doors out of the building.

"Be in touch if you come up with anything," he said.

"You too," I called after them, the irony not escaping me that I was asking the two people I'd wanted to see least in the world to "be in touch."

They walked out the door holding hands, and I watched them go, still thinking about the last name they mentioned. *Claude*.

CHAPTER 10

I sat back down on the couch and my shin screamed at me again. I took a look. A pale shade of chartreuse had developed beneath a one-inch scrape. I pushed my thoughts past my bruise to think about the possible suspects I had so far. As much as I hated to admit it, Pearce was right. I had to include my own neighbors on that list. Claude lost his job because of Chocolate Bliss, but how did he poison the chocolates? Jasmine had opportunity, but what was her motive? I didn't buy that she hated the changes to the shop. She and Duncan seemed friendly when I saw them working together yesterday. Who else could want to sabotage Chocolate Bliss?

I heard the door buzz again, and A. J. emerged from the police station. Finally! Normally, he was as alert as a border collie, his focus on everything around him, even during a conversation. Now he kept his chin low and walked with purpose toward the security complex doors. I popped off the couch to intercept him.

"A. J.!"

He started as if I'd zapped him and pulled me over to the floor plant, scooting behind it.

"Shh!" He shushed me harshly. "Are you trying to get me killed?"

"I think we already established that I'm not. Besides, we're in the security complex. You can't get much safer than this."

"It's the last place I would expect to be ambushed, which means I *should* expect it." He scanned the lobby, attempting to shield himself behind the plant.

"What are you talking about? Did the police say someone was after you?"

"It's obvious, isn't it? Those chocolates were meant for *me*. Someone messed with them, so I'd be killed."

"Who would want to kill you?"

"Tons of people. I walk our listeners through every suspect in my cold case podcast. Someone obviously didn't like being mentioned."

"Have you gotten any death threats?"

"No. Whoever it is must've not wanted to alert me."

I'd spent time thinking through different scenarios and only came up with an outside chance that A. J. was the target. "I don't know, A. J. How did a random criminal know about the chocolates meant for you and have access to poisoning them?"

"I don't know, and I don't want to find out." He flipped up the collar of his Salvation Army jacket and lowered his head.

"I'm worried about Deandra. And myself, frankly. She and I are persons of interest," I told him.

"I am too, thanks to you. They think *I* gave Kevin the chocolates." He suddenly looked introspective and said to himself, "Suspect or Victim? This could make a good podcast."

"You're blaming *me* for this?"

He pivoted from thoughts of the podcast to me. "You left the chocolates on my desk with that note."

"I know. I'm sorry about that, but I had no idea they were poisoned. We have to find out who did it and why. Let's go to your office and talk this out. Come up with some possibilities."

"They said the building is still cordoned off for forensics. The chocolates might've been tainted right at my desk.

I hadn't considered that.

"Someone was bold." He shook his head. "I'm going under."

"Under?"

"Undercover. It's too dangerous right now to be me."

I shook my head. A. J. loved the idea of playing big-city games in a small town, and it usually worked in my favor. But this time I needed his noir paranoia to take a back seat to what was really happening here. I didn't see how he could be the target unless someone from Chocolate Bliss or the cakery was out to get him. Still, I couldn't cross it off the possibility list entirely. Was A. J. supposed to be the one murdered?

"Wish me luck," he continued and slipped away from the cover of the large, waxy leaves.

I followed him out the door and caught up with him, my short legs making my shorter strides work double time to keep up.

"Listen, Pearce thinks Chocolate Bliss was the actual target," I said when I caught up to him.

"Sabotage?" A. J. asked. His strides didn't slow.

"Yes. That makes more sense, doesn't it? Now we just have to figure out who would want Chocolate Bliss to fail."

A. J.'s eyes peeked out from over his collar at me. "You, for one."

I *tsk*ed at him and accompanied it with a dirty look. "Not helping! Who else?" The orange figure in the pedestrian signal crossing indicated we had the right of way. We crossed Pleasant Avenue and continued down the sidewalk toward the Gazette. "I was thinking Claude could be a possibility."

"Trevor," he mumbled.

"One of the candy guys?" In my mind, I always thought of Gil and Trevor, who owned Sweet Tooth Vintage Candy, as the candy guys. Ugh. I hated to consider them. I liked them both, especially Trevor, who was a fairly regular customer with a penchant for our French-inspired linens and picnic accessories.

We stepped off the sidewalk to circumvent the few people in line at the Let's Talk Tacos truck. We both glanced over at the building where crime scene tape was X'd over the door. A. J. stuck his head so far under his collar, he looked like a turtle.

"You know, they didn't look so happy when I saw them at the grand opening," I continued, reminding myself that I had to be open to suspecting my neighbors, as much as I hated to do so. You could be right."

"I don't think I am," he replied.

"But you just said—"

"I know 'em. They're good guys. I think someone was after *me*."

We reached the parking lot to the Gazette building and A. J.'s Jeep Renegade.

"So you're not going to help me?" I asked, astonished. He was always the first to want to share information on a case.

"Okay, I'll help you. Go back to the taco truck."

I glanced at the food truck, incredulous. "What—I get you tacos and you give me information? Is this how you're going to play it?"

"I don't want tacos. Trevor was in line."

"What?" I looked back again but couldn't spot him from my vantage point.

A. J. hopped into his car and closed the door before I could say more.

If A. J. was telling me the truth, it looked like Trevor was going to be the first suspect I questioned.

CHAPTER 11

I walked past the smattering of picnic tables to see that A. J. was right—Trevor was waiting for his tacos. He was clean-cut and good looking like his husband, but with a wider waistband and a thicker head of hair.

I caught his eye as he picked up his order and turned from the truck, and we shared a smile. He lifted the bag, as if it wasn't obvious why he was there.

"My second day in a row. I can't resist," he said.

"Why resist?" I kidded.

"Hear! Hear! Life's too short. Speaking of . . ." Trevor lowered his voice and leaned in for some conspiratorial gossip, "Did you hear what happened over there last night?" He nodded toward the Gazette building.

"I sure did. It's awful. Did you know the journalist who died?"

"He was in the shop all the time. He had a bad sweet tooth. Bad for him, good for us. It made me wonder if he went into some kind of diabetic coma or something, but now the crime scene tape's on the door. What's that all about?"

I hesitated. I wasn't going to be the town crier,

especially since I was one of the persons of interest. "I'm not sure."

"I thought you'd get some inside info from Detective Tall, Dark, and Handsome. He's still your guy, isn't he?"

I felt a bubbly tingle at the mention of Heath. "We're dating. Nothing official."

"Gil and I knew we were meant for each other right away. Neither of us would've been able to handle the whole 'just dating' thing."

"We're both pretty used to being independent," I said, wondering how the heck I was going to steer this conversation away from my love life and back to the murder case. Besides, it wasn't completely up to me. Heath had been widowed and was treading slowly. Pushing him to declare a commitment to me never seemed right. Or maybe I was just scared.

"Reel him in, Willa! Or someone else'll grab him up."

I smiled politely, wishing he wouldn't remind me that Heath was still up for grabs.

"I'm sorry, I sound like my mother. I just want everyone to be as happy as Gil and I are. I got lucky that finding love was easy. It's the business part that's tough. I guess you need to prioritize one or the other. That's where you've got a leg up. Your shop seems to be doing really well."

"Thank you," I replied because of the compliment but also for giving me an opening to talk about their candy shop. "Your shop looks great. You've been in business longer than I have."

"It's been a struggle every year, though." His bouncy demeanor from earlier had deflated.

"It probably doesn't help with a new chocolate shop opening in town, huh? You two didn't look so happy at the grand opening yesterday."

"Neither did you. What was *that* all about? You and the chocolate grand master seemed to be getting into it on the sidewalk."

I felt my cheeks warm in embarrassment and shook my head as if it were nothing. "I kind of know him."

"Ooh, do tell! You have dirt on him?" He chucked me lightly with his elbow to spur me on.

How did this get turned around to me? "No, I don't have any dirt. I just don't much like him."

Trevor's grin collapsed. "Oh. Well, that makes three of us. No wonder Hope kept the whole thing a secret. Gil thinks it was out of guilt because we gave her the idea."

"You gave her the idea to pair with a chocolate shop?"

"Of course not! We told her about six months ago we were making changes to that extra room we've never used so we could start doing chocolate-making classes. We need to do something to bring in a little extra. We even talked with her about possible cross promotion once we got it going."

"Really? And then she partnered with a chocolatier?"

"Exactly! And we were friends with her! Or we thought we were, but she never even gave us a heads-up about it when she signed the contracts with the Chocolate Bliss people. Going into business side by side doesn't happen overnight, especially one that needs a liquor license."

That didn't sound like Hope. There had to be an explanation.

"Anyway, I've gotta get back with lunch. Lucky there

wasn't a line, or Gil would be hangry by the time I got back," he continued.

I looked behind him, noticing the lack of customers. He was right. It had to be lunchtime by now but there were only three people getting tacos. The line would usually snake down the sidewalk at this time of day.

I heard a *ding, ding* emanate from Trevor's pocket.

"See? I bet you it's Gil wondering if I ate his tacos and had to go back for a second round. It wouldn't be the first time." He giggled as he took the phone out of his pocket, but as soon as he looked at the message, his laughter was extinguished.

"Is everything okay?" I asked, worried that something had happened to Gil.

He didn't look up from his phone. "Gil says there was some community notification on his phone earlier that he missed. I don't even sign up for those things," he said as he scrolled the message. "He copied it for me. Oh my gosh. It says not to eat or drink anything you may have received from Chocolate Bliss or Hope's Cakery yesterday, but to bring it immediately to the police station. If you feel ill, see your doctor or go to the hospital immediately." Trevor looked up at me, questioning.

I pulled out my own phone and looked at the warning. It came out while I was in the interview room without cell service. It was titled Poison Warning.

"What does this mean?" Trevor asked, alarmed.

I panicked, knowing exactly what it meant—that everyone in town was now aware that the Chocolate Bliss chocolates had been poisoned.

CHAPTER 12

I walked back to Curds & Whey with the hollow feeling of what happened to Kevin Wallace overshadowing my former excitement about the birthday celebration for my shop. The first time I'd been a person of interest in a homicide investigation was around the time of my shop's grand opening event, and now here I was on our second anniversary facing something similar. This time was different, I reminded myself. I trusted Heath to clear my name. But that didn't mean I didn't want to get to the truth on my own.

I could feel myself beginning to seethe again when I thought how different today would've been had Pearce and Riley not come to Yarrow Glen. But was that fair? Would someone have found a different way to kill Kevin or was it about the chocolates? Or was A. J. right in thinking he was the target? I prayed nobody else had been a victim of any more poisoned chocolates.

I paused on the corner where Curds & Whey was and looked down the street at Hope's Cakery. As if the community notification wasn't bad enough, a police cruiser was still parked in front of her shop, announcing to anyone who hadn't already heard that something was amiss. Poor Hope. Her brand-new business got taken down along with the poisoned Chocolate Bliss chocolates. Would it ever recover?

I had to put aside my thoughts as I approached my shop. It was time to make this the best birthday party possible.

My mood was immediately uplifted when I walked inside and saw Mrs. Schultz. It was Switzerland hour and, despite being one person down, she had still managed to change into a blue dress with an abundance of faux lace at the collar, a half apron, and white stockings. I chuckled to myself, wondering how many doilies from Beatrice's thrift shop were sacrificed for that collar.

Mrs. Schultz and I shared a smile as she led a customer to the register where Claude awaited them. Mine soon faded, however, as I looked around the shop, which was surprisingly sparse of people.

I proceeded to our Cheeseboard Café at the rear of the shop where Archie was in charge of the raclette warmer. His outfit was just as impressive as Mrs. Schultz's. He wore a white shirt buttoned down the front and rolled up at the sleeves above his elbows. He'd added a tassel to the side of each leg of his khaki shorts, but it was the suspenders and knee socks that really put it over the top, and the Robin Hood style hat that I thought I remembered seeing him in at Christmas time when he'd dressed as an elf. A lone couple stood by the kitchenette's island, watching as he warmed the half wheel to just the right temperature and, with long motions, scraped the luscious cheese onto a bowl of potatoes. They sat at one of our bistro tables and June brought it over, along with two glasses of mead they'd ordered.

I waited until the couple was immersed in their meal

and conversation before I spoke quietly to Archie and June. "It looked like we were getting a crowd this morning. Has it been like this since I've been gone?"

"Didn't you get the community text?" Archie asked.

I sighed. "I saw it just before I came back."

"Word got around pretty fast afterward that the chocolates were you-know-what," Archie said, avoiding the word *poisoned*.

"I think people are afraid to eat from *any* shop now," June whispered.

"Oh great." The pit in my stomach was back. They needed to warn people somehow, but this was disastrous.

"Did either of you eat any? How do you feel?" I asked, suddenly anxious about much more than a drop in sales.

"I had Hope's cake sample yesterday, and I feel fine," Archie said.

"Me too. I don't like rum, so I skipped the rum crème samples," June said.

"Did you see Hope?" Archie asked. His concern for her was written all over his face.

"I didn't see her at the police station. Do you want to take your break and find her? It looks like we can handle this for a while without you."

"Thanks, Willa. I'd like to check in on her." He turned off the warmer and hurried to the front of the shop and out the door before I had the chance to remind him that he was dressed like a yodeler. Well, maybe it would cheer up Hope.

"I feel bad for Duncan too," June said. She tucked a strand of brown hair behind her ear that had escaped from her clip. "He was so excited yesterday when I saw him at the opening."

"That's right, you know him." I recalled her saying as much when she saw him.

She nodded. "His family's lived next door to mine since forever and our moms are good friends. I saw him around town the past few weeks, but I didn't know why he was back home. He's good at keeping a secret—he never said a word about them opening a Chocolate Bliss here. He seemed happy to be back home, though."

That aligned with what Pearce had said about this shop being Duncan's idea. Since he was from Lockwood, it made sense. "So you two haven't kept in touch?" I needed to get a better read on Duncan and hoped June could provide it.

"I only hear stuff about him through our moms. We didn't go to school together—he's older. My brother sometimes hung out with him, but Duncan left Lockwood after graduation. Now I guess he'll have to leave again. His mom will hate that. Unless this is going to close their main store too? Oh gosh." June shook her head at the thought.

Claude had left his station at the register and joined us in the kitchenette. "We're not serving Hope's cheesecake, are we? It could be poisoned!"

"Shhh!" I shushed Claude so the two customers we had at the café wouldn't overhear.

Too late. They already had their phones out and were talking in earnest. I got the sense the woman wanted to leave, but the man wanted to stay and finish his raclette and potatoes.

I walked over to them. "How is everything?"

"This cheese is awesome," the man said.

"We're running late, though. We really need to go. Don't we, Martin?" She glared at him so he wouldn't give the wrong answer.

He sighed with resignation, looking longingly at the blanket of raclette over his potatoes. "All right, but can I bring the rest with me?"

I was about to tell him he could when she stood and whispered loudly in his ear, "Not unless you want to end up in a hospital! I knew we should've gone to the winery instead. Come on!" She gave me a pinched smile and threw one last glare at him before he finally gave in and reluctantly left the shop and his cheesy potatoes.

"Sorry," Claude mumbled.

I let it go—I was pretty sure they'd gotten the news from their phones anyway.

"No, I'm not serving the cheesecake," I belatedly answered him. "It's at the police station."

June cleaned up after our quick-stop patrons and I gave Claude a second look, wondering if he could've really been the one to poison those chocolates just to get back at Hope. Was that why he didn't mind spreading the P-word around—to do as much damage to Hope's business as possible? If that was the case, he was now working for me, which meant I had to tread lightly.

"Archie's checking on Hope. I imagine you must be worried about her," I said to him.

"There's no coming back from this, is there? I think it's karma, don't you?" He leaned against the marble-topped island. "I warned her not to bite the hand that feeds her."

"What do you mean?" Was he admitting to threatening Hope?

"Rise and Shine was around for almost a quarter century when she inherited it. I don't think she appreciated what it takes to keep a place in business for that long or she wouldn't have been in such a rush to change it. I know for a fact she didn't appreciate what it took to run it day-to-day like I did the past two years. I kept that place humming while she took her little cake classes and went off to Paris, only to come back and decide she's not doing bread anymore."

I could attest that he wasn't exaggerating when he said he kept the place afloat without her, but his resentment made me even more suspicious of him. Under other circumstances, I'd have defended Hope—she was a little immature at times, but running a business was hard. I could never have done it on my own in my early twenties, as she was doing. But I had to keep that to myself for now. I wanted to hear more about how Claude really felt.

"It sounds like she left you in the dark," I said.

"She said she wanted to make it more of a cake bakery than it was, but she never told me she was doing away with bread completely. Personally, I think it's because she could never get herself out of bed before ten a.m. Remember when she had Archie opening the place for her? Poor lovesick kid. Glad he snapped out of it."

June, who was washing the wineglasses at the sink, spoke up. "I don't think making cakes is a . . . cakewalk either. It seems like she's pretty good at it."

"Yeah, okay, I'll admit she's got a talent for it," Claude replied. He screwed up his mouth, seemingly unhappy to concede the point, but his anger had deflated. "I sacrificed for years trying to get my bread business off the ground before I had to finally let it go. It's just frustrating to see her inherit a thriving bakery and throw it away the way she has."

He joined June at the sink to dry the glasses and I

gave up on the idea I'd get any more hidden truths from Claude.

As I left them to their task, I heard him say under his breath, "I'd have killed to be handed something like Rise and Shine."

I stared at the back of Claude, wondering how literally I should take his words.

"Happy Birthday!" The pronouncement was made with a flourish from the front door. Beatrice, in her late sixties, entered the cheese shop holding more costumes. As well as being an expert seamstress, she also owned a highly curated shop of thrifted and vintage items, many of which made their way into her own wardrobe, as well. Today over her tall, thin frame, she wore wide-legged jeans embroidered with vines of flowers and a short-sleeved collared sweater with green circles. She paired it with green high-tops. Her long silver hair was pulled back on either side with green gemstone combs and left to flow down to the middle of her back. Blue-framed glasses hung around her neck from a bejeweled chain. A few more steps in with a better view of the shop, her high spirits dimmed. "What happened? This place was packed when I stopped here this morning."

Mrs. Schultz and I took the load from her arms. They looked like the costumes for the Greek hour we'd scheduled for later today.

"Poisoned chocolates," Claude answered, joining us up front.

"Claude, would you mind taking these and hanging them in my office?" I asked, thoroughly fed up with hearing the word *poisoned*.

Claude dutifully took the costumes off our hands and brought them to the back.

"I heard! Scary stuff, but what does that have to do with you?" Beatrice asked.

"Apparently people are afraid to get food from anywhere in town now."

"I wonder how Lou's Market is doing," Mrs. Schultz pondered.

"That explains why the bookstore café was almost empty when I went in for a snack. It's starting to feel like a ghost town around here," Beatrice said.

"Did you try the chocolates?" I asked her.

"I wanted to, but I was working on the costumes yesterday. I didn't want Archie to have chocolate fingerprints on his pantaloons. I do love chocolate, though, especially with a dab of rum in it. What a shame."

Having visited with Beatrice in her apartment, I could attest to her fondness for rum.

"I guess I should get back to my shop, although I doubt there'll be anyone there but me and Sweet Potato," Beatrice said, referring to her plump orange cat. She walked out with a lot less enthusiasm than when she'd entered.

I scanned Curds & Whey. The celebratory decorations that had caused so much excitement when they went up were now imbued with disappointment. The fallout was affecting everyone, like a line of toppled dominoes. Would poisoned chocolates taint the reputation of every business in Yarrow Glen?

CHAPTER 13

By six o'clock, Archie, Mrs. Schultz, and I had already finished most of the closing duties and shut the door on our disappointing day just as Baz stopped in.

"I'm glad you're here. We need to have a Team Cheese meeting now," I said, locking the door behind him.

It was just Archie, Mrs. Schultz, Baz, and me—the original Team Cheese crew, a name we'd given ourselves whenever we'd get together to investigate a murder. We retreated to the hand-hewn picnic table that separated the bistro area from the kitchenette. Even with the changeover to the Cheeseboard Café and the addition of cute little bistro tables and chairs, I wasn't going to give up our favorite meeting spot. Archie and Mrs. Schultz had switched out of their costumes back to their regular clothes—him in cargo shorts and a T-shirt, her in a mid-calf-length floral dress, cinched at the waist.

"I take it this is about the poisoned chocolates," Baz said.

"So you heard the news?" Archie replied, throwing a leg over one of the benches, straddling it.

"Why do you think I didn't make it in this afternoon

for your birthday bash? Every client whose house I went to wanted to talk about it."

"Anyone with any interesting theories?" I asked.

"No, but a lot of them who ate one of those free samples yesterday or chocolates they bought went to their doctor today, convinced they'd been poisoned."

"That explains why the chocolates also poisoned people's desire to try *any* food in Yarrow Glen," I said glumly.

Archie sighed heavily, frowning. "Our birthday bash was a bust."

The weight of any bad circumstance hit me even harder when Archie was down, as it happened so infrequently.

"I'm sorry. That stinks! And not in, like, a cheese way," Baz said.

This cut a sliver of light into my dark mood. "Are you finally appreciating the funk of some of our cheeses?" I asked him. I'd been working on getting Baz to venture beyond cheddar since I'd met him.

"Let's not get crazy. I just didn't want to disparage the product while we're in the house of cheese."

I chuckled. "Much appreciated."

Mrs. Schultz continued to be serious. "Detective Heath brought Willa down to the station. You still haven't told us what happened there," she said to me.

"Uh-oh," Baz said, suddenly serious again too.

I stood from the bench. "This calls for a meal. Let's fire up that raclette warmer again and throw it on some prosciutto sandwiches. We have leftover crusty French baguettes from Lou's Market."

"I'm in!" Archie popped off the bench and set up the raclette and warmer.

"I wonder if Lou's feeling the pinch too," Mrs. Schultz

said almost to herself, concerned about Lou once again. "It was nice of him to stop by for the birthday bash today."

"It was," I agreed, smiling to myself. I knew Lou's interest had little to do with our celebration.

All four of us stood at the island making the sandwiches assembly-line style: sliced baguettes warmed in the oven, swiped with whole grain mustard, topped with slices of prosciutto, and finally slathered with thick melty layers of raclette.

We worked in easy tandem while I told them what happened at the police station with Shep, A. J., and Pearce and Riley.

"Your ex-fiancé asked for your help?" Baz was so surprised, his focus even left the food for a moment.

"That man's got some gall playing on your sympathies!" Mrs. Schultz harrumphed as we sat at the table with our sandwiches. Archie brought over a ramekin of cornichons from the fridge.

"I have mixed feelings about helping him, but I do want to help all our other shop owners, me included. And I'd like to get off the person-of-interest list. I should've never taken those chocolates to A. J. Maybe Claude was right about karma." I'd suddenly lost my appetite.

"You think Hope deserved this?" Archie looked up from his sandwich, eyes widened.

"No, not at all. I didn't mean karma for Hope, I meant for me. I originally wanted to bring A. J. those chocolates so I could try to sway his opinion before his review by telling him about Pearce and Riley. That's not a nice thing to do, regardless of how I feel about them personally. I'm sure they've worked hard to get to where they're at. Their chocolates might've deserved an incredible review. I was willing to let my personal vendetta get in the way of that."

Mrs. Schultz patted me on the shoulder. "Who could blame you?"

"The police, for one. Revenge is a motive. What happened did ruin their chances here in Yarrow Glen. Possibly at their shops back in Oregon too." My appetite hadn't returned but eating anything cheesy had little to do with my hunger level—cheese helped in almost any situation. I picked up the sandwich, trying to figure out the best way to eat it. It was as messy as this case.

"Well, we know *you* didn't kill him. Let's figure out our suspects." Baz had no problem with the sandwich, allowing any excess cheese to ooze onto his plate.

"We should do a murder board!" Archie added, already on his second napkin.

"Can we call it something different, please?" Mrs. Schultz asked. She was all for the drama of an investigation, but of the more cozy kind.

"We don't have a board for it anyway. But let's go through the possible motives. Pearce thinks it's sabotage," I said.

"Who would want to see Chocolate Bliss go down?" Baz asked.

I thought about this. "I hate to say it, but the obvious suspects might be the candy guys, Gil and Trevor. They seemed pretty upset at the opening."

"They sell those retro candy bars, so the adult customer base could overlap," Mrs. Schultz said, nodding. She rubbed her light linen scarf between her fingers, a sure sign her investigative brain was working overtime.

"Not only that, but they'd told Hope they planned

to start making some chocolate and holding chocolate-making classes, and she turned around and partnered with Chocolate Bliss. I talked to Trevor this afternoon, and he didn't deny that he and Gil were upset with her about it. They feel like she kind of stole their idea for it and their opportunity."

"Hope wouldn't do that," Archie said. "She must've already had this in the works."

"The bottom line is, they blame her, plus Chocolate Bliss encroaches on their business, which makes them pretty good suspects," Baz said, trying one of the pickles.

"But how could they have known about those chocolates for A. J. in order to poison them?" Mrs. Schultz asked.

We all agreed they might have motive, but no opportunity.

"Hope was really hoping it would work out and Chocolate Bliss would stay permanently. She's been worried about money lately. She wouldn't admit to it, but I think all that time she spent in Paris depleted a lot of that inheritance she got from her father's family," Archie said. He put down his sandwich, his eagerness about the case tempered by thoughts of Hope.

"How is Hope doing?" I asked. Archie had looked pretty down when he'd returned from seeing her on his break earlier, so I'd wanted to give him some time before asking about her.

"She's a wreck. Everyone's canceling their orders. And the ones who still want cakes, she's not even sure if she can deliver on. The police made a mess of her kitchen."

"That's awful. Poor Hope," Mrs. Schultz said, patting Archie's hand.

"She's scared too. She has no idea why anyone would do this."

"So far we don't have any suspects if the motive is sabotage, except Gil and Trevor who don't have opportunity."

"What about Claude?" I ventured.

"Claude from the bakery? The guy you just hired?" Baz asked.

"I talked to him, and he seemed kind of mad that Hope changed the bread bakery. He and Pearce also butted heads for the short time they worked together. Pearce didn't seem to like him either," I said.

Archie, Mrs. Schultz, and I glanced at each other, gauging our thoughts on the matter.

"He could still have a key to Hope's cakery," Mrs. Schultz said tentatively.

"She uses a code lock on the back door where employees come in. If she hasn't changed the code, he could be the one with motive *and* opportunity," Archie agreed.

"Let's write his name down," I said, reluctantly.

"What if the motive wasn't sabotage? If it was simply a case of murder, who was it directed at, Kevin the reporter, or A. J.?" Mrs. Schultz wondered.

"That's a whole separate motive category, Sabotage or murder?" Baz said, working on the last of his sandwich.

"We need a board," Archie contended again. He left the table and opened one of the drawers from the kitchenette. He came back with a pad of sticky notes and a pen. "We'll use these on the table for now."

He handed them to Mrs. Schultz who had better handwriting. She wrote "Sabotage" on one and "Murder" on another. Archie stuck them on the table.

"Write down Claude's name and the candy guys. I'll put their names under *Sabotage*," Archie said.

Mrs. Schultz wrote "Claude" on one sticky and "Trevor and Gil" on another, with "No opp" underneath the candy guys' names.

"We need one for Kevin, the reporter, and another one for A. J.," he continued.

Mrs. Schultz made notes for them too, which Archie placed under *Murder*.

"Wait, that doesn't make sense. Are we doing possible suspects or possible victims?" Baz asked, staring at the notes on our murder table.

"New category!" Archie announced. "These are in the wrong spot."

Mrs. Schultz used another note to write "Possible Victims."

"Okay, so we have two choices for possible victims," she said, handing them over to Archie.

I was silent, staring at the sticky notes before me, which brought my mind back to yesterday at the cakery. "Maybe three possible victims," I spoke up.

"Who's the third?" Baz asked.

"Me," I squeaked out, almost afraid to voice the scary thought I just had.

"You?" they uttered at once.

I told them about the mix-up of my order at the cakery and how A. J.'s chocolates had looked like they were meant for me. "If someone tampered with them while they were in the cakery . . ."

"Who would be after you? Pearce? Riley? Surely not!" Mrs. Schultz said.

"I don't wanna make you nervous, Wil, but it does seem like a big coincidence that your exes showed up here. Maybe it wasn't just to open a shop," Baz considered.

"Basil, that's just silly. Don't worry Willa like that."

Mrs. Schultz used Baz's full name, the only one who could get away with doing so.

"He's not, Mrs. Schultz. It's gone through my mind, but I can't understand why they would. We've had no contact since he broke off our engagement. And if they did have a problem with me, wouldn't they poison my cheese instead of their own chocolate?"

Archie and Baz held their mostly eaten sandwiches in their hands, and both froze, staring at them.

"Oh, come on, not you too! My cheese hasn't been poisoned. Someone had opportunity with the chocolates. They were either poisoned at Hope's Cakery or at the Gazette after I left them on A. J.'s desk."

"So let's narrow it down from there. Who was working at Hope's that day?" Baz asked.

"Jasmine. She could've felt the same as Claude and resented Chocolate Bliss coming in and practically taking over," I said.

"I don't know. I can't imagine Jasmine hurting an innocent person because she was mad at Hope," Archie said. He knew Jasmine better than the rest of us.

"And it's jeopardized her job now. Wouldn't it have been easier just to quit?" Mrs. Schultz added, reluctantly writing Jasmine's name on a sticky note.

"We have to put everyone on the board—or table—just in case," I said, recalling what Pearce had pointed out about the necessity to suspect our neighbors. I took the note and stuck it under Suspects.

"The manager of Chocolate Bliss must've had access to the chocolates," Mrs. Schultz said, tapping her pen on a new sticky note.

"Duncan," I provided. "June grew up next door to him. She said he's been working at the Chocolate Bliss shop in Oregon for a long time."

"Was he unhappy about a new shop opening here in Yarrow Glen?" Archie asked.

"Pearce and Riley said it was his idea. It's near Lockwood and June said he was happy to be back home," I replied. "I'll have to see if there's anything more she knows about him."

Archie had taken out his phone and been tapping at it for the past few minutes. When the table got quiet, he explained. "Baz said his clients thought they felt sick, so I was looking to see if the news reported that anyone else got sick or died from the chocolates. There's an article on it that says there's been no hospitalizations, but there was an uptick in urgent-care visits. Some people saying they had diarrhea—sorry—and others wanting to know if they could get their stomachs pumped because they ate one of the samples."

"I was almost done, but that finished it for me," Baz said, putting down the last of his sandwich.

"But nobody's been really sick? That's good. You can hardly blame people for freaking out that they might've been poisoned," I said.

"If none of the other chocolate was poisoned, then it was targeted. The poisoned chocolates were meant for either A. J. or Kevin." Archie moved their sticky notes to the top of the table. "Or . . ." Archie looked at me almost apologetically.

"Or me," I said what he couldn't.

"I thought we already decided that wasn't possible," Baz said.

I thought about it. "Maybe not probable, but it's possible. Duncan knew right away they weren't meant for me, but maybe someone put them by my cheesecake because they wanted them to come to me."

"Who could possibly want to kill you? What reason

could they have?" Mrs. Schultz asked, still not accepting the possibility.

"She's got a point," Baz agreed.

I was starting to feel better.

Baz continued, "I mean, sure, you get cranky when you're stressed, and you're a little manic when you've got an event coming up, and you're annoying when—"

"Okay! Okay!" I stopped him and kept myself from laughing.

Baz cackled—I knew he was teasing me. That was the kind of friendship we had. He could never fill the shoes of my little brother, but our relationship felt comfortably familiar to that one. He always knew how to make me feel better.

"Besides, if someone wanted you dead, poisoned chocolates would be the worst way they could try to do it. You'd never eat them," Archie added.

"Thanks, guys. You're right. There's no reason I would've been the target." I knew it was silly. Thank goodness for my friends.

Mrs. Schultz had been working her scarf in thought.

"What is it?" I asked her.

"If someone poisoned a batch of the chocolates when they were made, they might've not known *who* would eat them. Maybe it was like Russian roulette where it could've been anybody. If sabotage was the motive, the death would make the news no matter who'd been killed."

That was an even scarier thought.

CHAPTER 14

We needed more information before we could continue to speculate, so Team Cheese called it a night. Archie insisted on cleaning the raclette warmer before leaving.

"I've got to get to my penny poker night with the gals," Mrs. Schultz said, collecting the plates.

"You should've told me it was your poker night. We didn't have to do this tonight. You go on." I took the plates from her and brought them to the sink.

"No, this will work out fine. It's at Sylvia's tonight, and as much as I love her, I don't love being a guinea pig to the experimental dishes she whips up when she hosts. I hit my limit with her lime cabbage Jell-O mold."

Baz and Archie made a face.

"Not even cheese sounds like it could fix that one," I said.

"It was a lost cause, but we were polite about it, of course. It's a balancing act between not hurting her feelings but not wanting her to make it again," she said with a chuckle.

"I've got a few extra minutes. Do you want me to drive you? I can throw your bike in the back of my truck," Baz offered.

"No thank you, Basil," Mrs. Schultz said, already clicking her bicycle helmet on. "She lives on my street. I'll get there just in time to make it for poker and chocolate martinis. Good night! And Willa, please don't worry."

"Thanks, Mrs. Schultz. Be safe. Good night."

She left out the front door.

"Where are you off to?" I asked Baz.

"I've got a date at The Cellar tonight," he answered. The Cellar was the pub at the inn.

"With Constance?"

"No, not with Constance." He rolled his eyes at the mention of the inn's reception clerk, who seemed giddy whenever I saw them talking.

"Don't act like it's so preposterous. Every time I meet you to grab dinner at The Cellar, you two are chatting it up at her reception desk."

"She's easy to talk to and I like keeping her company when it's slow. You know we're just friends."

I knew, but I thought he was silly for not asking her out. "Well then, who's the date with?" I wasn't about to let him leave without getting *some* details.

Archie looked up from wiping down the warming machine, interested too.

"Her name's Sherry. Roman set me up."

Roman, the owner of Golden Glen Meadery across the street, was a friend of ours.

"He didn't want her for himself?" I asked, being snarky. I couldn't help it. Roman was known to have dated almost every single woman within his age range, me included for several months.

"No, and I guess I'm about to find out why," Baz said with a wink.

"Well, I hope it goes well."

"Don't get your hopes up. You know I don't have the best track record."

"Your track record for hilarious bad date stories has been above par, though," Archie chimed in.

"He's right about that," I agreed.

Baz chuckled. "Hey, Arch, you around later if my date night tanks?"

"No. I'm meeting June for a double feature at the Lockwood Cinema—both Godzilla versus Kong movies."

"Now that's a cool date," Baz said.

"It's not a date. A bunch of us are going together," Archie replied, now concentrating on his task.

"Cool. You got plans with Heath tonight?" he asked me.

"Not yet. Text me when you get back just in case."

"Will do. I gotta get showered. See ya." Baz followed Mrs. Schultz's path out the front door.

Archie moved onto washing the dishes.

"Leave them. You get home," I swatted his arm and offered him a dish towel to dry his hands.

"I'm practically done," he said, refusing.

I kept the towel and dried the plates.

"I'm glad to hear you and June still hang out. You two were fast friends right off the bat and then it seemed like it cooled off?"

"It hasn't cooled off. We're still friends. It went through some changes, you know, with her coming to work here." He began washing the plates in earnest. "And then with Hope coming back from Europe."

"Ah," I said, understanding. I didn't think her working here was the issue, as they were both excited about it at the time and always worked well together. The issue was Archie's ex-girlfriend, Hope.

He handed me the last dish and finally looked at me. "Yeah. June doesn't really understand my relationship with Hope."

"To tell you the truth, I'm not sure I do either. What *is* your relationship with Hope?" I asked, handing Archie the towel.

He dried his hands and sat on the farm table's bench. "I don't know. We're friends, I guess. She calls me when she wants to hang out or when she's stressed about something."

I leaned against the marble island in front of Archie. "I hope it's okay for me to say this, Archie, but that sounds like a pretty one-sided relationship."

He nodded slowly. "Yeah, I know. She was worried a lot when she came back from Paris and then she had so much going on with changing over the bakery, so I just wanted to help her through all of that. She shut me out the past few weeks, keeping Chocolate Bliss a secret, but now with what happened, she's scared. I don't want to feel like I'm abandoning her."

I sat on the bench beside him. "You're such a nice person. I wouldn't want to ever change that about you. I just don't want you to be taken advantage of, that's all."

He leaned over, forearms on his knees, and worked his hands. "You're not the only one who's said that to me."

"You do what feels right to you. Everybody does things in their own time."

"That's a nice way of saying I'll learn the hard way, huh?" he said with a slight grin, rising from the bench.

I laughed and gave him a hug. "I think we all do at one time or another. Especially when it comes to love."

He swiped his phone from the table, and we walked to the front door.

"Have fun at the movies," I told him.

"I will."

I walked outside with him to a chilly evening. The street was quiet. All the shops were long closed, The Kick Stand's bicycles put inside, the crates of produce from Lou's Market no longer under the awning. The shadows from the streetlamps shifted on the sidewalk with the movement of crape myrtle blossoms in the breeze. Our section of Pleasant Avenue was the last block of the downtown businesses—the street ended in a T at Hope's Cakery—so after business hours, there was little activity.

Instead of continuing on to his apartment across the alley, Archie stood outside the door staring down the street toward Hope's Cakery.

"Archie, what's the matter?"

"There's a car parked in front of Hope's, but her apartment and the cakery look dark." He plucked his phone out of his shorts pocket and glanced at it, then put it back. "She's been texting me all day since finding out about the murder, but I haven't gotten any from her in the last hour."

Archie stepped off the curb to get a better look at the recessed part of the cakery, which was where Hope's apartment was located.

"I can check on her if it'll make you feel better," I said.

"That's okay, I've got time. I'll stop over."

"If something's up, you shouldn't be there alone. Let's both go."

I quickly locked the door to Curds & Whey, and we walked the now nearly deserted street to the cakery.

We approached the car parked in a diagonal spot directly in front of Hope's. It looked like an older model sedan. A quick peek revealed it was unoccupied. Archie was first to the front door of Hope's apartment. Not a single lamp shone in the windows. Archie knocked on her door. We waited, but the only sound was a car in the distance. While Archie knocked again, I went to the front of the cakery and took a look through the rectangle of paned windows beneath the awning. Inside was dark except for the low lights in the display cases, but I saw a glow through the round window of the swinging door to the kitchen.

"Does she keep a light on in the kitchen?" I asked.

He left her apartment door to join me. "I don't think so."

"I bet she's in the kitchen then." I knocked on the front door of the bakery.

Archie stuck his nose to the shop door's window and cupped his hands to his face to get a better look. "She told me the police and forensics team ruined it, and she'd have to get it professionally cleaned."

"There ya go. She's probably cleaning it and isn't checking her messages."

He looked at me skeptically. "Hope? Cleaning? And why is there some random car parked here?" He called her phone while I rapped on the door. I heard the phone ring from his end three times until her voicemail picked up. "Hey, just checking on you. Give me a call to let me know you're okay." Archie ended the call, even antsier than before. He kept his gaze trained on the round window of the swinging kitchen door. My pulse was picking up pace too, but I told myself to be logical. There was no reason to be worried. Was there?

"Did you see that?" Archie said. "I just saw someone pass by the window. Someone's in the kitchen!"

Now *he* began rapping on the door, but still no one appeared inside.

I wrapped my hand around my phone, ready to call 9-1-1. Although my tingly senses told me something was up, logic prevailed. If Hope was immersed in mopping, the last thing she needed was more police in front of her shop.

"Let's see if her car's even here." I left the front of the shop.

With one last look inside, Archie followed me to the back of her apartment. The delivery van she'd recently swapped her car for was missing from her private parking space, which was separated from the lot behind the cakery that could accommodate a couple of dozen cars. A lone car sat in the lot, parked in the shadows.

"Maybe Pearce and Riley are here," I said.

"They shouldn't be here without Hope." He trotted over to the back door of the cakery.

"Archie, wait a sec—"

Too late—he pressed the buzzer.

We waited expectantly for the door to open. I slipped my hand in my pocket and wrapped it around my phone. I looked around the parking lot, barely illuminated by a single weak light and the bulb over the door that was attracting moths. I looked at the car again, which seemed to be waiting in the shadows—smallish, maybe a spoiler on the back? Was I imagining it or was someone sitting in the driver's seat?

The sound of the cakery's back door clunking open startled me. Duncan appeared on the other side.

"Hey man, what's up?" he said to Archie.

"I was looking for Hope," Archie replied, trying to peer past him.

"We're having a little meeting," Duncan replied, not stepping aside to let us in.

"Really? Because her van's not here," Archie said in a stony tone, starting to push his way in. I'd never seen Archie like this.

"Archie, is that you?" a voice called from inside.

Duncan finally stepped aside as Hope approached. Jasmine appeared in the corner of the kitchen, looking like she'd rather be somewhere else.

"Hi, guys. What are you doing here?" Hope asked, brows furrowed in confusion.

We stepped all the way inside, and the door closed behind us with another clunk.

I sensed Archie's relief at seeing Hope. My tension eased, as well. We'd overreacted.

"We saw lights on, but your van isn't here. We just came to make sure everything was all right," Archie answered. He still sounded uncertain that it was.

Her face lightened, but just as quickly creased in misery. "The police took my van overnight. They must think I was the one who poisoned those chocolates because they're doing their tests on it."

"I'm sorry," I said.

"Better they rule you out right away," Archie said, trying to look on the bright side.

Hope pushed up the sleeves of her cropped sweatshirt. "I hope they don't make as much of a mess as they did in here."

Her distress was evident with a glance at the kitchen. Gray powder was left on the surfaces and faint footprints marred the tile floor. The metal shelves of cake pans were in disarray. A shelf on the opposite wall of the kitchen stood empty. The police must've also confiscated Chocolate Bliss's molds.

"I'll help you clean it," Archie offered.

"There's no way I want to clean this. It makes me too sad. I spent so much time and money renovating this kitchen. All new stainless tables, new blenders, a new oven, everything but the walk-in freezer. I even bought all new cake pans. But look at it now."

She barely looked before she turned and headed toward the swinging door on the opposite end of the kitchen. She went through it to the front of the shop. The four of us looked at one another and followed. She'd flicked the lights on and was standing on the other side of the counter like a customer, staring up at her neon Hope's Cakery sign.

"Sorry, I can't stand to see the mess in there," she said, wiping her eyes.

Archie went to her side.

"I know it's hard," Duncan spoke up.

She scratched her head, mussing her pixie-style hair, then straightened it again with one swipe of her hand. She stood straighter, seeming to want to move on from the pity party. "Duncan, you've met Archie, right? And this is Willa from the cheese shop across the street."

We gave each other a quick smile.

"You guys met yesterday," Jasmine said.

Duncan's eyes sparked recognition. He pointed at me. "Right. You were the one who took the chocolates to the Gazette."

Was I being too sensitive, or did he say it with an accusing tone? I took a beat and channeled Mrs. Schultz's investigative motto: you catch more flies with honey than with vinegar. I ignored the perceived jab and said, "I hate to be attached to this, even peripherally. I can imagine how hard this is for you."

He stuck his hands in his jeans pockets. "Can you?

If it was your cheese that was poisoned, how would you feel? This obliterated my future."

Was he threatening me?

"Hey, dude, she's trying to offer you sympathy," Archie spoke up.

"I don't need sympathy from the person who might be responsible."

"What?" *He was accusing* me*?*

Duncan continued, "Pearce and Riley told me about you. They said you hate them. Did you poison the chocolates to try to get back at them?"

I was too stunned to speak.

Hope went to Duncan's side and entwined her arm in his, as if physically restraining him would hold back his words. "I know you're upset, but Willa wouldn't do something like that," she told him.

I was relieved to hear her defend me. "Thank you, Hope. No, I wouldn't. And I didn't. Regardless of my past with Pearce and Riley, I'd never do anything to hurt someone, much less kill them."

Duncan sighed and looked at the floor, running a hand through his hair. "Then I'm sorry. My life went from the best to the worst in less than twenty-four hours."

Hope stepped away from him. "You're not the only one, you know."

He softened. "I know. I'm sorry, I'm just trying to figure out who did this so I can salvage my business. *Our* businesses," he corrected.

"I can assure you, it wasn't me," I said.

He glanced at me, and I wasn't sure if he looked apologetic or uncertain.

"We're going to have to do this another time," he said to Hope. "Jas, do you need a lift home?"

"No, I'm meeting my friends at The Cellar," Jasmine replied.

Duncan strode to the front door.

"You don't have to go," Hope said to his back, but he turned the bolt lock and walked out.

"Duncan!" Hope followed him out, closing the door behind her.

The three of us looked at one another uncomfortably.

"Guess the meeting's over," Jasmine said. She shrugged and started toward the door.

"Jasmine." I put my hand out to signal her to wait a moment. "If you guys were having a meeting, why aren't Pearce and Riley here?"

"Duncan wanted to brainstorm ways to get the business up and running once the case is closed. Pearce and Riley were just here to get it started, but it was supposed to be Duncan's shop. That's what he and Hope had planned."

Archie looked as surprised by this as I was.

"Did Pearce and Riley know this?" I asked. All they'd said to me was that they were letting him manage it.

"Of course. That was the deal they made. He was supposed to take over the Ashland shop, but something happened with that, so he had to look for another place. That's when a friend told him about Hope wanting to rent out some of her space."

"It didn't seem like Duncan's shop at the grand opening," Archie said.

I remembered how Pearce introduced it as his and Riley's shop and had to agree.

She shrugged again. "That's Pearce."

That I understood.

"Did you see anything suspicious when they were making the chocolates?" Archie asked Jasmine.

"I wasn't here. They did everything the day before and that morning before I got in at one o'clock."

"You didn't see who put the box of chocolates with my cheesecake?" I asked.

"No, sorry."

Hope came through the front door, and I heard Duncan's car pull away, his headlights splashing across the shop's interior through the window before it left.

"I'm sorry I broke up your meeting," I said to her, feeling responsible.

"It's my fault. I'm the one who wanted to come," Archie said.

Hope put an arm around Archie's waist. "You're always here for me."

Archie smiled and wrapped his arm around her shoulder in return.

"I'm out. Have a good night." Jasmine held up a peace sign as she continued to the front door.

"Sorry to waste your time, Jas. Thanks for coming," Hope called after her.

When she left, I said to Hope, "Thanks for defending me. I'm glad you don't think I poisoned those chocolates. Do you have any idea who might've done something like that?"

"I wish I knew." Her gaze went to the swinging door that led to the kitchen. "My brand new cakery's a mess, in every sense of the word. I was hoping this would be a new beginning for me. I should've stayed in Paris. Everything was so much better there."

Archie's arm slipped from her shoulder. I was sure that hurt him to hear, but I hoped he would take her comment with a grain of salt—she was going through a lot right now. The sooner this case was figured out, the sooner we could all get back to normal, which would hopefully mean Archie and Hope could have a straightforward discussion about their lopsided relationship.

"Were you around when they made their chocolates for your grand opening?" I asked Hope. I wanted some blanks filled in to help the investigation.

"Yeah, we shared the kitchen the day before when I made my cakes, and they made their chocolates."

"All three of them?"

"Yes. Duncan and Pearce did the chocolate, and Riley and Pearce did the crèmes. Except for the rum crèmes. Those were made entirely by Pearce, and he didn't want anybody touching them. He made a big deal out of it, which is the only reason I remember it."

"That's interesting," I said. Archie gave me a look that indicated he thought so too.

"Those are his signature chocolates. He doesn't think Duncan can make them as well as he can." She rolled her eyes.

"So what's the process of making their chocolates?"

"I don't know the exact process. I was busy making my cakes. I know they make the crèmes and put them aside. Duncan and Pearce make the chocolate and put it in the molds, then the crèmes go in, then they cover them with more chocolate, and they go in their refrigerator."

"So the crèmes might've been unattended for a while before they went in the chocolate molds?"

Hope placed her hands on her hips, her long pink nails on display. I wondered, not for the first time, how she made cakes with those. "You're trying to figure out if the chocolates were poisoned in my kitchen, aren't you?"

"Well . . ." The answer was obviously *yes*, but I wasn't sure how she would take it.

"That's what scares me. Whoever did it could've poisoned my cakes instead of the chocolates. But who would do either? None of them would ruin their business. It doesn't make sense!" She shook her head and looked again toward the kitchen.

"Somebody could've snuck in overnight and messed with the chocolates. Archie said the back door is code locked?"

"It is and we all have the code."

"You, Pearce, Riley, and Duncan?"

"Mm-hmm."

"Would any past employees know the code?" I didn't want to point the finger at Claude outright.

"We changed it after the renovations. We had too many workers coming in and out. I didn't even give it to Jasmine until the day of the grand opening just because she hadn't been around."

Hope forced my hand. "What about Claude?"

She looked surprised. "Claude? No, he quit before we changed the code. Besides, Claude wouldn't do anything."

"I know, I just like to be thorough."

I wasn't as sure about Claude as Hope was, but unless he got the code some other way, that dropped him off the suspect list.

"Do you know if the chocolates for A. J. were made separately?" I continued questioning.

"I don't think so because that was another whole fight."

Archie and I glanced at each other, eyebrows raised.

"What happened?" he asked.

Hope continued, "Pearce wanted them to be all rum crèmes—he wanted to make sure that's what A. J. reviewed, but Riley said there should be a variety in the box so A. J. could try their top sellers. It sounded like Pearce just wanted the recognition for himself. Duncan and Riley were always on the same side with any tiffs they had with Pearce—and believe me, they had plenty in the weeks they were here."

"Really?" It was interesting to hear that Riley and Duncan would side against Pearce.

"Yeah. Anyway, Duncan agreed with Riley, as usual, so with two against one, Pearce gave in."

"So they all knew those chocolates were going to A. J.," I confirmed.

"Of course. You don't think one of *them* did it, do you? That doesn't make sense. Why would they? I know Duncan didn't do it." She crossed her arms. "It was going to be a long summer working with Pearce, but then it would've been perfect once Duncan took over. Nothing seems to go right for me."

Archie reached out for her, and she wrapped her arms around him.

"I'm sorry this is happening to you, Hope. You don't deserve it," I said.

"Thanks. Thanks for not being mad at me about Pearce and Riley being here. I had no idea they knew you until after everything was in motion. I knew there was nothing I could do about it, but I didn't expect them to be here for long. Like I said, Duncan was the only one who was supposed to stay permanently."

"Don't worry. I don't blame you. I'm not mad," I assured her.

"I'm glad to hear you say that. I wish Gil and Trevor felt the same way. They're furious with me.

"Trevor mentioned that to me. I think they're hurt that you didn't say anything about Chocolate Bliss, especially after they told you they were planning to start making chocolate at the candy shop."

"They mentioned doing classes, that's all. Chocolate Bliss doesn't do classes, so I didn't see the conflict. I'd been thinking about sharing the bakery space with someone else and then Duncan called me when he heard about it, and it took off from there. I didn't want to say anything in case it fell through, and then Pearce said they wanted to keep it a secret for a bigger reveal. I thought it was a fun idea, especially because everybody kept telling me how much they didn't want me giving up the bread. I wanted to do what *I* wanted to do for once." She looked up at her sign again. "Maybe everyone was right. Look where it's gotten me."

"None of this is your fault," Archie said.

"Archie's right. This is just bad luck," I said.

"I need a change of luck then." Hope went behind the counter and pushed open the swinging door to switch off the kitchen lights. "Let's get out of here," she said to Archie.

"Archie, do you need a ride somewhere?" I asked quickly, as a reminder that he had plans.

"I've got a little time before I have to leave," Archie replied.

"Where are you going?" Hope asked him, clicking off the shop lights, leaving only the display cases illuminated.

"I'm going with some friends to see the Godzilla double feature."

"Godzilla?" Hope wrinkled her nose in distaste.

"That's why I didn't ask you to go," he said.

"You know me so well. You sure you can keep me company for a while?"

"I'm sure," he replied.

That was my cue to go and leave Archie to his own decisions. I followed them out the front door when something occurred to me. "Why did Duncan offer to drive Jasmine home?" I asked Hope.

"He drove her here. Her place is on the way," Hope answered.

She locked the door behind us, and we parted ways. Archie gave me a wave without looking back—not wanting to see any judgment, no doubt.

I started across the street to go home but stopped at the corner of her building. If Duncan's car was the one parked in front and Jasmine didn't bring one, whose car was parked in the lot?

I walked back to the parking lot, hurrying my steps. I'd dismissed the idea of someone being in the car the minute Duncan opened the cakery's back door. I'd just make a quick check to satisfy my curiosity.

I rounded the back of the building. The car was still there! Suddenly, the headlights snapped on, blinding me. The car powered past me noiselessly and sped out of the lot too fast, making a quick left away from downtown and then a right onto the adjacent street with barely a brake tap. Someone had been watching Hope's Cakery and didn't want to be seen.

CHAPTER 15

I let myself into my cheese shop, still thinking about the car. There was no engine sound, so it had to be electric or hybrid. I was pretty sure I saw a spoiler on the back as it disappeared down the road. Was my imagination on overdrive because there'd been a murder, or did someone involved want back into that kitchen?

I couldn't pinpoint who it might be, so I let the possibility go. With everything that had just transpired inside Hope's Cakery, I had enough to think about. Duncan was ready to blame me. It worried me that others might find out about my past with Pearce and Riley and think so too. I didn't doubt Heath would prove I wasn't involved, but that kind of gossip could cause a lot of damage quickly. It wasn't just me I was worried about—all our shops were in jeopardy if we didn't discover who poisoned those chocolates.

It didn't sound like all was rosy between Duncan and Pearce and Riley. Riley was quick to defend Duncan when I'd asked her and Pearce about him. Pearce was not. And Jasmine said Duncan always sided with Riley in arguments with Pearce. Were Duncan and Riley closer than Pearce wanted them to be? Could something have happened that would make one of them sabotage their own business?

I jumped at the *rat-a-tat-tat* on the door, my body instinctively in fight-or-flight mode. Through the door's panes, I saw Heath. I immediately eased, mentally kicking myself for that silly car jangling my nerves as I unlocked the door and opened it.

"Didn't mean to scare you," he said, entering.

I locked the door behind him and melted when his soft lips found mine. After the kiss, he wrapped me in his arms, and I stayed there, my head resting on his chest, comfortable in the security of his embrace. When we eventually loosened ourselves from each other, I looked up at him. "I needed that."

"Me too," he replied, keeping an arm around my waist as we walked to the rear of the shop.

"You okay?" he asked, rubbing my back.

"Just a little on edge. Do you need something to eat? Drink?" I watched him sink into a bistro chair. He looked tired.

"Nah, I'm okay."

I sat across from him. "How's the investigation going?"

He paused, then said, "Chief Jeffers is overseeing this one closely."

I felt a thread of panic pull at my throat. The Yarrow Glen chief of police was well-known for proclaiming that his police department was a well-oiled machine, which was another way of saying he took long lunches while Heath ran the investigations. At least Chief Jeffers knew how to hire the best people for the job to make his own easier, which was why he hired Detective Jay Heath who used to work for the San Francisco Police, where a much higher crime rate prevailed. The arrangement suited both of them, which was why the chief's change in attitude about this case was concerning.

"Is it because of me?" I asked.

Heath looked at me and reached across the small round table to put his hand in mine. "Obviously none of us thinks it's you."

"Bu-ut . . ." I knew there was more.

He nodded. "But . . . you had the chocolates in your possession before delivering them to the Gazette. You wrote the note that was found by the victim's body. You have a past with Pearce and Riley, which gives you motive for sabotage. And you were overheard getting in a heated argument with Pearce the morning of the murder."

"I wouldn't say *heated*" was my only lame reply.

"You were also overheard at the Chocolate Bliss grand opening saying, 'I could kill him.' Is that true?"

I didn't want to see Heath's look of disappointment. I scrunched my eyes shut, then squinted one eye open. "Off the record?"

His hand slipped out of mine and he lifted his face to the ceiling, as if asking for divine help. "Willa!"

I opened my eyes to face the music. "How was I supposed to know someone would poison his chocolates? All of those things happened before I knew! Who would be stupid enough to initial a note and put it in a box of chocolates, knowing it would incriminate them?"

"Listen, you're preaching to the choir here, but on paper it looks bad. You'd be amazed at how stupid some criminals are." Heath sighed. "I read your interview transcript. You told Shep everything?"

"Yes! Everything! Oh, wait, there was one thing."

Heath took his mini notepad and pen out of the

inside breast pocket of his suit. "Start from the beginning."

Even though my friends and I had dismissed the idea, I told him about the mix-up with my ticket on the box of chocolates. We debated about the implications of that.

"It doesn't make sense. We've coexisted just fine these past ten years. Why would they open a shop here just to try to use it to kill me?"

"You're right. That doesn't make sense. But it's still worth noting." He finished scribbling what I'd told him onto the pad.

"And then there's the car I saw tonight," I said.

"What car?"

I proceeded to tell him about going to Hope's with Archie and about the person I thought was watching Hope's Cakery. Heath jotted down a few things, but he didn't appear excited by this new development.

"You think it's nothing?"

"It could be something, but it could also be a couple of teenagers hooking up in the back seat and not wanting to get caught. Right now, it's best if we stick to investigating what we already have and not go off on tangents."

I agreed, but inside I pouted. I wanted something to go on, even if they were tangents.

"Is Claude Bentley one of the people you're looking at already?" I asked.

"The former manager of Rise and Shine bakery?"

"And our newest employee," I said timidly.

Heath threw up his hands. "Of course he is," he said sarcastically.

"He's upset with Hope for changing the bread bakery

to a cakery, and he felt pushed out by Pearce, so he definitely has motive."

"Did he have access to the chocolates while they were here at the shop?"

"No, but he knew they were going to A. J." A thought popped into my head, something I'd missed at the time. "The next day at the taco truck I saw Trevor—one of the candy guys who own Sweet Tooth Vintage Candy. He said it was his second day in a row getting tacos, which means he could've been there with Claude after Claude saw me taking the chocolates to the Gazette. Maybe the three of them made a quick plan?"

Heath said nothing as he jotted down notes while I considered the possibility that Claude was in cahoots with Gil and Trevor, and they were all after one thing—revenge.

"What do you think?" I asked him.

He looked up from his notepad. "I think I'm keeping notes, and we'll check it out."

I sighed. I should've known better than to think he'd speculate. He liked to have all the facts. I needed some more facts too. "What kind of poison was it? Where can you get it?" I asked. "That could be a clue to the type of person who could get their hands on it, wouldn't it?"

"Good observation, Detective Bauer." He barely suppressed a smile.

He was half teasing me, but I still reveled in the compliment. "And the answer?"

"The toxicology report showed the unusual substance that showed up in the victim's bloodwork was tetrahydrozoline."

"What's that?"

"It's one of the substances in over-the-counter eye-drops. It can be found in almost any store that has a health and personal care section. Perfectly safe if used as directed in the eyes, but if ingested in large quantities by mouth, it can be very harmful, even deadly, as was the case here."

Something so easily accessible didn't help me narrow down my suspect list.

"What did you find out about Kevin Wallace? Do you think he was the target?" I asked next.

"Nothing in the deceased's background stands out. The only person his housemate mentioned he might've had a problem with was Deandra."

"Oh no. Could his housemate be deflecting?"

"Always a possibility, but we checked him out and he seems innocuous too. It's unlikely the perp was someone outside the Gazette building or Hope's Cakery, since the chocolates weren't meant for the victim, they were meant for A. J. There's no way they could've known the victim would eat them."

"Any chance he drank the eyedrops himself as some kind of high? Like I've heard how some people abuse that cold medicine—you know the kind—that people take at night?"

"No. Nothing addictive or mind altering about it."

"You're sure the poison was in the chocolates?"

"Traces of the chocolates detected in his mouth had the tetrahydrozoline. The report showed he wasn't microdosed over a period of time—it entered his bloodstream all at once, which once again brings it back to the chocolates he swiped from A. J.'s desk. We think it was *in* the chocolates rather than *on* the chocolates because there was no significant trace of it in the box or on your note."

"So you're saying someone didn't pour it on the chocolates after the fact."

"Based on the lack of it anywhere else, that's our conclusion."

"That leaves out my quick-plan theory by the disgruntled Claude, Gil, and Trevor."

"We've been conducting our own less than scientific tests to see how the poison could've got into the chocolates."

"And?"

"The most likely scenario is that someone put it in the crème fillings before they were covered in chocolate."

"That means it was done while they were being made in Hope's kitchen."

"Or the ones in the box on A. J.'s desk were switched with poisoned chocolates, but again, that would take planning."

I nodded, taking in this new information. "Do you think all the chocolates from the shop were poisoned or just the ones in that box?" I thought of Mrs. Schultz's Russian-roulette theory.

"We don't know yet. Some people have brought the chocolates they'd bought yesterday in for testing, but so far, they all test clean. Nobody's brought in the rum crème samples that were given out—they likely all got eaten at the time."

"Those are Pearce's specialty."

"He admitted that he made all the rum crèmes—for samples and for sales—and Riley confirmed that two of the rum crèmes were included in the box of eight that went to A. J."

"If someone wanted to ruin Pearce, that would be the place to put the tetra-whatever in."

"Tetrahydrozoline. For the amount that was in the victim's system, he would've had to consume a lot more than just two. All eight chocolates were eaten, and we think all of them were tainted.

"That's a lot of chocolate to eat at once." My hand went to my stomach, which felt suddenly queasy at the thought.

"We've learned Kevin Wallace had a major sweet tooth. It would help to know definitively if the tetrahydrozoline had been in any of the other chocolates or just the ones in that box. No deaths or injuries reported so far, just people complaining of an upset stomach, but whether that's true or psychosomatic, we don't know. In very small amounts, it wouldn't show up in anybody's bloodwork."

"And Hope's baked goods? My cheesecake?"

"All clean."

"So we should concentrate on the people who were in Hope's kitchen making the chocolates."

"That's who we're focusing on. We haven't found any connection between any of them and A. J."

"He'll be relieved to know that." I felt relieved too until my next thought hit. "So that leaves only me as the possible target."

"You know I'll look into that, but the more likely motive is sabotage. Now, whether the person was willing to take your life or A. J.'s for it, that I don't know."

A cold chill tapped at the back of my neck and trickled down my spine.

"Hey." Heath reached for my hand again and I put mine in his. "I'll find out."

I had faith in him, but the more hands on deck, the better. I took myself out of the equation for a moment to focus. "Sabotage. That's what we theorized."

"We?"

"Baz, Mrs. Schultz, Archie—"

"I know who *we* are. Why are you theorizing?"

"Two reasons. One, I might've been the intended target. And two, if it's sabotage, then it doesn't bode well for me as a suspect."

"If you get too involved, it won't bode well for you in either scenario," Heath shot back.

I popped out of the chair in frustration, letting go of his hand. "What am I supposed to do? Wait around for you to save me like I'm Lois Lane?"

Heath remained calm in the face of my quick bout of hysteria. "I'm no superhero, but I *am* a detective and it's my job. Besides, I kind of have a personal stake in this one." Still seated, he pulled me in. He looked into my eyes and gave me his off-duty smile that always made me forget whatever it was we were talking about.

I wrapped my arms around his neck, and we kissed. In the safety of his embrace, I was happy to let him do his job. I ran my fingers through his thick head of black hair.

He offered another smile, as dreamy as his kiss. "I hate to end this, but I have to get back. More files to go over. More interview transcripts. I've got hours more work to do."

I exaggerated my frown. "Superman's work is never done, huh?"

He chuckled and released me from his arms. "Something like that."

I stepped back and let him stand from the chair.

"There's always tomorrow," I said, giving him another kiss.

He looked unsettled.

"What's the matter?" I asked.

He hesitated. The look on his face caused a ping of anxiety in my chest.

"While this investigation is ongoing, I think we'd better keep our distance," he finally said.

"Keep our distance?" The ping turned into a boulder.

"I don't want to, but like I said, the chief is keeping a close eye on everything."

"Including you and me?"

"Well, I know he's watching *me* on this one."

I could feel the pumping in my chest and the heat flushing my cheeks as my heart battled against this decision that I knew I had to accept. I swallowed any selfish feelings. "I understand. It could put you in a bad light."

"It's not that, Willa. I don't want him taking over the case. As long as I'm in charge, you'll be protected. If he takes me off, you're another person of interest, same as the others—or worse, at the top of the heap."

A knot of fear tightened in my gut. "Should I be worried?"

He held onto me. "I'm not telling you this to worry you. I just want you to understand why I won't be stopping by for a while."

I knew this was the right thing, but I still hated it. "I'll miss you, but I understand. Will you still be able to call me?"

He kissed me on the forehead. "I think it's best if we have as little contact as possible right now. No questions about the investigation. No texting either, okay?"

I nodded, the lump in my throat making it hard to verbalize my answer. This case could drag on for months. Just as much, I hated the thought that Heath was putting himself on the line for me.

He forced a small smile. "I'll walk you to your apartment door, though. Make sure you get home safely."

"That's okay. I . . . I want to finish cleaning up." I always preferred ripping the bandage off quickly. "I'll be fine making it the twenty steps to my apartment, I promise," I said, faking light-heartedness while I walked him to the front of the shop.

We stood at the door.

"Be careful, okay?" he said, staring into my eyes.

"I will. You too."

He kissed me one last time, but it was little more than a peck and left me wanting more. Against everything in me, I let him leave. I locked the door behind him and stared out the window, watching him walk away, his usual assured gait faltering.

This case had to be solved, and soon. There was too much at stake.

CHAPTER 16

The tears came as soon as his outline disappeared into the darkness. Sure, we were never official, but in my mind, he was my guy. Now we were back to pre-dating status. Even worse—I couldn't even talk to him. What if he decided he was better off without me? After all, I was putting his job in jeopardy. Maybe he'd come to think I was too much trouble to bother.

I wiped the tears from my eyes. The pity party would have to be put on hold. I had to find a murderer.

I turned off the lights and went through to the stock-room to grab some empty boxes from the week's deliveries. I pushed open the heavy side door, which led to the back of the alley, carrying the boxes with me. The cool air tingled on my skin and gave me goose bumps. I threw the cardboard into the large recycle dumpster. The noise it made reverberated down the silent alley. I looked around me. The harsh lights from the building directed at the pavement only cut two circles in the darkness. Why did I feel I wasn't alone?

I hurried those twenty steps to the back of the building. The automatic spotlight clicked on, illuminating the exterior creaky wooden stairs that led up to my apartment door. I had one foot on the bottom step when a figure came out of the shadows under the deck and grabbed my wrist.

I yelped and whipped around on him, ramming my elbow hard in his chest.

"Ouch!" he cried.

Now under the full blast of my spotlight, I clearly saw the person, in a long trench coat and a fedora pulled down over his eyes, who was now rubbing his chest where my elbow had connected. I immediately recognized the curly hair sticking out from under the hat. *A. J.*

I came this close to elbowing him again, my adrenaline still pumping, even though I now knew I wasn't in danger. "A. J.! What is wrong with you?" He made a habit of sneaking up on me, but this time was a doozy.

"Shhh!" he said, looking around. He tugged on the brim of his hat. "You trying to get me killed? Again?"

I wasn't going to hear the end of that poisoned chocolate delivery, was I?

"Why are you here?" I demanded.

"Can we go upstairs?"

I grumbled resolutely and tromped up the stairs, trying to expel my vexation with each hard step I took.

I'd no sooner unlocked my door and pushed it open than A. J. barreled past me inside it. He stopped short when he caught the flicker of the TV—I'd left *Chopped* on for my betta fish Loretta with the volume turned off. "Oh, jeez, that scared me," he had the nerve to say.

"Seriously, A. J.?"

I closed the door behind us, and he bolted it, not looking as contrite as I would've liked.

"What has gotten into you? Has something else happened?" I asked, tossing the keys in a small basket on my kitchen counter. I grabbed the fish food for Loretta.

He slung his hat next to the basket and took off the trench coat, revealing his usual white T-shirt and jeans. He draped the coat over my living room chair and slumped in it. A vague imprint of the hat was left in his mane of black curls.

"I'm sorry for the *intruder*, Loretta," I said to my fish, giving A. J. the side-eye, as I sprinkled her dinner into her bowl.

"I'm sorry I scared you. I didn't mean to. I just didn't want anybody to see me," he said.

His fingers nervously tapped the armrest. I could tell he wasn't himself, so I let him off the hook. My prior nerves and bad mood had nothing to do with him. "You want a drink or something?"

"Nah. I'd better stay sharp."

I turned off the TV and sat on the love seat catty-corner from him. "Are you okay?"

He paused before admitting, "It's a lot, you know. Finding a dead body."

My guard came down. "Yeah, I do know."

"That's right, you do know. But did you ever think one of those dead bodies could've been you?"

With the mix-up of the ticket on the box of chocolates, I *had* been thinking about that. "You're right, that adds another level to it. I'm sorry you're going through this."

"At the same time, I feel guilty for being glad it wasn't me." He looked at his lap, not meeting my gaze.

"That's natural. Don't beat yourself up about it."

He nodded.

A. J. and I didn't do big emotions with each other, so this display of vulnerability caught me off guard. He must've really been struggling, and I wanted to find a way to help. "I just talked to Heath, and the police don't think you were the target. Unless someone at Chocolate Bliss or Hope's Cakery has a vendetta against you. Nobody knew you were getting the chocolates except them."

"And Deandra."

"You don't think *Deandra* did this just because she was mad about Kevin, do you?"

He paused, the doubt on his face vanishing. "No, I don't. I know the old notion that poison is a woman's weapon, but Deandra would be more satisfied by knocking Kevin out with that big purse of hers. And knocking me out too, while she's at it."

I laughed and nodded in agreement, relieved to hear him use some logic.

"The police took Kevin's laptop to see if there's something on it that can give them any clues as to who might've wanted him dead if he was the target. Hopefully, Deandra didn't put her disdain for him in writing," he said.

"What was he doing at the Gazette after hours?"

"Trying to earn brownie points from me, no doubt. Hey, listen, I didn't love him as much as Deandra thought I did. I just liked that he was willing to put in the work. Our staff is half part-timers, half volunteers. I don't have a lot of go-getters. It was nice to be around someone who had that journalistic fervor that I do, you know?"

"Fervor is nice, but so is longevity and loyalty," I reminded him.

He paused to take that in for only a moment then changed the subject. "Did Heath tell you about the tox report? Tetrahydrozoline. It's an unusual one for killing someone," he said.

I let him go on and tell me about it to see if there

was anything new that I hadn't gleaned from Heath. In turn, I told him about the uptick in doctors' visits.

After considering it for a moment, I said, "How many of those stomachaches at the urgent care were real, I wonder? Maybe if the chocolates were meant for you, they were only meant to give you a stomachache, but because Kevin ate the whole box at once, it killed him."

"Huh. That's a good point, Willa."

"Well, you don't have to act so surprised!"

The automatic spotlight clicked on again outside the window and I heard footsteps on my creaky steps. I immediately went to the window to see who it was. A. J. left his chair and ran to the kitchen, hiding behind the counter.

"It's just Vera from the taco truck. I wonder if Baz got back early and ordered something."

"No, that's mine. I ordered delivery but put your name on it just in case."

"Just in case of what?"

Vera knocked on my door.

I left the window to answer it. "Did you tip her already?"

"Of course I tipped her."

I opened the door. "Hey, Vera."

"Hi, Willa."

A. J. stayed out of sight in the kitchen while Vera swapped the food for thanks, and I closed the door.

I placed the bag and drink on the butcher block, and we sat on the island's stools. He pulled out his food and dug in, while I sat there, taco-less. The savory aroma tried to trick my full stomach into thinking it was hungry.

"Let's get back to the case since you're staying for dinner," I said, staring at him.

Mouth full, he mumbled, "Oh, did you want one?"

I chuckled. A. J. had obviously lived alone for too long. "No thanks, I've eaten." I went to the refrigerator and retrieved a bottle of water for myself. "Why did Kevin eat the chocolates in the first place? Did he swipe them to write the review himself? That tracks with who he was."

"It does. And he had a mean sweet tooth. I would've given the review to him, anyway, if I knew he wanted it. He took the pictures for the grand opening story."

"I saw him there. If the samples were tainted, he could've had some of them yesterday afternoon too, which means there would've been tetrahydrozoline in his system before he even had the eight chocolates in the box. That's a lot of chocolate to eat at once, even for a story. Are they that good?"

"I don't know and I'm not going to find out now."

"You and everyone else in Yarrow Glen, which is why the police are thinking the motivation was sabotage. The box didn't even have your name on it, so if it was someone outside of Chocolate Bliss or Hope's that poisoned them, they may have not cared *who* ate them."

"But how did they do it?"

I shrugged. I'd been thinking about it all day and seemed no closer to a conclusion.

"The people with the most obvious motivation—the candy guys or Claude—didn't have access to the chocolates, and the people who did have access to them wouldn't want to tank their own business. At least that's what it looks like from the outside," I said.

A. J. wiped his mouth and went in for a second taco. "What do you mean? Do you have some insider info?"

"Hope mentioned Duncan and Pearce and Riley argued a lot. Were they your run-of-the-mill colleague tiffs or was there more to it? That's what we need to find out."

"I'm a reporter, so they're not going to tell *me* anything," A. J. said, giving me a meaningful look.

I took another swig of my water. "I already talked to Pearce and Riley."

"And?"

"They didn't have much to say. They thought maybe Jasmine."

"Jasmine?"

"I know. She's not my top suspect, but frankly, nobody is at this point. Hopefully the police will have more to go on soon."

"That sounds like you're taking a back seat. You're not investigating this?" He unwrapped the last of his tacos.

"I am. I'm just at a loss as to where to go next."

"Is it because Detective Heath's your boyfriend now? Is he putting pressure on you to stay out of it?" He stuffed about half the street taco into his mouth.

"He's not my boyfriend," I said, blinking away the tears that threatened to appear at the mention of Heath. "I just trust him to solve the case, that's all."

A. J. swallowed his large bite, then his hands flew to his neck. His face suddenly reddened.

"What's the matter? Are you choking?" I ran to get behind him and threw my arms around his torso, fists clenched for the Heimlich maneuver.

He shook his head and eked out, "No, not choking. I-I think I've been poisoned."

"What? I'll call poison control!" I grabbed my phone off the counter and ran to the fridge where the number was on a magnet.

He came after me. "Don't call. I'm fine," he said in his regular voice. "But see? Someone could strike again! Don't you want to help me?"

I felt like my mind had whiplash. "Not now I don't! What kind of a joke was that?" I pushed him away from me and stomped into the living room.

He followed me in. "It wasn't a joke. I need your help, Willa. Usually, we can help each other on a case."

"Weren't you the one who drove away from me when I asked for help this afternoon?"

"I had to go incognito first!"

"Incognito? You stand out more than ever looking like a detective from one of those old black-and-white noir mysteries."

He looked over at the hat. "Hey, I saw the fedora at Bea's thrift shop. I couldn't pass it up." He looked at me with a little smile, hoping I was done being mad at him.

I wasn't.

"Listen, I'm sorry I scared you, but I'm freaked out. That could be me in the morgue right now. Don't give up so soon. I need your help, Willa."

The memory of Pearce's plea echoed in my head.

I sighed. Why was I such a sucker for someone in need? "I'll find out what I can."

"Great. I, uh, I appreciate that." A. J. looked away. He was never comfortable saying thank you. "Why is your fish looking at me like that?"

I looked over at Loretta too. Her red fantail gently wiggled, keeping her iridescent blue body in place as one eyeball stared, presumably at A. J.

A. J. squinted his eyes at her. I couldn't tell if he was trying to determine what she was doing or trying to intimidate her.

"She's judging you, for sure," I said. Loretta liked to flirt with new people, but she didn't like them to overstay their welcome. "I think it's time for you to go."

"Go? I thought we'd start on the case tonight."

I was about to protest, but the reason my nerves were frayed to begin with had to do with that parked car behind Hope's Cakery that peeled out as soon as the driver saw me. And after agreeing not to even talk to Heath for who knows how long, I had a feeling I'd be spending the evening pacing my apartment.

"Maybe we *can* do something tonight," I said.

A. J. happily flopped into the living room chair again, and I told him what had transpired with the car. "It could be nothing," I finished.

"Could be something. Or some*one*, like Claude."

"Why would Claude be staking out the place?"

A. J. thought for a moment. "If he snuck in overnight to poison the chocolates, he could've accidentally left something behind that could be incriminating."

"Hope said they changed the door code after she did the renovations, because they had too many people coming and going."

"Was that before or after Claude quit?"

"Hope said it was after." As I thought about my talk with Hope at her cakery, another thought came to me. "The front door is a key lock. He ran that place while she was in Paris. He must have a key to the front door."

A. J. nodded. "Even if he gave it back, he could've made a duplicate."

"She didn't say anything about changing the front door lock. Do you think he'd chance it by sneaking in again? The police already went through the place. Besides, anything of his that they did find there, he could brush off as something he left behind before he quit."

"Criminals get paranoid."

He had a point, but I still wasn't set on Claude. "If we're considering all the possible suspects who could've been in that car, what about Gil and Trevor?"

A. J. frowned—I could tell he wasn't happy to be considering them. "If the chocolates were poisoned the day before the grand opening, it leaves them off the hook. They didn't know about Chocolate Bliss."

"What if they're in on it together—the three of them?"

A. J. was quiet while he considered this. "Why would Claude put himself in the crosshairs like that? He'd be the one with access to the cakery, so he'd be the one suspected."

"True."

"Don't forget, the car could also belong to your former musketeers."

"Pearce and Riley?"

"Maybe they found out about the meeting and weren't happy Duncan was having it without them. Or they could just be keeping an eye on him."

"Hmm. I wonder." I stood, too antsy to sit.

"The only thing to do is see if one of them drives that car," A. J. said, also getting up from his chair.

"I didn't get a perfect look at it. I'm not even sure of the color."

"Yeah, but you said it was hybrid or electric and it may have a spoiler on the back. That'd be easy to rule some people out, right?"

"You're right. Let's do it."

He shrugged into his oversized trench coat and stuck

his fedora on. He had to tug at it to get it to stay on his overabundant curly hair. "I'll drive."

"Why? My car's right here."

"So's mine. You really ought to be more observant, Willa."

"I was too busy recovering from my elevated heart-rate!" I shot back.

"I almost gave you a heart attack and you almost poisoned me with chocolates. Call it even?" He held out his hand.

I stared at it for a moment, then shook it. "Deal." Anything to get him to stop reminding me that I almost accidentally killed him.

CHAPTER 17

I changed out of my work blouse and khakis, opting to leave my cheese-pun shirts on their hangers for this night mission. I returned to the living room in jeans and a dark long-sleeved shirt. We made a quick detour back into my shop from the alley to look up Claude's address from the employment forms he'd filled out. I paused at the doorway to my office.

"What's the matter?" A. J. didn't hide his impatience.

"I don't feel right using his information this way."

He rolled his eyes. "Let me get this straight. You feel okay suspecting the guy of murder, but not using his address to prove it?"

Now it was my turn for an eye roll. "You're so annoying!" I hated it when he pointed out things I'd rather not admit to. I continued in and copied Claude's address. "What about Gil and Trevor?"

"They live above their shop, just like you."

"All right, let's go."

A. J.'s Jeep was parked in the back of my building like he said. A short drive up Pleasant Avenue took us past the inn and candy shop. We took a left turn on Hyland Street, then another left into the public parking lot attached to the no-outlet road that accessed the rear of two blocks of businesses located on Pleasant Avenue. Patrons at The Cellar usually kept the lot full on a Saturday night, but tonight it was half-empty.

"Don't tell me people are even too spooked to go to The Cellar," A. J. said, thinking the same thing as I was.

He sunk down a few inches in his seat as he slowly drove past the first row of cars. People who were staying at the inn parked in this lot, so Pearce and Riley's car was the first one we sought out.

"I'll look on this side and you do that side," he said.

"Do you think it'll be easier to look on foot?" I asked.

"And be out in the open? You're welcome to, but not me." He pulled on the brim of the fedora.

"Be careful. You still need to see where you're going."

His Jeep crawled past the parked cars as he peered over the steering wheel. "Do you think whoever's after me would know my car? Maybe we *should've* taken yours."

"I think we'll be fine, A. J. If you do have disgruntled podcast listeners, they couldn't have known about the chocolates," I replied, scanning the license plates.

By the third row, I'd started to think Pearce and Riley had gone out and it was all for naught, when I spotted it. "Bingo!"

A. J. stopped the car. "Oregon plate?"

"Not only that." I pointed to the vanity plate that read CHOCLT.

"That's him for sure."

Our excitement for having found Pearce's SUV was replaced with disappointment. "The car I saw was definitely not an SUV. More like a Prius."

"That's one down." He pulled his car out of the lot and drove along the dead-end road. The back of the candy shop with Gil and Trevor's apartment above it was tucked between two rows of trees, giving it some privacy from the adjacent inn to its right. A small hardscaped patio with a firepit and two Adirondack chairs made for a cozy outdoor space. To the left, there was barely enough room for the portico situated between the building and the row of trees. Tucked into the darkened portico was a vehicle.

"Is that it?" A. J. asked.

"It could be. I can't tell from here."

A. J. made a loop where the road ended at the library book drop-off, then passed the inn's temporary check-in parking, and stopped the car behind Sweet Tooth Vintage Candy. "Get out and look."

"Because that's not suspicious," I said sarcastically. "What if they happen to be looking out their window?" There was a light shining behind curtains on the second floor where their apartment was, not to mention a light above the shop's back door.

He reconsidered and drove back to the parking lot where he pulled into a vacant spot and shut off the engine. "Let's go. I'll keep a lookout," he said.

"Thanks."

I stopped him as he was unbuckling his seatbelt. "You're going to keep the Sam Spade thing going on?"

"If any situation calls for being undercover, it's this one."

He had a point. I wouldn't have minded a trench coat and hat, myself.

We crossed the street and followed the narrow sidewalk until we came upon the back of the candy shop again. We stayed in the shadow of the trees on the lefthand side where the portico was, hoping they didn't have any motion-sensitive lights in place.

I still couldn't tell what kind of car it was, but it was the right size, and I was pretty sure it was a dark color. Just ten more steps would get us close enough for me to get a better look at it.

The sound of a car's engine drew closer. We pulled back into the trees to wait for it to pass, when the beam of headlights flashed across the narrow drive.

"It's them!" I harshly whispered, pulling A. J. by his coat into the trees, sending us both to the ground, caught among the sticky needles of pine.

The headlights straightened out as the Subaru pulled behind the portico, directly in front of where we were hiding. I decided breathing was no longer a good idea under these circumstances. Why was it so quiet back here? We heard the engine cut and saw the driver's side door open. I couldn't see his face, but his stocky profile in the car's ceiling light behind him told me it was Trevor. He held a bottle—wine?—and proceeded up the steps to their deck, humming. From our vantage point on the ground, we could see over the roof of the car to their small deck. We waited for Trevor to go inside, but Gil came out onto the deck to greet him. He had two champagne flutes in his hand.

Oh gosh, were they going to sit on their back patio and drink champagne?

They started back down the steps. I crab-crawled backward as A. J. turned and did a commando crawl. Their voices carried, letting us know they were, indeed, coming back down the steps to their patio. Once we'd extricated ourselves from the branches and were in the adjacent alley, we fumbled our way to our feet and hightailed it back to A. J.'s car in the parking lot.

We sat there for a minute, catching our breath, mostly from the pumping adrenaline more than the short run.

"Two people suspected of poisoning chocolates sneaking around a candy shop at night probably wasn't the brightest idea we've ever had," he said.

"No kidding." I noticed he was bareheaded. "You lost your hat."

His hand went to his head. "Oh no."

"We're not going back to get it," I said before he could even suggest it. "Look for it tomorrow. While you're at it, you can find out what kind of car was parked in their portico."

He silently agreed.

CHAPTER 18

~⚘~

"Where are we headed next?" A. J. pushed the button to turn on the car's engine.

"Home? I don't think we should press our luck. I can wait until Claude comes to work tomorrow to take a look at his car."

"We've come this far. Let's finish it up. Where am I driving?" He stared at me, his hands on the wheel, ready to go.

I reminded myself why this case needed to be solved ASAP. Hopefully, Claude's house would just require a drive-by. I checked my phone where I'd noted the address and conveyed it to A. J.

"That's the area I used to live. It's mostly affordable rentals." He started driving.

"You moved?"

"Yeah, just a couple months ago. I hope my publisher doesn't decide having an editor who's a murder suspect is a bad look for the paper. I can barely afford the new place, as it is.

"You're not a suspect, you're just a person of interest."

"Just?" he emphasized.

There was no *just* about it—I knew that as well as

A. J. But I was trying to make us both feel better about the reality of our situations. "You were also almost the victim. Your boss has got to keep that in mind too. Besides, this'll sell more papers, don't you think?"

"Now you're talking like one of us journalists, Willa. When did you become a cynic?"

"I use my cynicism for optimistic reasons, like believing you won't get fired."

"An opti-cynic. I like it." A. J. smiled and we drove the rest of the way to Claude's neighborhood in silence.

We slowly rolled down his street until a mailbox indicated we'd arrived at the right place. The front stoop was unlit, but it didn't hide the fact that the lawn needed to be mowed. An enclosed breezeway connected the small 1950s home to the one-car garage that was slightly leaning to the right. A light glowed from above the garage door, revealing the outline of a car inside.

A. J. slowed his Jeep parallel to the curb on the opposite side of the street and put it in neutral. "What do you think? Does it look like the car?"

"It could be the Batmobile for all I know—it's too dark in that garage to see anything. Again!"

A faint yellow glow emanated from a downstairs window.

"He's got to be home. I'll just check on his car tomorrow when he comes to work."

"We came all the way here. There's no chocolate here, so nothing to be scared of. Do you want to figure out this case or not?"

A. J. had no idea how much I wanted to figure out this case, send Pearce and Riley on their way forever, and see Heath again.

He pulled up farther so as not to park directly across

from the house and turned off the engine, making his decision clear. He looked at me again for my consent.

"Fine, let's check it out," I agreed, exiting the car.

The rhythmic thumping of a basketball from a kids' pick-up game at the other end of the street carried all the way down a half dozen houses. I tried to shut the door without slamming it as I exited the car, which only partially closed it. I attempted it twice before A. J. slammed his shut without care and did the same to mine.

"The only way we won't stand out in people's memories is if we act normal," he said. Proving his point, he walked confidently to Claude's driveway.

The glare of the garage light on the driveway pavement didn't help me identify the car. We'd have to get closer. Regardless of A. J.'s theory, I slunk down the short driveway like a cartoon cat burglar. If I could get a glimpse of a spoiler even, I'd be willing to bet Claude was the one at Hope's Cakery. All I'd have to do was find out why.

A dog's insistent bark from inside the house froze my steps. Even A. J. halted his confident stride. I heard a door swing open and shut. It must've been from the recessed breezeway. Footsteps. The barking became more insistent. The dog was likely waiting for the command to attack.

Claude came around the corner holding some kind of club.

"Claude! Claude! It's just me!" I said, surrendering with my arms in the air. I looked over at A. J. and saw his arms in the same position.

"Bree, shush," Claude commanded gently.

The dog quieted immediately.

Claude and his dog were now in the driveway where

we could see each other properly. Bree was nothing more than a vocal golden retriever.

A. J. and I relaxed our arms.

"Sorry if we scared you," I said.

"No worries, you didn't. I came out to see why Bree was barking. It's usually just a racoon."

"Brie? Like the cheese?"

"Short for *brioche*," he said. "Good girl!" He patted her on the head then broke off the end of what I took as a club in his hand and fed it to her.

"Is that . . . a baguette?"

He looked at it, like it was normal to be carrying a baguette. "I've been experimenting all evening."

So then, not waiting to sneak into Hope's. A. J. and I shared a quick, knowing look. Not our guy.

"It looks good," A. J. told him.

Claude held it up. "It's a little flat. I'm trying to perfect low sodium bread. I wanted to sell some at the bakery, but I worked so many hours, I never had time to play around with it." Bree finished her piece and used her paw to ask for another. "That's enough." Then to us, "So what brings you by?"

"What brings us by?" I repeated. *Good question.* "We saw your car in the garage, so we figured you were home." This prologue gave us an excuse to get closer to his car and take a proper look. It was a small Chevy hatchback. No spoiler. Not electric.

I looked at A. J.—Mr. Act Normal and We Won't Get Caught—but he avoided eye contact. I'd have to get us out of this one myself.

"I have one more tax form for you to fill out," I pulled out of thin air.

"Oh, okay."

I inwardly sighed in relief. That was easy.

"Where is it?" he continued.

Why does there always have to be a glitch in the plan? I felt my face flush, and I hoped he'd think it was my foolishness and not my half-baked lie that was to blame.

"Did I leave that in the car, A. J.?" I made a show of asking.

"I think you left some forms on your desk," he responded. "Sorry, I didn't know they were important."

"Not important. It can wait. I'll see you tomorrow, Claude," I said, already starting to walk away.

"Okay. Yeah, see ya," he said, sounding confused.

A. J. and I walked back to his car. Claude and his dog were already back inside when I waved, not that he could see me, but I was still adhering to the act normal edict. But what was normal about thinking your new employee might be a murderer?

CHAPTER 19

The next morning was Sunday, and the shop opened late, which meant I could sleep in, but of course, I didn't. In fact, I hardly slept at all. Visions of poisoned chocolates danced in my head like a murderous version of *'Twas the Night Before Christmas*. Last night's car caper was a useless outing, but at least it felt like we were doing *something* and kept the restlessness at bay.

I reached for my phone, my stomach twisting at the memory of my conversation with Heath last night. The funny thing was, he and I weren't connected at the hip. When things got busy for either of us, we'd often go a day or two with only a quick check-in, knowing we'd have downtime to reconnect soon. At thirty-five, I was used to my independence and my own apartment. Heath was older than me—he'd just turned forty—and had been married when he lived in San Francisco. He was already a widower when he'd become a detective here shortly before I arrived, so he was accustomed to being on his own since living in Yarrow Glen. But what lay before us felt very different. Knowing I wouldn't and *couldn't* see him or talk to him made me yearn to do so, right this minute. If he was my boyfriend, this might feel differently, but he wasn't. I'd convinced myself that I was okay not labeling what we had, but I could've really used the assurance of something more now. I checked my texts. I was prepared for there to be nothing from Heath, but it didn't soften the smack of disappointment. Nothing from Baz either, darn it.

When friends aren't available, there's always cheese. I threw on my usual spring morning attire of yoga pants that had never been through a day of yoga in their well-worn existence and an oversized University of Oregon hoodie, then padded into the bathroom to use the toilet and wash my face. I started to tackle my ratty hair, which had worked its way into a nest at the top of my head overnight, but I didn't want to deal with looking at the stubborn early gray hairs that insisted on popping out from my scalp like groundhogs. "I'll deal with you later," I told my disheveled reflection in the mirror. I had more important things to do, like forage for cheese.

The uneven hardwood floor felt chilly on my bare feet as I padded through the short hall to the living room, which was separated from the kitchen by a small butcher-block island with a trio of stools tucked under it. It was a cozy space, just right for me and my flashy betta fish, Loretta.

"Good morning, Loretta," I greeted her as I crossed the room mostly furnished with leftovers from my grandmother's farmhouse. Loretta's bowl was situated atop a tall metal stool draped with linen, which I referred to as Loretta Island. I removed the lid with the warming light, and she raced to the top to greet me. She looked much better this morning than I did, her iridescent blue body and red fantail just as vivid as always. I could feel her judgment at my bedhead and morning attire. "Not everybody can wake up as beautiful as you, Loretta. Don't be so judgy." I swear, if she had shoulders, she would've shrugged one at me. I took it down to her being hungry, and obligingly sprinkled food into her bowl. I turned on the nearby TV and clicked on Food Network's *Chopped*, her favorite. She wiggled her magnificent fantail as soon as her crush, Ted Allen, appeared on the screen.

With Loretta enjoying her breakfast with Ted, I checked my kitchen for my own. Alas, my cupboards and fridge were pitiful. I'd have to go downstairs and swipe some of my inventory.

I slid into my shoes and went out to my deck, the chilly air reminding me that it was still April. Baz loved his sweet coffee drinks, hot or cold, but he couldn't get them until the used bookstore café opened at nine. He usually hung out on his deck wrinkling his nose at a very light beige cup of coffee that he found a new way to complain about every morning. Unfortunately, Baz wasn't there giving his coffee dirty looks.

As I descended the stairs, I noticed a car—a boxy Honda Element, not the one I'd been in search of— parked next to his. Ah, *that* was the reason—his date must've gone well.

That put a smile on my face as I took the alley door into my stockroom and through to my shop, fragrant and gleaming. It was another sunny day in beautiful Sonoma Valley, but it wasn't until later in the morning that the sun would peak the surrounding mountains of Yarrow Glen and fully stream into the front of the shop.

I turned up the lights. I knew just what cheese I wanted—Deer Creek Creamery's Moonrabbit Cheddar. The Chartreuse liqueur the Wisconsin cheese is bathed in adds a delicate herbal bouquet with hints of clove, citrus, rosemary, and thyme that complements the cheese's creaminess. I cut off a chunk before returning upstairs, but I wasn't in a rush. My shop was my feel-good place, so I lingered, eventually moving to the front windows to fuss with the display. I rearranged some of the well-known Italian wedges—Asiago, Romano, Pecorino Locatelli, Parmigiano-Reggiano. It was meditative, tweaking each cheese wedge so it sat in harmony with the others—not too aligned like soldiers, but not too chaotic as to look messy. It was a quiet skill to achieve a measured disorder of cheeses.

An insistent series of *meows* from the other side of the glass broke me out of my place of zen.

It was my shop neighbor's cat, Pudge, a large tabby with a clipped ear, a sign that he'd been a stray who was captured, neutered, and released again. He'd hung out in the alley by Carl's Hardware enough that Carl had begun feeding him, giving him the name Pudge and the physique to fit it. Pudge still preferred roaming at night, but he spent a good deal of his days inside the hardware store, often taking naps on the shelves. If you went into the store for something he happened to be ly-ing on, you were out of luck—you'd have to return an-other time.

Pudge also seemed to know the days of the week. On days our shops opened late or not at all and Carl wouldn't be proffering food at the appointed hour, Pudge would slink down to my shop door, having tapped me as an early riser no matter the day.

I hurried to the kitchenette and opened a can of cat food, a stash of which I kept in my cabinet, and filled a cup with cold water, then took them out the front door. Pudge waited beside the door, looking like a replace-ment for my cow mascot Guernsey.

"Here you go, Pudge." I set down his food by the

building. He dug in immediately. I dumped the old water into the street that I kept for any furbabies who needed a drink throughout the day and refreshed the bowl, setting it next to his food. He tolerated a few strokes of my hand down his back, but then paused nibbling at the canned Seafood Galore to stare at me. His chartreuse eyes said *Thanks, but I'll take it from here.* I got the appreciation from Pudge, but not the devotion.

I left him alone to enjoy his breakfast in peace. However, *my* peace was interrupted when I realized the two people coming my way down the sidewalk were Pearce and Riley. *Great.*

"Hi, Willa," Riley said in a tone reserved for funerals. She pushed her excess curls away from her face. She looked worn out.

Pearce gave me a once-over I probably wasn't supposed to notice, and I suddenly remembered I had a bad case of bedhead. He looked more appropriate for seeing others in public—obviously showered and wearing jeans and a long-sleeved shirt, but his glasses barely hid the bags under his eyes he didn't have yesterday.

"I'm glad you're here. Can we come in?" he asked.

I wanted to hear new information they might have about the case, but my insides balked at allowing them into my shop, my sanctuary. I went against my emotions and reluctantly allowed them inside. "We don't open for a couple of hours. I'm assuming you're not here for cheese?" I awkwardly kidded.

Riley managed a half laugh. "No." She scanned the shop. "Can we sit down?"

I silently led them to the café area, feeling strange to be doing so. I left my Moonrabbit Cheddar where it was—this might even be too big of a job for cheese to de-stress me. They sat side by side at one of the bistro tables. Across from them, I pulled my chair out from the table to keep more distance between us.

Riley stopped biting her lip long enough to say, "This is a really nice shop, Willa. Good for you. You did it." She gave me a nervous smile.

"I had no doubt you would. You're type A, like me," Pearce added, somehow sounding like he was taking some credit for it.

"Thanks," I replied, although it came with a sour taste in my mouth. They didn't come here to discuss our past, did they? I hadn't thought I could be more uncomfortable than talking to them yesterday, but here we were.

Riley spoke again. "First, let me just say . . . I'm sorry. I'm really, really sorry how it all went down with the three of us. I never meant—"

Oh my Gouda, it was going to get worse.

I put my hand up. "Listen, the reasons don't matter anymore. It happened ten years ago, as Pearce pointed out yesterday." I took a moment to decide what I wanted to say. "Am I still hurt by it? It'll always sting to be betrayed by the two people I thought were my best friends, but we don't need to rehash any of that. The only thing I need an explanation for is why you brought Chocolate Bliss to Yarrow Glen."

"I told you, it was Duncan's idea," Pearce said.

"Yes, but it's *your* business. You had to have looked into it and seen I was here, if you didn't already know."

"I wasn't involved in it. It was between Pearce and Duncan," Riley stated. But she stared at Pearce, silently prompting him.

"Yeah okay, I knew, but Duncan was psyched about it, and it seemed like the perfect thing—we wouldn't have to commit a lot of money until we felt more certain about it." He shrugged. "It was just a business decision. It had nothing to do with you."

My mouth popped open. *Nothing to do with me?* Apparently, Pearce had never found that sensitivity chip he'd been missing all those years ago. I realized I wouldn't get any answers from him that would satisfy me, so I didn't bother to argue the point.

"Hey, I'm not the only one who's ever put business first," he said.

"What's that supposed to mean?" I shot back. "You said the same thing yesterday. Obviously, there's something you want to get off your chest."

He looked at me like I was being obtuse. "Come on, Willa. Once you came back from France with that cheese shop idea, you went full steam ahead with it. After we graduated, you left for months at a time doing your cheese*managering* thing."

"Cheesemongering," I corrected, keeping myself from rolling my eyes. "It was for my certification. I thought you were both excited about the idea."

"We were excited by the idea of being entrepreneurs, but cheese was *your* passion. I knew it would be your baby all the way. We might've been the three musketeers, but it wouldn't have been one for all and all for one when it came to the business," Pearce said. "You have to admit that."

I looked to Riley to contradict what he was saying, but she wouldn't look me in the eye. Had I really steamrolled them into the idea of owning a cheese shop together? Or was that the narrative that made them feel most comfortable about what they'd done? I didn't want to revisit the past any longer. It was time to get answers for the present.

"So is that how it is for you two and Duncan? All

for one and one for all?" I asked, wanting to know more about their dynamic.

"Well, no. Duncan's an important member of the team, but Riley and I own Chocolate Bliss."

"But you let him decide where the potential third Chocolate Bliss was going to be."

"And see where that got us? This is what happens when I'm not in charge of making all the decisions." Pearce looked at Riley as if reminding her of the fact.

"You were for it too?" I asked her.

"Well . . ." She started to shake her head.

"Oh come on. You were the one who kept pushing me to let him do it with only a promise that he'd have the money," Pearce said to her.

"He wanted the shop really bad," she explained.

"So you knew all along it was going to be Duncan's shop then?"

"We were still hashing it out on paper," Pearce said with less conviction. Riley gave him a dubious look.

"So it wasn't a done deal? If he thought he might not get it after all, don't you think that could be motive for him to sabotage the shop?" I asked. It seemed obvious to me.

"Not Duncan," Riley piped up. "He wouldn't do that."

Pearce seemed to be considering what I said. "Wait a second, Ri. Willa's got a point. He tried to get you to soften me up and give him better terms for the franchise, remember? He wasn't happy with us. Maybe he wanted to throw in the towel and get back at us at the same time."

Riley stuck her elbows on the table and clutched at her mane of curls. "This is a nightmare. Everything we've worked for, everything that's been put on hold because of this business, and now it's all for nothing!

Our reputation is ruined and now we're batting around which one of us is a murder suspect? None of us would sabotage our business. We've all worked too hard!" She began to cry.

Pearce pulled her to him and wrapped his arms around her. "Hey, we'll get through this."

Oddly, I felt pleased seeing him care for her. Maybe it was the reminder that I needed that the man I used to love was indeed, loving. Or maybe I needed to see that things had worked out the way they were supposed to.

"Can I ask you something else?" I said, once they'd untwined themselves.

"Shoot," Pearce answered.

"If the chocolates for the editor of the *Gazette* were so important, why was I mistakenly given the box?"

"What do you mean?" Riley asked, wiping under her eyes and checking her fingers to see if her mascara had run.

"That's how I found out the chocolates were going to A. J. The box was with the cheesecake I'd ordered, and Jasmine brought both to me."

They looked stumped.

"It must've gotten misplaced in the shuffle. It was a crazy day," Riley explained, sniffling.

I could relate to the madness of an opening day.

"Hope's not the most organized. It was harder than we thought sharing the space and we didn't have it quite as worked out as we thought we did," Pearce added.

I wasn't buying that Hope was to blame, so I kept it moving. "Can you go over how the chocolates were made?"

They had no hesitancy going through the process with me, pretty much confirming what Hope had said but in more detail.

"I would've noticed right away had anything been poured on or added to the chocolate. The simplest thing can mess up the way a chocolate looks. I know for a fact they were all glossy and pristine, just like every other time we've made them," Pearce said with conviction.

Riley nodded.

"Then the poison had to have been put in the crème fillings," I echoed what Heath had believed.

Pearce fiddled with his glasses. "It's not impossible Duncan could've slipped something in before we poured the fillings into the chocolate molds," Pearce suggested, looking to Riley to back him up.

Riley shook her head stubbornly. "The police said none of the chocolates brought to the station were poisoned. We unmolded each kind of chocolate, then took two from each batch of our top sellers to give to A. J. The forensics would've found it in the other chocolates they examined. That proves it couldn't have happened in our kitchen. I bet somebody switched them once they were at the Gazette."

That possibility put me and A. J. in a terrible position, and I hoped it wasn't true.

"So we're no closer to finding out who did this," Pearce said.

I felt the same way. Everything I'd heard kept sending me in circles. I felt no closer to getting to the truth.

Riley's face crumpled in despair once again. "Oh, Willa, this is such a mess. Have you found out anything since we talked yesterday?" she asked.

They looked at me expectantly.

Everything I'd discovered was conjecture and I wasn't about to throw one of my neighbors to the wolves without being certain. "I'm afraid not. I'm sorry," I told them.

Riley slumped even farther in her chair.

"Isn't the detective on this case your boyfriend?" Pearce asked, catching me off guard. How had he known that?

"We're dating, but I don't have any influence when it comes to his investigation."

"You could go to bat for us," Pearce suggested.

Go to bat? I didn't say that out loud, but my look did.

"I know, that's a lot to ask, but Chocolate Bliss has been our life. We've waited on marriage and kids . . ." Riley said in a quivering voice.

"And that picket fence you've been going on about forever," Pearce said with affection.

Riley looked down, seemingly embarrassed. When she looked up, her eyes gleamed with tears. "If we lose our business and our good name, all that sacrifice will have been for nothing. Pearce has worked so hard."

"You have too, Ri." They locked hands.

"He doesn't talk about the investigation with me." *To say the least.*

"You know we're not murderers, Willa," Riley continued to plead. The fingers of her free hand nervously played with her flowy boho skirt. "Can't you at least talk to him?"

I had to concede that in my heart of hearts, I didn't believe they did this. I sighed. "I'll do what I can."

"Thank you," she said, wiping a tear that bubbled over.

"If you find out anything, let us know. We're heading back to Oregon on Monday," Pearce added.

"You're allowed to leave?" I asked, surprised.

"They can't make us stay. They know where we are. We have to check on our other shops and do damage control."

They rose, and Riley paused as if to wait for me to stand so she could hug me. I took a moment too long to decide if that was something I wanted to do, so she followed Pearce to the front of the shop. I let them out and locked the door behind them, then bolted toward my Moonrabbit Cheddar. My cheese would be working overtime.

CHAPTER 20

I took my cheese and left out the alley door to return to my apartment. I heard footsteps on Baz's side of the stairs as I headed up mine directly across from his. We met on our respective decks on top.

"Baz!"

"Hey, Willa." He was holding two sugared-up cold coffee drinks with whipped cream.

"You had a good date last night, huh?" I eyed the door where I assumed the second coffee was going.

"It was the opposite of a good date. She saw her ex at the bar."

"Uh-oh. What did she do? Talk about him all night? Make a scene?"

"She left with him."

"No way! I'm sorry. No wonder you're consoling yourself with a double dose of sugar and caffeine. I'm doing my version of the same." I lifted my Moonrabbit Cheddar in explanation.

"Well, actually—" He was interrupted by his door opening.

Out stepped Constance Yi, the receptionist from the inn, in slightly wrinkled work clothes and a fresh-scrubbed face. "I thought I heard voices. You're a life

saver. Thanks." She took the coffee he held out for her.
"Hi, Willa."

In my head, my mother's voice reprimanded me to close my mouth before I swallowed a fly, so I picked my chin off my clavicle to say hi back. I gave Baz a hidden smile.

"It's not what you think," Baz said.

"I slept on his couch. It's very comfortable by the way," she told him.

"She refused the bed," he added.

"Okay, TMI!" I said, waving my hands in front of me. I liked details about Baz's dates, but not *those* kinds of details.

"I mean she refused to let me sleep on the couch instead of her." He rolled his eyes at me.

"I've got two murder suspects staying at the inn, so I was freaked out at work. Baz was nice enough to talk me down. Once I clocked out, I needed dinner, so we came back here and had bologna sandwiches and a bottle of wine and decided it wasn't a good idea for me to drive home."

"Your famous bologna sandwiches. You know how to treat a girl," I ribbed.

"Have you ever had them fried? They were delicious. Hits the spot when you get off work late!" Constance said with conviction.

Baz beamed.

It sounded like Baz had found the perfect girl for him, one who'd been right under his nose.

"I'm glad you had Baz to make you feel better. For what it's worth, I used to be friends with Pearce and Riley, and I don't think they're murderers."

"No offense, Willa, but do you remember the last time friends of yours stayed at the inn?" She was referring to former cheese shop colleagues who'd come to Yarrow Glen for the Northwest Cheese Invitational, after which a murder occurred, and they all became suspects.

"You have a point," I had to admit.

"I should've listened to Gil and Trevor and told Pearce Brenner we were all booked up."

That confirmed my observation that the vintage candy guys weren't happy about Chocolate Bliss. "What did they say?"

She continued telling the story in her usual quick clip. "They told me the Chocolate Bliss people were bad news and if they came to the inn, I shouldn't be nice to them. Of course, I couldn't do that. I have my job to think about. It didn't matter anyway because I never saw them. I only saw their manager, Duncan, go to The Cellar once in a while, and I didn't know who he was at the time. I thought Hope had found a new guy, and I was going to warn her because he'd come in with Gia a lot too."

Gia. She was with Duncan at the grand opening when I picked up the cheesecake and chocolates. I must've been right when I thought they'd looked pretty cozy, but I thought she and Roman were together.

"Anyway, I'd started to think Pearce and Riley were going to cancel their suite reservation, but they finally showed their faces after the grand opening." She took another sip of her coffee drink, having finished her story.

"Wait, are you saying Gil and Trevor told you this *before* Chocolate Bliss's grand opening?"

She looked off in thought for a moment. "It was a couple weeks before."

"I wonder how they found out."

Constance shrugged.

The *how* didn't really matter, but the *when* sure did. This meant they had time to plan something, like somehow sneaking into Hope's to poison the chocolates or switching out the chocolates box meant for A. J. The warning to Constance might've been because they knew what was to come.

Constance was friendly with Gil and Trevor, so I didn't want to voice my suspicions about them. "Well, I'll let you two enjoy your coffee," I said.

"I've actually got to get going." She turned to Baz. "Thanks for last night. I hope we can do it again."

I searched my pockets for my keys to unlock my door and allow them a private goodbye, but I wasn't quick enough.

"Yeah, we'll do it again. Hopefully without looming murderers next time," Baz said.

This brought a nervous titter from Constance. "That would be even better. Bye, Willa!" She scurried down the stairs as I opened my door, finally realizing I hadn't locked it in the first place.

I said goodbye, then waited in the doorway before speaking until two quick beeps of her car horn indicated she was gone. "Tell me everything."

I stepped back onto the deck as Baz, who'd watched her drive off, turned to face me.

"What do ya mean? We already told you what happened." Even a mound of whipped cream couldn't hide his smile as he sipped his froufrou iced coffee.

"Uh-huh." I pressed my lips together but didn't hold back my smile either.

He swatted his hand my way. "It's just Constance. We're not dating or anything. She's just a fr—"

"Friend. I know. And what could be worse than

dating someone you already know you get along with?" I asked sarcastically.

"I thought you, of all people, would be the last person to razz me about this. People always think something's going on between me and you, and we both know how annoying that is."

"Yeah, but that's me and you. That would be weird."

"I know. Like dating one of my sisters." He pulled back his lips and flared his nostrils like he'd just gotten a whiff of rotten eggs.

"You don't have to make that face. I'm not *that* bad."

He chuckled. "I was thinking of my actual sisters. You're a lot more fun than they are."

"Good move, complimenting your way out of that one."

He lifted his sugary coffee in a "cheers" and took another sip.

"What about Constance? Do you think of *her* like a sister?" Yeah, I wasn't letting this go so easily.

"And we're back to Constance." He leaned on the railing. "Okay, she's cute. She's fun. There's never an awkward silence between us. And no, I don't think of her like a sister. You happy now?"

I smiled. "As a matter of fact, I am. I think you two make a great couple."

"We're not a couple!"

"That can be remedied."

"And you wonder why I never talked to you about her!"

"I *do* wonder that. This is what best friends do. Am I not the best wingman, er, wingwoman?"

He raised his eyebrows and looked down his nose at me. "All right, bestie, you really wanna go there?"

He'd allowed me to pretend for a very long time that

I wasn't into Heath when we both knew darn well that I was. It wasn't until Heath and I started dating that I actually admitted it out loud. But the thought of what was going on with Heath twisted my stomach. I took the heat off myself and kept the focus on Baz.

"Point taken. I'm happy for you, by the way. I had no idea you were such a player. Showing up at The Cellar with one woman and leaving with another."

He choked on his coffee. "Yeah, that's me. A player."

We laughed.

"Can we change the subject?" he said.

"If you insist. After what Constance just told us, I think it might be a good idea to pay a visit to Gil and Trevor. They might've had time to plan a candy swap. They're such nice guys, I hate to suspect them, but what do you think?"

"I guess we have to keep an open mind. I'm in. Are you taking that squirrel with you?"

"What squirr—?" I saw his gaze was focused atop my head. I threw my hands over my nest of hair as he broke out into laughter just before I swiped at him. He knew it was coming and jumped back, saving his arm from my backhand. I didn't want to give him the satisfaction, but I couldn't help but laugh along until I remembered I'd looked like this all morning. All I'd wanted was to sneak downstairs for a little cheese!

"What's the matter? You know I'm just teasing you," he said.

"It's not that. I went downstairs to get some cheese"—I once again lifted the chunk of cheese I'd proffered from my shop—"but Riley and Pearce came to see me."

Baz's eyes widened. "What did they have to say?"

"Wouldn't you like to know?" Fair play for teasing. "What's your schedule like today?"

"It's a Sunday. Unless I get an emergency call, I'm off today."

"I'm going to shower and eat my cheese, not necessarily in that order, and then open the shop. If it's a quiet day, which I have a sinking feeling it will be, we can walk up to Sweet Tooth, and I'll tell you everything then."

"What are we going to say to Gil and Trevor?"

"Hmm, I'm not sure yet. I'd love to get a look at one of the private areas of their shop to see if they could've made a poisonous batch beforehand and switched the chocolates out."

"How are we gonna get them to show it to us?"

"I'm not sure, but I think we might need some Team Cheese reinforcements."

I went inside, plans already ruminating in my head.

CHAPTER 21

After making myself presentable and eating not as much of my Moonrabbit Cheddar as I'd have liked, I opened Curds & Whey. Mrs. Schultz had brought in fresh parsley and chives from her herb garden and got busy making a dip her friend had brought to poker night, using the mild and buttery Jarlsberg, along with mayonnaise, red onion, and lemon, as well as the herbs.

"I can't wait to try it," Archie said.

"It reminds me of pimento cheese—not much to look at, but a bit addictive nonetheless," she told us.

"Sounds good to me," June said.

The three of us left Mrs. Schultz to finish the dip while I oversaw June and Archie's selections for today's cheese boards. We moved to the front of the shop to take a look at what we had. There were plenty of Swiss cheeses left over from yesterday's birthday bash, and since Mrs. Schultz had chosen a Swiss cheese dip for our sampling counter, we decided to stick with a Swiss theme. For the Swiss cheeseboard special, we agreed on the mild, well-balanced, and slightly sweet Rothenbühler Swiss; the bold, nutty, sharp, and aromatic L'Evitaz; and of course, the ever-popular delicate and fruity Emmental. Although I left June and Archie to discuss the salty accompaniments, it still somehow felt too quiet in the shop.

Mrs. Schultz eventually joined us at the sampling counter. "It needs some time in the refrigerator for the flavors to meld. I hope you like it."

"I'm sure we will," June said.

"We'll see—it'll be hit or Swiss!" Archie exclaimed, chuckling at his pun.

Mrs. Schultz and I laughed with him. June stayed unusually silent.

"How was *Godzilla*?" I asked.

Archie shuffled his feet. "I didn't go."

Without comment, June kept writing the day's cheeseboard combos on the chalkboard in her neat handwriting. Now I realized why the shop felt out of sorts—it wasn't filled with their usual friendly chatter.

"I know, I should've gone. It would've been fun. I'm sorry." He directed the comment to June.

June gave Archie a half smile for the apology. "It's okay. You're forgiven. You're the one who missed out—it was an awesome double feature. My friends and I roped Duncan into going. He needs to take his mind off of everything that's been going on," she said. "By the way, he told me what happened at Hope's, and he feels really bad about what he said to you, Willa. I told him what a cool person you are."

"Thanks, June. It's okay. I've been known to accuse people wrongly. I don't hold it against him." In fact, he was still on my suspect list, but I wasn't going to tell her that. "Has he talked to you about working at Chocolate Bliss at all?"

"Not really. When I first saw him in Lockwood, I thought he came back home because he'd finally quit."

"What do you mean 'finally'?"

She stopped writing to think for a moment. "It was like a year or two ago—his mother told my mother who told me that they weren't appreciating him at his job and that the owners he works for were bad people."

"What did they do?" Archie asked.

June shrugged. "I didn't get the details. I just remember his mother told him he should leave, but I took what she said with a grain of salt, because she's been wanting him to move back to Lockwood forever. But now after what you said about them and what's happened . . . I wonder if those two he works for really *are* bad people."

It made me wonder too.

June took the chalkboard to the café area to hang it.

"Archie told me what happened at Hope's last night," Mrs. Schultz said, once June had gone.

"And Heath came by when I got back." I continued to speak quietly and made sure June was out of earshot when I told them about the substance that had killed Kevin Wallace.

"Anybody could have that," Mrs. Schultz said, wide-eyed.

"I know. Heath said Kevin Wallace ingested the equivalent of several vials worth, which is why the police believe it had to have been put in the crème when the chocolates were being made, not poured on afterward or injected into them. He said there wasn't any trace of the substance in or around the box."

"That means they were poisoned when they were made," Archie said.

Mrs. Schultz picked up the thread. "Which means it was Pearce, Riley, Duncan, or Hope."

"And we know it wasn't Hope," Archie said.

"Right. Or there's another possibility. The chocolates were switched out," I said.

"You mean by Gil and Trevor?" Mrs. Schultz asked, recalling our discussion last night. "But they didn't even know about Chocolate Bliss until that afternoon."

"I found out this morning from Constance that they *did* know. Weeks ago."

Archie's and Mrs. Schultz's mouths popped open in surprise.

"Trevor or maybe both of them might've been at the taco truck after Claude saw me with the chocolates that I was bringing to A. J. My guess is that Claude clued them in. They could've already made the poisoned chocolates and planned to infiltrate the shop at another time but decided to use the opportunity of switching A. J.'s chocolates."

"But that would mean Claude was in on it too," Archie said.

"Potentially. Or he could've been commiserating with them without knowing what they had planned. I wonder if he was the one who told them about Chocolate Bliss in the first place. *He* knew about it before the grand opening."

"I wonder what Claude keeps in his medicine cabinet," Mrs. Schultz pondered, tapping a polished nail to her chin.

The three of us flinched when Claude came bounding through the door with greetings.

"Morning, Claude," I said, trying to brush off my suspicions about him. Having an employee you currently think could be involved in murder was awkward at best.

"Good morning, almost afternoon. What's got you spooked?" he asked me.

"Uh, nothing!" I said too cheerily. I toned it down. "I guess it's been too quiet—we haven't had any customers yet."

Hands on his hips, he scanned the shop as if to confirm. "Ah, are customers still staying away because of the poisoning? Geez, I wouldn't have expected that." He looked introspective.

Mrs. Schultz retrieved Claude's Curds & Whey apron from under the counter and ambled up to him. As she handed it to him, she stuck her face close to his and peered at him. She was as tall as he was, so they were practically nose to nose. After a handful of seconds, she stepped back and smiled at him as if the odd interaction had been like any other. She began straightening one of the already perfect displays on the table next to her. Archie and I looked at each other. What was Mrs. Schultz up to?

"Do I have something on my face?" Claude wiped his cheeks and his goatee.

"No. I was just admiring your eyes. They're such a nice shade of . . . uh . . ."

"Brown?" he filled in, skeptically.

"Yes. Brown," she said with her toothy smile.

He nodded, seeming to consider the compliment. "Nice thing to say. Thanks."

I had an idea that she might be conducting her own red-eye research, which got me to thinking that we could use her bravado at the candy shop.

Mrs. Schultz retrieved her dip from the refrigerator and brought it to the sampling counter. I opened some salted mini pretzels, and we all had a taste. Mrs. Schultz was right—I could easily polish off a whole bowl of it in one of my evenings on the couch watching my favorite Hitchcock movie, *Rebecca*.

Since everyone was gathered round, I spoke to my crew. "I have an idea, and I want to see what you think. What's happened at Chocolate Bliss has really messed things up for Hope's business. I was thinking we could surprise her by all meeting at her cakery tonight to clean her kitchen, so she doesn't have to hire professional cleaners or do it all herself. The police made a mess of it."

"That's a great idea," Archie said with a wide smile on his face.

"She could sure use some community support. I'll ask some of her other friends too, like Gil and Trevor," I added. It would be a bonus to have an excuse to see them.

Claude snorted. "Good luck with that!"

"I know they were upset with her about Chocolate Bliss, but you think they still hold a grudge after everything that she's been through since yesterday?" I asked him. I was hoping Claude had the inside track to how mad they were at Hope.

"You'd have to ask them," he said with his palms out, as if he didn't want to get involved. "But I wouldn't doubt it. She still did them dirty, even if it did end up in disaster for her."

"What about you, Claude? Do you still hold a grudge?" Mrs. Schultz asked him.

"Me? Nah, I'm good. Life's too short. But I don't think I'm available tonight. I've still got my bread research to do. Hey, wasn't there another form you wanted me to sign?" he asked me, quick to change the subject.

It took me a second to remember the fib I'd told last night in his driveway. "I ended up having your signed one after all. It was stuck to the back of one of the other forms," I answered with a wave of my hand, hoping to wave it from his memory as well. I returned to our conversation. "Nobody's obligated to come, but if you want to, we'll meet at Hope's Cakery at seven tonight. Claude, do you mind inviting Jasmine for us?"

He shrugged. "I'll let her know," he said in a tone that didn't hold a lot of promise for her attendance.

Archie put his arm around June, giving her shoulders a shake to rouse some enthusiasm. "Come on! It'll be fun. We'll crank up some music."

I didn't blame her for not being up for it. After all, it seemed that Archie's lingering feelings for Hope were the reason their blossoming relationship had stalled.

She broke into a smile. "Yeah, I'll come. I do feel bad for her."

"Great! Thanks, guys," I said. Not only would we be helping Hope, but maybe having everyone there would bring some answers to the surface.

"What's on tap for today since it's dead in here? Oop. Sorry, bad choice of words," Claude said.

I ignored it and took out my tablet, handing it to June. I said to Claude, "June can show you how to do the inventory list. It'll get you acquainted with some of our cheeses. Do you mind, June?"

"No. I'd rather have something to do . . . as long as it's not cleaning." She playfully stuck her tongue out at Archie and gestured for Claude to follow her to the refrigerated case where we kept our goat and feta cheeses.

"All right, I deserve it," Archie called after her.

"June's a good friend, you know, Archie," Mrs. Schultz reminded him.

His smile lingered as he watched her. "I know. She's the coolest."

"Does *she* know you feel that way?" I asked.

"Sure she does. Why wouldn't she?"

Mrs. Schultz and I glanced at each other. Why were guys so clueless?

"What?" he asked, visibly perplexed.

"You'll have to figure this one out for yourself, Arch," I said.

I spotted Baz through one of the large front windows just before he entered Curds & Whey. "Hey, guys. Is this a good time?" he asked upon entering.

"What do you think?" My arm swept the room like a game show hostess showing off a new car.

Baz nodded at the shop, vacant of customers.

I took off my apron. "I have to run a Team Cheese errand with Baz. I'm going to need you, Mrs. Schultz."

Her eyebrows rose in surprise, but she loosened her apron without asking questions.

"You want to come too, Archie?" I asked.

He leaned in and said quietly, "You know I'm always up for investigating, but I don't think I want to leave June here alone with Claude. He's still one of our suspects, right?"

"Good point. All right. We won't be too long. I have my phone if you need me. You're in charge. If we're not back in an hour and it's still like this, you three can enjoy Mrs. Schultz's dip."

"Did someone say dip?" Baz scanned the sampling counter and made a beeline for it.

I snagged him by the arm, and Mrs. Schultz and I pulled him out of the shop while he made a show of looking longingly after the dip and pretzels.

Headed in the direction of Main Street, Mrs. Schultz asked, "Where are we going?"

"To Sweet Tooth Vintage Candy," Baz said.

"Gil and Trevor?" she asked, leaving the rest of the question unspoken.

We need you to find a way into the back of their shop to look for evidence of chocolate making while Baz and I distract them."

Baz nodded in agreement at his role.

"This is the first time I don't *want* to find anything. We do have other suspects," I said as we walked up the street.

"Especially after what June said about Duncan having a problem with Pearce and Riley for quite some time," Mrs. Schultz added.

I filled in the blanks for Baz about what June had told us.

"Didn't you say Pearce was pointing the finger at Duncan this morning?" Baz asked.

"Yup. There's definitely a fracture in that trio. Enough to give one of them motivation to kill in order to seek their revenge?"

The three of us glanced at one other. We didn't have an answer.

"So that's why we need to pursue all avenues, including the possibility that the candy guys swapped A. J.'s box of chocolates for poisoned ones. Are you up for it, Mrs. Schultz?" I asked her.

Mrs. Schultz squinted her blue eyes and looked off in the distance. After a few moments, her attention returned to me. "I will be when we get there."

CHAPTER 22

We crossed Main Street at the library and walked another block to the inn, walking in silence as Mrs. Schultz discovered her "character's motivation." Next door to the inn was Sweet Tooth Vintage Candy. The red-and-white peppermint swirl awning above the entrance to their shop left little question that there would be sweets inside, even without the large window displaying a bubble gum machine filled with colorful orbs of gum, large red-and-white swirl lollipops, and chocolate Easter bunnies on post-holiday sale. A man was sitting on a bench in front of the window lost in his cell phone.

A tinkling bell attached to the door announced our arrival. Gil, who was at the register with a woman and her young son, smiled and nodded to us in acknowledgment. Inside the small shop, a path of stickers that looked like oversized peppermints led to classic vintage candy—Pop Rocks, Necco Wafers, Sugar Daddy pops, Chuckles . . . and on and on. Glass jars offered various flavors of Old Fashioned Sticks, like cinnamon and tutti fruitti. Unfortunately, there was no display case to indicate they'd gone ahead with their plan to make their own chocolate.

Mrs. Schultz stopped at the gumball machine, and Baz and I scoped out the shelf of vintage chocolate bars. I took a few wrapped ones—Goobers, Marathon bars, Charleston Chews—out of their boxes. I wanted to see if any of them could've been poisoned and switched out to resemble the ones made by Chocolate Bliss, but none were the right shape.

I left the chocolates and waited for Gil to be done with his customers at the register. The boy, about seven, was bargaining with his mom for licorice.

"Wouldn't you rather have this stuffed toy for a souvenir instead?" his mother said. She was holding a plush replica of a Circus Peanut, hoping to persuade him. It was a good likeness, but not a very exciting toy.

"I want licorice. Please, Mom?"

"Not licorice. You'd have this for much longer. You can keep it in your room." It was obvious she didn't want him to have candy. I knew it would be a lost cause. There was a reason for the phrase *Like a kid in a candy shop.*

"I'm sorry we ever came in here. It's torture!" he cried dramatically, leaning heavily against the counter, as if the weight of being denied licorice was too much to bear. I was ready for him to drop to the floor at any moment.

She sighed and turned to Gil behind the counter. "I guess I'll take two licorice sticks."

"Two? I want six!" he said, still not satisfied.

"Two will be fine," she told him calmly.

"It says six!" He pointed to the sign that said "Six licorice sticks for two fifty or fifty cents each."

She sighed. "All right, but you're only allowed to eat two now."

Gil had no sooner handed her the small bag of licorice when her son snatched it and dug his hand in. "I'm going outside to see Dad," he replied, scurrying out of the shop with the ends of three sticks already in his mouth.

"Just two!" she called after him futilely as she completed the transaction.

Once she left, I noticed two colored sheets of paper taped to the register. One of the signs offered candythemed birthday parties and the other was for a class to learn to make hot chocolate bombs. The date was for tomorrow afternoon. What luck!

While Baz was enthralled by the vintage candy bars, Mrs. Schultz was pretending to peruse the items on the opposite wall, all the while inching her way to the door leading to the back of the shop with the sign above it that read Private. I needed to keep Gil distracted. I approached the register.

"What brings you by, Willa? I don't think we've seen you in here in a year or more," he said.

"Guilty, as charged. I guess I'm not much of a sweets person."

"That's okay. I'm not much of a cheese person. Trevor just buys everything else in your shop," he said with an affectionate resignation.

I chuckled along with him. "I came by to see if you and Trevor would be willing to help us clean Hope's kitchen tonight. She's been through a lot."

He froze for a split second, then straightened the licorice jar next to the register. "I'm not sure if we're going to be free tonight."

I nodded. "I understand. Just thought I'd ask since I know you all are friends."

"That friendship's taking a little hiatus right now. Baz, I didn't see you there. Can I help you find something?" Gil was done talking about Hope.

"Hi, Gil. I'm working my way through," Baz answered, showing both hands gripping multiple chocolate bars.

Mrs. Schultz was at the end of the long counter to Gil's right, perilously close to crossing beyond the counter into the area customers shouldn't go. I had to keep his attention on me and Baz so Gil wouldn't see her. I pointed to the sign at the register. "What are hot chocolate bombs? Now *they* sound amazing!"

Instead of helping Gil's mood, his mouth puckered like he'd just eaten one of his own Warheads sour candies. He stood on his toes to look over the register and reached around it to tear off the sign. "They're chocolates with marshmallow inside that you melt in a hot chocolate drink. We received too many cancelations, so the class is off."

That's too bad." I was more disappointed than he knew.

Out of the corner of my eye, I saw Mrs. Schultz just about to go through the swinging door into their back room when it suddenly opened, almost clocking her.

"Whoa!" Trevor, with his arms stacked with boxes of wrapped candy, pulled up. "Mrs. Schultz! I'm sorry! Are you okay?" he said, putting the boxes on the counter so he could better assess her.

Mrs. Schultz was busted.

She covered her mouth and mumbled, "Bathroom?"

"I'm sorry, we don't have a public restroom, but they have one next door at the inn," Trevor suggested.

With her hand still covering her mouth she continued to speak as if her mouth was full of something, and added pleading eyes too. "Bubblegum. Dentures."

Trevor's face reddened. "Oh! In that case, let me take you to the one in our new room where we do our classes." He led her past us and beyond the last rack where Baz was choosing more candy to a doorway with a vertical-striped curtain across it that I hadn't noticed. He pushed the curtain open, and they went through.

I smiled to myself. Mrs. Schultz didn't wear dentures.

"Can I get you anything?" Gil asked as I continued to stand at his counter.

"Oh, uhhh—"

Baz joined us with both hands full of chocolate bars, which he deposited on the Formica counter. Gil began to ring up the purchase as they chatted amiably. My gaze kept pulling toward the curtained doorway.

I was relieved when Trevor walked back through without Mrs. Schultz. *Good! Mrs. Schultz would have some time to snoop.* He picked up the boxes he'd brought out before the run-in, saying hello to us and re-stocking some of the items by the counter.

"So that's where you have the chocolate-making classes?" I asked.

"We were lucky the space was already there and had the plumbing and electricity. We just never used it. Who knows when we'll use it again, thanks to that pop-up poison shop," Gil said.

"Gil! You can't say stuff like that." Trevor left what he was doing to go behind the counter and be by Gil.

"Why not? We spent a lot of money to outfit that room, and you spent a lot of time and effort decorating it."

"It was a fun project. You know how I love an

excuse to shop," Trevor said to us. "I even helped Hope buy some things for her new cakery. That was before we knew she stabbed us in the back, of course." He sighed. Trevor may not have been as demonstratively angry as Gil, but it was apparent he wasn't any happier about Chocolate Bliss than his husband was.

"Willa wants us to help them clean Hope's kitchen tonight," Gil told him.

Trevor stared at me with his hand on his chest. "Now, Willa, I'm a friendly neighbor, but even Mr. Rogers might have a hard time with that request."

"I know you're upset with her about bringing Chocolate Bliss to town, but don't you think she's paying for it more than anyone right now? Her cakery could be ruined forever."

Trevor and Gil looked at each other, then at the counter, but didn't make eye contact with us.

"Have you asked about her reasons for choosing Chocolate Bliss? Or when she decided to do it? Maybe things were in motion before you told her about your chocolate-making plans," I said.

"All I know is that she kept it a secret, didn't she? That was out of guilt," Gil said unapologetically.

"You didn't know about it before the grand opening?" This was my chance to see if they'd lie about it.

They glanced at each other, a seemingly quick silent agreement whether to tell me.

"Claude came in a couple weeks before asking us hypothetically if he left the bakery, would there be a position open here? It didn't take much for him to start complaining about what was going on at Hope's," Trevor said, confirming what I knew and what I suspected about Claude.

A clang sounded from the other room, followed by a cascade of crashing metal. *Uh-oh*.

We ran into the chocolate-making room to see Mrs. Schultz in front of a free-standing cabinet with its doors open, along with several pots, baking sheets, and silicone chocolate molds on the floor at her feet.

"Oops!" she said, her toothy grin in full view. She began to pick up the bakeware. I ran over to help so I could inspect the chocolate molds more closely, but Trevor was too quick and took everything out of my hands and placed them by the sink.

Mrs. Schultz did a little eye batting. "Thank you, Trevor. You'll have to forgive me. This room is so cute and neat, I just couldn't help a little snooping."

"Now you know my secret—I pile everything on top of each other. I told you we needed to replace this cabinet with something bigger," Trevor said to Gil.

"We might not need to replace it at all with the way things are going," Gil replied. "Look at this. New sink, new stove, new furniture. All for classes we can't even sell tickets for."

"The police will solve the case soon and things will go back to normal. People have short memories these days," I said, hoping to convince myself of it too.

Gil closed the cabinet door. "How short? We might still have Chocolate Bliss to contend with."

"I can't see Chocolate Bliss doing business in Yarrow Glen after this, no matter how the case turns out. I don't think you guys have anything to worry about," Baz said.

"Can you say that louder, Baz? Gil's such a worry wart. I told you Chocolate Bliss is done for." Trevor affectionately squeezed his husband's shoulders.

"It's not like I don't have reason to worry," Gil replied.

A look passed between them, making me wonder if his concern wasn't about a competing candy shop but rather about the investigation.

We had no choice but to follow Gil and Trevor out of the room without any further snooping. Baz paid for his inordinate amount of candy bars, and we said our goodbyes.

"Willa, hold up a second," Trevor said as we started for the door. He went behind the counter and reached under it, placing the item he'd retrieved on the shiny Formica surface. It was A. J.'s fedora.

A tiny gasp escaped my throat that I prayed they didn't hear. "A hat?" I said, hoping it covered the sound of my surprise.

"Found it out back last night. It's A. J. Stringer's, isn't it?"

I was at a loss for what to say, which might've worked in my favor. "Could be?"

"Beatrice said she sold it to him or one like it, anyway. We know you two *hang out* together."

Why did he seem to emphasize "hang out"?

"You want to give it back to him?" He held it out for me.

With each step forward, my guilt magnified. Was this their way of telling me they'd seen us last night or was I being paranoid?

"I'm sure if it's his he'll appreciate it," I said, plastering a smile on my face.

I did my best to casually stroll out of Sweet Tooth Vintage Candy with A. J.'s hat. As soon as the shop's door closed behind us, I bolted down the sidewalk.

"What was that all about?" Baz asked when I finally

stopped in front of the inn and he and Mrs. Schultz caught up.

"Sorry, that spooked me. Do you think they saw me and A. J. last night?"

"Wouldn't they have come out and asked you?" Mrs. Schultz said.

"Not if they're guilty of something. Did you find anything before we came into the room?"

"Just what you saw. They have chocolate molds, but of course they would. If they did make poisoned chocolates, I don't think they would've left any evidence lying around in a place so accessible."

Although I hadn't held out much hope of finding anything incriminating, it was still disappointing our efforts didn't produce anything but paranoia on my part. I had to find a way to check the candy guys off my list.

"I've got one more thing to check out," I told Baz and Mrs. Schultz.

Baz looked at his phone. "Sorry, Carl sent me a job. I gotta run."

"That's okay. I won't need your help. Mrs. Schultz, you can head back too. I won't be long. If we still haven't had much business, tell Claude he can go home."

"Gladly," Mrs. Schultz replied.

"We'll catch up later," Baz said to me.

They continued to the Main Street crosswalk, and I took a right at the inn.

CHAPTER 23

I climbed the three porch steps but instead of continuing into the inn, I walked down the side porch around to the back. Maybe I should've had Baz and Mrs. Schultz stay at the candy shop and keep Gil and Trevor occupied while I did this last errand, but I hadn't thought of it until now. In the daylight, I'd be able to see the car in their portico without having to get so close.

I left the porch and continued past the inn's drop-off area where the trees still created a privacy barrier to Sweet Tooth Vintage Candy. Once on the sidewalk, I boldly walked next door. Both cars were there, the Subaru behind the one I'd yet to identify. I only had to take a few steps onto the property before I saw it—a Volkswagen with a hatchback. No spoiler. Gas engine. I mentally crossed Gil and Trevor off my suspect list.

"What are you doing here?"

I turned with a start. A. J., of course. He'd dispensed with the trench coat and was back to his usual attire of green Salvation Army jacket, white T-shirt, and jeans.

"Sneaking up on me *again*, A. J.?"

"Hey, I was the one who was supposed to come back, remember?" His face brightened. "You found my hat!"

I pulled him with me off the property and we went

back in the direction of the inn toward the library on the corner. I handed him his hat.

"I didn't find it. Gil and Trevor did. And they knew it belonged to you."

"How?"

"They figured it was a thrift shop find, so they asked Beatrice."

"Beatrice blew my cover? Dang. I should've told her what I bought it for." He trudged silently beside me.

A. J. was not at all acting like himself. He usually walked at a fast clip, and he talked at the same pace if he wasn't trying to pry information from me. But not today.

"Is it the hat or something else? You don't seem yourself. What's going on?" I asked.

"I just got out of another interrogation at the police station."

"Why?" The last time I talked with Heath, he was focused on someone in the Chocolate Bliss kitchen having committed the criminal act.

He stuck his hands in his jacket pockets. "They read what was on Kevin's laptop. He'd started writing the review on Chocolate Bliss, so our hunch about why he took the chocolates was on point."

"That's no surprise. What does that have to do with you? Did Deandra say something else?"

"She didn't have to. It was all on his computer. He had a whole plan to take over my position as editor in chief. Not only was he trying to be a one-man show, which I was stupidly encouraging, but he had a whole manifesto to make me look incompetent. He'd planned to use my podcast against me and tell the publisher I was shirking my newspaper duties for the podcast. It was all there in black and white."

"Wow. He really wasn't a nice guy."

"Deandra never liked him. I should've listened to her. I thought she was just jealous."

"Lesson learned the hard way," I mumbled.

"Yeah, well, it might cost me my freedom. The police think I saw what was on his computer, and that gives me motive. I know I've moved up on their person of interest list."

I stopped walking. "No way! Oh, A. J., come on. They know you."

"'They know me' won't hold up as a defense in a court of law." He continued walking, veering to the library's butterfly garden, where he plopped himself on the bench. I followed him.

The spark of excitement I always saw in his eyes was gone. The old A. J. knew how to annoy me, but I didn't like this new, defeated A. J. I understood what it was like to have your freedom on the line, and I didn't wish it upon anybody, certainly not a friend and a good sleuthing partner. I had to do something to turn this around.

I sat down next to him. "Do you have an alibi?"

"I was at Apricot Grille, but the server says he can't be sure what time I left. They're saying there's a window of time where I could've gone to the Gazette and poisoned him and then called the police, pretending that I'd just gotten there and found him."

I scoffed. "That sounds very willy-nilly."

"Willy what?"

I waved my hand. "It's an expression I've heard Mrs. Schultz use. I mean, it's not very concrete. That doesn't seem like a strong case against you. If you knew all that, why wouldn't you have just fired him?"

He shrugged. "Revenge?"

"That's ridiculous and anyone who knows you knows that. You'd have rather made a story out of it."

The corner of A. J.'s mouth turned up. "Thanks, Willa."

"I'll talk to Heath." *Somehow.*

"I appreciate it, but I don't know if your sexual wiles are going to be enough to make him ignore the evidence."

"A. J.! I mean I'm going to tell him about the other suspects he should be investigating more closely."

Heath said they didn't believe the poisoning was done spur of the moment, because there weren't any traces of the substance found in the box. I knew this would make A. J. feel better but I didn't feel comfortable sharing Heath's information with anyone but Team Cheese.

"If we could prove the substance was put in more chocolates than just the ones Kevin Wallace ate, that would prove it was done at the cakery and would get you *and* me off the hook," I told him.

"How are we going to do that? As far as we know, all the chocolates from that day have been turned in to the police or eaten, and nobody else has been poisoned."

"That's what Pearce and Riley keep saying, but it doesn't make sense." I shook my head in frustration.

"Just because we want it to be so, doesn't mean it is." He slouched on the bench and leaned his head back to look at the sky.

"The A. J. I know would never give up on a story until he's pursued all the leads."

"My usual sources have all clammed up. Go figure. They don't want to talk to a suspect."

"We still have plenty of possibilities without your police sources' inside information."

I told him about my conversation with Pearce and Riley that morning and also what June knew about Duncan. With each piece of information, he sat up a little straighter.

By the time I was done, he was scribbling notes onto a notepad from his messenger bag.

"Well?" I said.

He clicked his pen and returned it to the bag. "Okay. Let's see what we can dig up!"

The spark was back.

CHAPTER 24

We left each other at the corner—he headed one way down Main Street to the Gazette and I headed the other to the security complex. I was determined to speak with Heath. I felt nervous about my decision, but this was official business. He'd want me to give him the information I had.

I passed the post office and Ron's Service Station before coming to the newer glass-fronted building I'd been in yesterday. Through the lobby, I walked up to the bulletproof partition stenciled with POLICE at the top. The no-nonsense security officer was seated behind it, the one who reminded me of a young, tough Bruce Willis. Even though he'd seen me often enough since I lived in Yarrow Glen, he never made small talk.

"Hi. I'm here to see Detective Heath."

Without a greeting, he put the landline phone to his ear to call Heath's office. After a few moments, he put it back in its cradle. "Detective Heath's not in his office."

"Oh." I was about to ask for Shep when I saw Heath emerge with the chief of police, a tall man with doughy jowls. I waved at Heath until he noticed me. Unfortunately, so did Chief Jeffers. They continued talking, so

I stepped back from the partition to wait until Heath was free.

"Have a good lunch, Chief," I heard the security officer say before the door buzzed, and Chief Jeffers exited. He looked me over with a neutral expression and continued through the lobby and out the door. *Uh-oh.*

I looked through the partition, expecting Heath to be at the door to allow me into the secured police department, but he'd disappeared. Even without Chief Jeffers there, he didn't want to see me. I checked my phone. No text that he was coming out or that I should come in. Oh no. Would he think I was ignoring what he said last night and came just because I wanted to see him?

"Is Shep in? Officer Shepherd?" I corrected myself.

The security officer checked his computer. "He's not in."

I sighed in disappointment. "Okay. Thanks." I scanned the room on the other side of the partition one more time, still hopeful that Heath had just been waiting for Chief Jeffers to leave the building before coming to see me. Silly me. He wasn't coming.

I walked away from the partition to the lobby but was reluctant to leave the building. I looked at my phone again. Would a phone call or text from me make it worse? Probably. I stuck my phone back in my pocket.

The buzz of the security door sounded, and I turned, expecting to see Heath after all. It was Duncan.

He exited the police department and saw me.

"Do the police want to see you too?" he asked, approaching me.

"No, I'm uh, waiting for a friend." I didn't feel comfortable telling him I'd intended to give the police a piece of information, even if it wasn't against him. "Are Pearce and Riley here too?"

"They must've been here before because the police had more questions about making the chocolates." He shifted from one foot to the other. "Hey, listen, I'm sorry I went off on you last night. June vouches for you and she's a pretty good judge of character."

"That's okay. This is a really stressful time for everyone, all of you at Chocolate Bliss, especially."

"I just don't get why they think one of us would've done it." He glanced around and saw we were alone and gestured for us to take a seat on the firm, straight-backed sofa. "June said you've helped the police solve murder cases before?"

"That's been exaggerated," I said, trying to brush it off.

"Why would I ruin my chances to make a success of this shop? I didn't think any of us would, but now . . . I don't know if I trust Pearce and Riley anymore."

"What do you mean?"

"The police asked me about the contract that I wouldn't sign. Nobody but Pearce and Riley knew about that. I think they're trying to make it look like I was mad about it and sabotaged the shop." His voice was tight with emotion.

Sitting this close to Duncan, I saw the stress around his eyes, his clenched jaw, the vein visible in his taut neck.

"Why wouldn't you sign it?" I asked.

"Because it wasn't what we'd agreed to. I was stupid to put everything in motion with this new Chocolate Bliss over a handshake. Pearce kept putting off drawing up a contract, saying it was just formalities. He waited until a week before the shop opened to finally give the contract to me. He knew how bad I wanted this. He thought I'd sign it just to have it, even if it gave them most of the profits. He said the only way he'd change the contract was if I could front everything myself. I almost walked away right then, but . . . I don't know." He leaned over, resting his forearms on his knees, and shook his head. "I'm stubborn, I guess. I wasn't willing to give up on my dream. This was the closest I was going to come to it. I've been trying ever since to find a way to get the money."

Duncan sounded sincere. If he was telling the whole truth, that left him without motive. But if he'd given up the dream and instead decided to seek revenge . . .

"I told that detective I applied for a loan. He can look that up and see that I'm telling the truth. I wouldn't do that if I wanted to tank our business," he continued.

"Are you planning to go back to Oregon?"

He huffed. "Pearce tried to convince me I was better off going back, but that was just to make himself feel better that he was cheating me out of the new shop just like he did in Ashland. There's nothing left for me there. This *had* to work out, that's why I took Pearce's help to come down and open it with me. I knew that with him to back me up during the first few months, we'd do well enough to make it a permanent location. I moved out of my apartment in Eugene, and Riley already hired my replacement. I risked it all on this." His head dropped into his hands.

I wasn't sure what to do. Pat him on the back? Say something reassuring? He seemed sincere in his desperation. Then again, so did Pearce and Riley. Maybe it *was* the candy guys and/or Claude after all.

I had to start narrowing down the suspects. Everyone possibly had opportunity, so it all came down to motive. Duncan could've been mad at Pearce for duping him about the contract. The candy guys wanted

Chocolate Bliss to fail, and they were mad at Hope for partnering with another chocolate shop behind their backs. Claude not only wanted Chocolate Bliss to fail but also the cakery, so it could go back to being a bread bakery. Pearce and Riley? I didn't have a motive for them yet. They had the most to lose, but that apology out of nowhere this morning felt like they were trying to cover all their bases since they'd found out I was dating the detective on the case. Were they just desperate to clear their names or were they trying to manipulate me because one or both of them were guilty?

Somebody was lying. I had to find out who.

CHAPTER 25

Duncan walked to his car, and I started back to Curds & Whey. I'd been gone too long, so I checked my messages.

There was one from Archie he'd sent only ten minutes prior: *Don't rush back. Still slow. Claude's gone home.*

Not what I wanted to hear, but at least I didn't have to feel guilty for being away from the shop. I had to get a better handle on who to believe, Pearce and Riley or Duncan. I felt like I knew Pearce and Riley, but it had been more than ten years. And the only thing I knew for sure was that they were good at keeping secrets, like they had about their relationship when I was engaged to him. June said good things about Duncan, but was it for the same reason I wanted to believe Pearce and Riley? Having a history with someone was a strong influence. Pearce and Riley—well, Pearce at least—seemed ready to believe it might be Duncan, but that could've just been for self-serving reasons. Who else could tell me more about Duncan?

The meow of a cat brought me out of my ruminations. I looked around. Pudge was pacing in front of Bea's Hive of Thrifted Finds. I crossed the street to see if he was okay. This time of day, he was always snoozing in Carl's Hardware, as far as I knew.

"Pudge, are you okay?"

He stopped at the window to the shop, looked up at it, and gave another loud wail. I looked to see what was bothering him. Beatrice's shop only had standard-sized windows in the front, so the contents of the store were mostly unknown until you stepped inside and found yourself in a maze of vintage curiosities. The only things I saw were a few cute buildings from a light-up Christmas village and two O-mouthed carolers towering over it.

The door to the shop opened with the sounds of a cuckoo clock, and Pudge ran in before Beatrice even stepped a foot onto the sidewalk.

"Pudge!" I yelled, surprised.

"It's okay." Beatrice waved off my concern. Today, her blue-framed glasses hung from their bejeweled chain over dark denim overalls and a T-shirt. "He's been coming to visit Sweet Potato. Who am I to stand in the way of true love?" Sweet Potato was Beatrice's orange tabby cat.

"Oh my! He really *is* an alley cat, even neutered. How did he find her?"

"It was the case of the drunken carolers. I'd see them knocked over every morning and kidded that they must get tipsy on wassail at night after I go upstairs. Sweet Potato never had an affinity for the window and always stayed upstairs at night with me, so I couldn't imagine that it was her. Then one night I heard Pudge outside, serenading her. I came down and there was Sweet Potato, my own Juliet, pressed up against the window. It wasn't long after that night that he came inside on the heels of a customer. I thought it would be a disaster—Sweet Potato has never liked other cats—but Pudge was different."

"Aw, that's so sweet!"

"He's not happy to stay inside, though. Thirty minutes tops, and he's meowing to get out. I don't blame him—Sweet Potato can be a handful."

I chuckled. "Well, young love can be volatile," I played along. "I'm glad all is well. I was just checking on him."

Beatrice stepped all the way outside. "Any developments from your detective boyfriend on the chocolate poisoning?" she asked before I could leave.

"I'm afraid not. I'm sure they're making progress; he's just not informing me of it."

"It was heartening to read that no one else fell ill."

"It's a relief, for sure. It looks like the box of chocolates the journalist ate was the only one poisoned." Although that meant bad news for me and A. J., I was still thankful no one else had gotten sick or worse.

"Unlucky fella."

We nodded in sad commiseration.

"Will you be around about five o'clock tonight? We'd like to return the costumes from yesterday," I said.

"I'll be here."

I moved aside so an older man could walk around me on the sidewalk, but it looked like we were both in his way—he wanted into the thrift shop. Beatrice opened the door for him with a flourish and a smile, waving her arm to usher him inside. The door again set off the cuckoo clock, which had been revamped to "cuckoo" three times when the door opened. Now *that* would drive me cuckoo.

"Good afternoon, Fred. Shopping for more vintage electronics?" she asked.

"They don't make radios like they used to, Beatrice," he replied with a smile of his own, going through the doorway.

Beatrice wiggled her fingers at me in goodbye and followed him inside.

I found myself thinking about Pudge and Sweet Potato as I continued down the sidewalk. Why couldn't love be that easy for me? Ironically, Golden Glen Meadery was up ahead—Roman's shop. He was my first unsuccessful relationship in Yarrow Glen. Gia worked there. She seemed pretty close with Duncan when I saw them together at Chocolate Bliss, and Constance mentioned how she'd seen them together more than once at The Cellar. How well did Gia know Duncan?

There was little hope of Gia talking to me, seeing as how I was not her favorite person, to say the least. But last I knew, she and Roman were still working together and possibly still dating. Maybe he could get some information about Duncan from her.

I had to make one last stop—the meadery.

CHAPTER 26

I entered Golden Glen Meadery with a purposely pleasant look on my face—something between a smile and my resting face—in hopes of not ticking off Gia the moment she saw me. This might've been a *Mission Impossible* task, but I always gave it a go whenever we crossed paths.

Besides the tension I had with Gia, the meadery was an inviting shop. The beamed ceilings were painted gray and the floor was poured concrete, but the exposed brick between the horizontally stacked shelves of mead warmed the room. Whereas Curds & Whey tapped all of a patron's senses, this starker palate allowed for the mead to be the star of the shop. Sleek, long-necked bottles contained a spectrum of crisp golden hues from clear morning sunshine to a deep brandy brown. Some of the Golden Glen labels read Blackcurrant, Pear Nectar, Dry Honey, and Rosemary—all flavors Roman made himself.

The meadery was vacant of customers and of Gia. Maybe I'd get to talk to Roman without first enduring her scowl.

This thought no sooner crossed my mind when the tasting room's barnlike door at the rear of the shop slid open and she emerged. Her polite smile vanished when she recognized me. She walked over to me wearing her usual work attire—a meadery shirt, a mini skirt, and sky-high heels. Once again, I admired her endurance. I had one pair of black heels in my closet that had moved with me to my last eight apartments and had only been worn to two weddings and a bar mitzvah.

"Hi, Gia."

She returned to her polite barely there smile. "Can I help you?"

"I'm here to see Roman. Is he in the tasting room?"

"He's in his mead-making room."

"Thanks." I'd been in that windowless basement-like room before, which was located off the tasting room. It was where he aged the large tanks of mead until the drink was ready to be bottled and also where he kept his bottled inventory. The small section of Enora's wine he sold came from his family's winery in northern Sonoma.

"You're going to disturb him anyway?" she said as I started past her.

"I guess I am," I replied and kept going. She didn't follow.

I walked through the doorway into a cozy, softly lit room, the transom windows on the back wall adding natural light. I'd been here plenty of times to deliver cheese platters to pair with Roman's mead for scheduled customer tastings and always appreciated how his tasting room exuded a very different feel than the industrial aesthetic of the front of the shop. A horseshoe of round, high-top cocktail tables hugged the walls, partially framing a grouping of comfortable-looking worn leather chairs and a sofa in the center.

I went around the bar with stools for eight to the

corner where I knew his mead-making room to be. Opening the door, I announced myself so as not to startle him. I found him at a counter in the back with some large jars that looked more like science experiments than beverages.

Roman turned and greeted me with a crooked smile that formed a dimple on his cheek. I was still getting used to seeing him clean-shaven. "Hey, Willa!" he said, moving to the sink to wash his hands.

"Hi, Roman. Am I disturbing you?"

"No, I was just playing around with some new flavors." Roman was as laid back as his T-shirt, jeans, and cowboy boots.

"This is what it starts out looking like?" I made a *yikes!* face, slightly revolted by the contents on the counter.

"You know how they say don't meet your heroes? I say don't meet your mead before it's ready. Fermentation is not a pretty sight unless you're one of us brewers. These are just experiments. Sometimes they work, sometimes they don't, but most great mead ideas start that way." He turned off the water and dried his hands with a paper towel. "I stopped in for your birthday bash yesterday, but Archie told me you were at the police station because of the poisoned chocolates. How did you manage to get involved in that?"

"I always manage to, don't I?"

He laughed with me, knowing all too well. *Funny/ Not funny.*

"It looked like the poisoning affected your big day. I'm sorry," he said, as we walked out of the mead-making room.

I sighed, the disappointment of that day seeping in again. "Yeah, it fizzled out as soon as the news hit."

"Same here. I had two private tastings, both canceled. I might have to cancel the cheese plate I ordered for next week's tasting. We'll see."

"I understand. I might have to adjust next month's mead order for the café." When I'd decided to open the Cheeseboard Café, it was a no-brainer to serve Roman's mead and his family's wine. He'd always supported my business, and he even helped me through the process of securing a liquor license for the café. Although we were no longer dating, we were still entwined in business and in friendship. The initial awkwardness of returning to a friendship without the flirty banter had finally subsided for the most part. Roman was a natural flirt.

He went behind the gorgeous, handcrafted black walnut bar, and I took a seat on one of the stools that lined it. On the olive wall behind the bar hung a large rendering of Roman's Golden Glen label. His mead was simply showcased on a single glass shelf below it.

"I know it's work hours, but I'd like to get your opinion on my latest creation. I was going to have the group who was coming today give it a try as a bonus since we're not selling it yet. It would've been nice to get a dozen mead drinkers' opinions, but someone with a developed palate like yourself would be helpful too. If you don't mind?"

"Twist my arm," I said. It was true, I never partook during the workday, but after what I'd been going through lately, a few sips of mead certainly wouldn't hurt.

From under the bar, he lifted a fat clear jug with a beautiful translucent cranberry red mead inside. The mead didn't go into the sleek mead bottles that were found on the shelves until it was ready to be sold.

"I'm not sure if it's what I want it to be." He poured the mead—just enough for a few sips—into two wine-glasses. He slid one to me.

"What kind is it?" I asked.

"I don't want to say until you try it. People can be influenced into thinking it tastes a certain way just because I tell them what it is. The color might tip you off enough."

I sniffed, and caught the whiff of berry and a hint of something else. We clinked glasses and I took my first sip, smacking my tongue against the roof of my mouth. Once my tastebuds got over the surprise, I sampled again. "By the color, I expected it to be sweet, but it's got a hint of smokiness to it. I like the balance. A berry with peppers. At first, I thought cranberry because of the color, but it's lighter than that without the bite cran-berry has." I took another sip, finishing it off. "Is that chipotle pepper?"

His smile grew. "Raspberry chipotle. That's it! I knew you'd be the right one to ask. You have a good palate."

"I usually save it for cheese, but I'm glad I can help. It's really good, Roman." It really was. If I wasn't going back to work, I'd have had another glass.

He offered me more, but I reluctantly declined. He drank his in one swig, nodding in satisfaction. "Thanks. I wanted to make sure the chipotle was coming through enough."

"It's just right. You get the berry, then the smoki-ness slides in. Your group that canceled missed out." I shook my head and lamented, "This Chocolate Bliss murder seems to be affecting everyone."

"You, especially. They're *the* Pearce and Riley, aren't

they?" He extended a sorrowful look, while capping the mead bottle.

Roman and I had been friends even before we'd dated, so he knew about Pearce and Riley. I hadn't expected him to remember who they were to me.

"Yeah, that's them. I had no idea they planned to open a Chocolate Bliss in Hope's new place. Did you hear anything about their pop-up before they opened?"

"I heard rumblings. Gia's been hanging out with Duncan since he's been here—a month or so now. I had no idea who he worked for."

"So you know Gia and Duncan are friends?" I treaded lightly. Gia not only worked at Roman's meadery but she and Roman had been dating for the past year, as far as I knew. Even though she and Duncan looked kind of cozy when I saw them at Chocolate Bliss, I didn't want to pass along my assumptions about her relationship with him to Roman.

"They used to date in high school," he stated matter-of-factly.

My eyebrows shot up before my brain told them not to.

Roman chuckled. "We're not exclusive. Never were," he explained.

"Ah." I tried to stay out of his business with Gia. They'd gotten together almost immediately after he and I broke up, which had made me salty for quite some time. But I couldn't help but wonder how working at the meadery together and non-exclusive dating for a whole year worked out. I knew it wouldn't have worked out for me. *Not your business, Willa! And thank goodness.*

"What are you thinking?" Roman asked.

"What do you mean?" I could feel my face heat up in embarrassment. Were my thoughts about his dating life that transparent?

"There's been a murder in town, and you know some of the people involved. You don't usually let that slide."

"Oh," I said with relief. Oddly, talking about murder was much more comfortable than thinking about Roman's dating life. "You're right about that. I'm even more involved than you think."

He looked at me, his eyes questioning.

"I don't want to get into it now, but I do have reasons to try to figure this out. And Pearce has asked me to help him, if you can believe that."

"Does that give you more incentive or less?"

We laughed together again.

"The one thing I don't want to do is have to spend more time with him or Riley, but I would like to know more about Duncan. Has Gia said much to you about him?"

Roman chuckled. "That would be awkward."

"Yeah, I guess you're right."

"She probably knows him pretty well, though. You could ask her."

Easy for him to say. Two years ago, I'd accused the guy she was dating, Derrick, of murder. The outcome was one neither of us wanted. That, compounded with my close relationship with Roman, and well . . . let's just say, we wouldn't be besties anytime soon. And now I'd be questioning her about another friend of hers suspected in a murder? Probably not the best idea. But if Gia was close with Duncan, I wanted to know how close they were and how much she knew about what was going on at Chocolate Bliss.

"I don't know if what I need to ask Gia is going to sit well coming from me," I told him.

"If you need to ask me something, just come right out with it." Gia stood at the tasting room doorway, her arms crossed and a scowl on her face that did not invite questioning. Her heels clacked down the steps.

I guess I had no choice. I slid off the stool to meet her.

"It's about Duncan," I said boldly.

"What about Duncan?"

I started to lose my nerve but forged on. "I just talked to him at the police station. I think Pearce and Riley are turning on him and he's feeling a little trapped. Is there anything you can tell me that might shed some light on his relationship with them?" I recalled what Constance had said about Duncan and Gia often going to The Cellar together. "You've been hanging out with him for weeks. He must've talked to you about them and his hopes for this shop."

She scoffed at me. "Do you really think I would talk to *you* about Duncan so you can play Veronica Mars again and get involved in this chocolate poisoning? You must think I'm really stupid."

"Hey now, Gia . . ." Roman cautioned, coming out from behind the bar.

"Oh great, you're going to defend her now?" She shook her head, a look of disgust for Roman on her face. Then she focused on me. "Leave Duncan alone. I swear, if something happens to him, I'll be coming for you." She turned and strode out of the room to return to the front of the shop.

"That went well," I said, feeling a little shook.

Roman stuck his hands in his jeans pockets, looking

a little sheepish. "Sorry. She shouldn't have spoken to you that way. I'll have a talk with her."

"No, don't. I understand where she's coming from. I can't say I blame her." I still had some lingering guilt about whatever part I may have played in what happened to Derrick.

"I guess we're no help on this one," Roman said, taking my thoughts out of the past and plopping them into the present.

"That's okay. I knew it was a long shot."

"You've got Detective Heath for a boyfriend now, so that's got to help you out and get you some more inside information than usual."

"You know Heath. Or maybe you don't, but he goes by the book. I may be dating him, but he's not telling me too much."

He nodded. "At least it must be comforting to have him by your side instead of across an interrogation table. No more having to decide what to tell him and what to keep from him." Roman was referring to a case he and I had solved together that Heath was less than happy about. It had caused a rift between me and Heath for months.

"Hm," I answered, feigning agreement with a tight-lipped smile. I wished Heath was by my side, but ironically, I was on my own more than ever. "Well, I've been gone from the shop long enough." I went to leave when I realized I'd have to pass Gia again. I really wasn't in the mood for another confrontation. "Do you mind if I leave out the back door?"

Roman glanced toward the sliding barn door and immediately figured out why I made the request. "Yeah, that's probably best. I've got to work with her for the rest of the afternoon—let's not rile her up again."

Roman's default was laid back, so he didn't do well with *riled up*.

He walked me to the back door and pushed it open. He stepped outside and held the heavy door open with his back. "I'm glad you came by anyway. And thanks for your advice on the new mead."

"I'm glad you asked me. Let me know about the cheese order for next . . ." I trailed off as I noticed the two cars parked directly behind the meadery. One was a Mini Cooper with a MEADMAN vanity plate—Roman's car. The other was a gray Prius with a spoiler on the back.

"Whose car is that?" I asked.

Roman looked at the cars. "It's Gia's. Why? You look like you've just seen a ghost."

Not a ghost, but it *had* vanished into the night. And now here it was, belonging to someone who—let's not beat around the bush—despised me. Someone who was very close with Duncan, who could've had access to their kitchen and seen my name on the box of chocolates that were meant for A. J. Was Gia the killer?

CHAPTER 27

I stood staring at the car.

"What's up? Is something wrong?" Roman asked.

"Roman, can I ask you something?"

"Sure."

I lowered my voice. "First, can you shut the door so we can talk outside. I don't want Gia to overhear."

He let the door go and it closed with a clunk. Roman's brows creased in question.

"Has Gia ever talked about seeing the inside of Chocolate Bliss? I mean like, going into the kitchen or anything?"

He let out a quick snort and looked at the ground as he pushed the stones around with the toe of his boot. "Yeah, as a matter of fact, she got an intimate tour of the kitchen."

"Was it the night before the grand opening?" The thumping of my heartbeat faintly reached my ears.

"I don't know if she was there then, but the time I heard about was pretty soon after Duncan came to town, I think."

Okay, not conclusive, but that means she might've been back there more than once.

"What did she say about it? Did he teach her anything

about how they make the chocolates?" If she knew the process, she could figure out how and when to poison them.

He chuckled uncomfortably again. "No, it wasn't that kind of tour." He looked away at first, like he didn't want to tell me. "They hooked up there one night. I overheard her giggling about it on the phone with her friend during her lunch break."

"Oh." That wasn't what I expected to hear.

"Duncan's apparently staying with his folks and, well, she likes that kind of thing."

"What kind of thing?"

"Hooking up in public places, spur of the moment."

I recalled the time I caught Gia having a make-out session in Apricot Grille's dumpster enclosure with Derrick.

Roman continued, "Like here in the meadery, she used to like to—"

"Yeah, okay, I get it," I cut him off. I didn't need to hear more.

"Why are you asking about Gia? I thought it was Duncan you were interested in."

I hesitated to tell him. After all, he'd been sort of dating her for the past year, exclusive or not. He and I had a close friendship that spanned two years. Would he believe me or go straight to her with what I told him?

He stared at me, waiting for my response. I went with my gut.

"Last night, Archie and I went to Hope's Cakery to check on Hope. Hope, Jasmine, and Duncan were there having a meeting. I saw someone waiting in a car in the parking lot that looked and sounded just like Gia's hybrid."

"So? She was probably waiting for Duncan."

"Except she wasn't. Duncan was parked out front. She was parked in the dark, the farthest away from the lights in the back lot, and she was there even after everyone left. I didn't know it was her at the time. I wasn't even sure someone was in the car, but I thought I saw someone. I don't know, it just gave me a weird feeling, so when everybody left, I went back to the parking lot to see if the car was still there. She saw me and immediately took off in a hurry, like she didn't want to be seen. Why would she be there, hiding, late at night?"

He shrugged. "I have no idea. Why do *you* think she was there?"

"Like I said, I didn't know it was her, but I've been thinking that whoever it was had wanted to get back inside the kitchen. If they'd left something incriminating, they could've wanted to go back when no one was there and retrieve it."

Now Roman outright laughed. "You're not saying you think Gia poisoned those chocolates?" When I didn't laugh along, he quickly became serious. "Are you?"

"Shh." I looked around. I knew there was no way she could hear us. There were only closed transom windows on this side of the building. Still, I didn't want to chance it. "I'm not saying that! Okay, maybe I am. It's just a possibility. I know it's not much to go on."

"What reason would she have for doing that? She doesn't even know A. J. And she'd be ruining Duncan's business."

"I know the chocolates went to A. J., but when the box was at Hope's, it accidentally had *my* name on it. In fact, Jasmine gave them to me at first. Gia may have thought they were intended for me. Or switched it so the chocolates *would* be for me."

"Oh, Willa." Roman still had a smile on his face, more of an incredulous one than a happy one. "Sure, Gia doesn't like you, but she wouldn't go to those lengths. I know you don't much like her either, but I think you're reaching here."

"It's not about me not liking her. She's always blamed me for everything that happened with Derrick. Maybe this was finally her opportunity to get her revenge."

He stopped smiling and looked at me thoughtfully. I couldn't tell if he was considering what I said or disappointed that I was still pushing this theory. His hand brushed his jaw and moved to the back of his neck where he gave it a squeeze, rolling his head as if to release some tension. His gaze fell back on me. "I don't know what to tell you. I mean . . . I suppose it's possible. Not likely," he quickly added. "But possible. How are you going to try to prove it?"

"I don't know if I can. If I can find out if she was in Hope's kitchen around the time of the grand opening or earlier that day, at least I'd know if she's a viable suspect. I still don't know exactly when or how the poisoning occurred, which makes it more difficult."

"Do you plan on sharing this theory with Heath?" Roman looked a little nervous. He obviously cared about Gia more than just the physical attraction.

"No. I'm going to keep it to myself for now until I can find out more." Roman didn't need to know I wasn't allowed to talk to Heath. "You won't tell her, will you?"

He snorted again. "Me? No, I wouldn't want her killing the messenger. That's a figure of speech!" he added hurriedly, after realizing what he'd said.

"I know."

"Besides, I trust you. You've had the right instincts before."

"Thanks, Roman. That means a lot to me."

We stood there smiling at each other until it suddenly became awkward.

"Okay, I'm really going to go now. I'll keep you posted about what I find," I said.

"I appreciate that."

He used his keys to go back inside, and I walked around the building back to our street. Considering Gia as a new suspect made me wish I'd had that second glass of mead.

CHAPTER 28

I returned to Curds & Whey, where June, Archie, and Mrs. Schultz were around the sampling counter finishing Mrs. Schultz's dip from this morning.

"We hoped you wouldn't mind. Only an hour of work to go and too much dip left," Mrs. Schultz said. "It's a shame. It was quite good, if I do say so myself."

"It's really good," Archie said through a mouthful of cracker and dip.

"Baz might mind, but not me. I'm sorry to have been gone all day. Did you all get your breaks in?"

"We took turns. We had a handful of customers today, but overall, it was slow," June supplied.

I noticed Claude's absence.

"I feel bad hiring Claude and then not having work for him," I said.

"He seemed fine with it. He was talking about his bread the whole time he was here anyway. I think he was glad to get back home to it," June said. She left Archie to finish the dip. "Time for me to clock out too. The café's all cleaned." She untied her apron and began to take it off.

"Thanks. Before you go, June, has Duncan ever talked to you about Gia?" I asked.

"The girl who works at the meadery?"

"Yes."

Archie and Mrs. Schultz glanced at each other with a questioning look.

June thought for a moment. "He might've mentioned her in passing. I think he said something about going to dinner with her once."

Too bad.

"Why?"

"Oh. I, uh, was just chatting with her at the meadery and she mentioned she'd reconnected with him. They're friends from high school, so I thought you might know her too. Small towns."

Archie and Mrs. Schultz locked eyes again. They knew something was up. I hoped June wouldn't notice.

"Nope. I was in middle school when Duncan went to high school, so I don't know her personally, just know of her from the times I've stopped in the meadery."

I nodded. "Can I get in on that dip?" I asked, wanting to change the subject. I took a cracker and scooped some on it. As soon as the creamy cheese made its way to my stomach, it caused a grumbling, reminding me that I hadn't eaten since the paltry cheese I'd pinched for breakfast. I thought how one of Roman's meads would go well with this.

"It was a delicious dip. Thanks for making it, Mrs. Schultz," June said. She plucked her small handbag from under the counter. "I'm going to grab something to eat and then I'll meet up with you guys after closing to clean Hope's kitchen."

I'd almost forgotten about that. "That's so nice of you. Are you sure you want to stay for that? We'd understand completely if you want to pack it in for the day."

"Archie promised me ice cream afterward, so I'm holding him to it," she said with a grin.

"Nothing's going to make me veer from that plan, I promise! I owe you. Double scoop, waffle cone," Archie replied.

We said goodbye to June as she bounced out the door with a smile on her face.

Mrs. Schultz held up a finger. "That reminds me, Claude called Jasmine about tonight, but she was training all day at the bookstore café, so she passed on the cleaning party."

"She took another job?" I asked.

"Sounds like it. She probably couldn't afford to wait and see how Hope's Cakery pans out."

"I don't think Hope knows about Jasmine yet. I haven't gotten a text from her about it. She's going to be crushed," Archie said. The gleeful banter he'd had with June was no longer reflected on his face.

"Let's hope this surprise cleaning party cheers her up," I said. Poor Hope. One hit after another and everyone was abandoning ship, even someone she'd worked with at the bakery since before she first took it over.

"So what was all that about Gia?" Mrs. Schultz asked.

"Yeah, I've never known you to have a 'chat' with her," Archie added.

I filled them in on everything from last night's mysterious car sighting to finally finding that it belonged to Gia.

"Holy cannoli," Archie said, absently scooping another cracker into the dip.

"Do you think it's far-fetched?" I asked.

"Possible motive. Possible opportunity. She's a viable suspect. She should go on the list," Archie said.

"Although, I do wonder if she'd sacrifice her friend, Duncan, like that. And she knows Hope." Mrs. Schultz began rubbing her scarf between her fingers.

"Maybe she thought it wouldn't be so easy for the police to pinpoint the source of the poison. Or maybe she thought it wouldn't look like a murder at all. If I'd have accepted the chocolate and eaten it after dinner, it could've appeared to be a natural death or from something else I'd eaten. If there'd been no note, maybe murder wouldn't have even been considered."

Archie shuddered. "I don't like to think about you being the one who ate those chocolates."

"There was no chance I was going to take them home," I said, giving Archie a half hug.

"You're probably right that if it was her, her plan went awry. Gia's not the most pleasant person, but she *has* been Roman's friend for a long time." I could tell Mrs. Schultz wasn't happy about putting another member of the Yarrow Glen community on the suspect list.

"I don't like the idea of it either, but I have to pursue it."

"She would've had to have been there the morning of the grand opening to see A. J.'s box of chocolates. They said they assembled it that morning," Mrs. Schultz recalled.

"That's true," I agreed.

"But also, the night before when they made the crèmes. Wouldn't Heath have told you she was someone he interviewed? Surely, one of the others would've mentioned she was there." Mrs. Schultz's fingers were now rapidly working her scarf.

Mrs. Schultz was poking some serious holes into my

theory that Gia was the culprit. I felt deflated because I knew she was right.

"You're right, they would have told the police she was there. Pearce and Riley were desperately looking for someone else to blame it on before they turned on Duncan." I thought about what Roman had said about Gia's proclivity for public places and wondered whether Duncan had snuck her into the cakery, and that's when she was somehow able to taint the crèmes without him knowing. Then another thought occurred to me. "Or maybe it wasn't the crèmes she had to taint," I finished my thought out loud. Roman's mead had still been in the back of my mind. "What if it was the rum that was poisoned before it even went in the crème?"

"Why didn't we think of that?" Archie said, his eyes wide with excitement that clues were clicking into place.

"I hate to be a wet blanket again," Mrs. Schultz interjected, "but didn't Heath say it was much more than just two chocolate crèmes that killed him? It had to be in almost all of them that Kevin Wallace ate. There were only two rum crèmes."

I sighed. Archie's eyes dimmed. Mrs. Schultz was right again.

"That's always the sticking point, isn't it? That most, if not all, of those chocolates had to be tainted," I said with a sigh.

"It brings it back to A. J.'s box being the only chocolates poisoned," Mrs. Schultz said.

"Which means it had to be a secret chocolate swap," Archie took up the trail reluctantly.

They looked at me with concern, knowing what this meant.

I finished it out loud anyway. "With no evidence against Gil and Trevor, which leaves me and A. J. as the prime suspects." My prior optimism sank like the blue diamond Rose threw from the Titanic into the ocean. This was the worst possible conclusion, and I hoped the police weren't coming to the same one.

"First things first," Archie said, not one to stay down for long. "We have to see if Gia was in the kitchen the morning of the grand opening. If she's guilty, she had to have put the box with your cheesecake."

"Good plan, Archie. We'll work backwards from there. Let's not give up," Mrs. Schultz added, getting on board.

I felt a sliver of my optimism attempting to resurface.

"Okay then. I know I've been gone all day, but if Jasmine's still at the bookstore café, this might be my chance to talk to her about Gia."

"Go! We'll be fine here," Mrs. Schultz insisted.

"I can text Hope and ask her too," Archie said.

"Wait on that, Archie. I don't want this to get back to Gia. I'd rather we ask Hope in person so maybe it won't be so obvious that we suspect Gia. Can you see if Hope will meet us here just before seven? We'll talk to her before everyone else comes for the cleaning party. That part can still be a surprise."

"Good idea," Archie agreed.

I swiped another cracker into the cheese dip on my way out to talk to Jasmine. I had to be on the right track. Duncan could've told Gia about the important box of chocolates they'd be making for the editor of the *Gazette*. Gia was with Duncan when I went to pick up my cheesecake, so it's a real possibility that she had access to the chocolates in the kitchen. It was lucky for her I offered to take them to the Gazette—if I had eaten them, I'd be dead. If A. J. had eaten them, I'd be framed. There were several missing dots, but it was as close to connecting them all as we'd gotten so far. I had to be on the right track this time—mine and A. J.'s lives might depend on it.

CHAPTER 29

Next to Lou's Market was Read More Bookstore, the used bookstore and café owned by Sharice, who was also a talented illustrator and used the space to promote both authors and artists. Her shop exuded a fantastical quality, from the painted checkerboard floor to the ceiling light fixtures with drum shades made to look like classic book covers. The rows of shelves were overfilled with books, necessitating knee-high stacks at the ends of the narrow aisles.

The attached café that Baz frequented every morning for his sugary coffee drinks was cleverly hidden behind a chest-high hinged bookshelf. Its décor was more subdued than the book section but just as inviting with an eclectic mix of comfortable chairs in cozy seating arrangements around short tables. The Lending Library shelf located in the café was an important asset to a case Team Cheese had been thrust into the previous spring, so I always had a doubly warm and fuzzy feeling whenever I came here.

It was lucky for me that, unlike Curds & Whey, which had truncated hours on Sundays, Read More's café extended their Sunday hours to match the bookstore's. But my luck petered out there when I saw another barista, not Jasmine, was behind the café counter. I must've missed her. I stood for a minute deciding whether to appease my still-grumbling stomach with something from behind the glass display case. Besides coffee drinks, tea, and vegan smoothies, they had an array of prepared sandwiches, small salads, and desserts.

Plan B. I scanned the café to see if June had chosen it for dinner. Maybe over a meal, she'd open up more about Duncan and remember something he might've mentioned about Gia. But it was Sharice I spotted. In a distinctively artsy blouse of mosaic-like vibrant concentric circles over leggings, she was rising from one of the cushy chairs tucked in the corner. I now saw Jasmine was seated in the chair across from her. They shook hands and she gestured to Jasmine, who had a coffee in front of her, to stay seated. Read More continued to be my lucky charm!

She walked toward me to return to the books section of the shop, her magnificent natural black hair bouncing with her energized personality. Behind a nearly makeup-free face and cat-eye glasses, her brown eyes crinkled in friendly recognition as she passed, and we exchanged quick hellos.

I hurried over to the corner just as Jasmine was getting up from her seat with her coffee.

"Jasmine!" Unfortunately, I didn't have time to play it casual.

"Hi, Willa. Did you want the chair? I was just leaving."

Many of the chairs were taken by patrons. Most, however, were just using the café to read, without the accompaniment of drinks or food. The fear of the Chocolate Bliss poisoning still lingered.

"Actually, I was hoping to talk to you. Can you stay for another minute?" I asked.

She shrugged. "Sure." She returned her coffee to the low table and sat. I took the chair Sharice had just occupied.

"Is this about Hope? I'm sorry I won't be helping with cleaning her kitchen, but I've been training here all afternoon and working tomorrow, so I knew I wouldn't be up for it. I don't mean to be insensitive to her, but I need to make money, and who knows what's happening with the cakery? I took my vacation time while they did the renovations, but I can't afford to go another week without a paycheck."

"I understand. You have to think about yourself too. This isn't about Hope. I wanted to ask more about the day of your grand opening."

"Okay. I told the police everything, but go ahead."

"Did anybody pop into the kitchen at all throughout the day besides the five of you who were working?"

She reached for her coffee on the low table between us, giving me a better view of her exceptional sleeve of tattoos—steampunk images of gears mixed in with owls dressed in neo-Victorian garb with aviator glasses and scrolls. With her nose ring, I'd figured her more for punk rather than steampunk, but I liked it. She took a sip of her coffee as she considered my question.

"Gosh, it was so crazy that day, trying to get everything finished. After the first rush of customers, Hope did the baking and I mostly stayed up front."

I pushed on, more direct this time. "Did you happen to see Gia when she was there, Duncan's friend from the meadery?"

"Yeah, I know Gia." She all but rolled her eyes at the name. "She's been hounding Duncan ever since he first met with Hope. Hope used to tell me how Gia would always show up out of the blue whenever Hope had a meeting with him, or they were getting the shop renovated. There was obvious chemistry between Hope and Duncan, and Gia wasn't happy about it."

"Hope and Duncan have something going on?" I asked. I was sure Archie didn't know about this.

"No. There's chemistry, like I said, but they decided to keep it professional since they had to work together. I don't think Gia liked the amount of time they spent together, though. I do remember seeing her in the shop that day."

"Do you know how long she stayed or if she went into the kitchen?"

Jasmine looked off in thought, then shook her head. "I couldn't tell you if she went in the back. I didn't see her in the kitchen, but it was pretty crazy that day. She came in at closing time too. I remember Hope giving me a look when we saw her come in. Gia always wanted special attention from Duncan, but he didn't have the time for that."

I wondered if there was a time that morning before they opened that she could've slipped in the back and swapped out the box of chocolates for the poisoned ones. Swapping the chocolates is the only way that A. J.'s box alone was poisoned. Maybe her plan was just to plant a box of chocolates for me, but she saw A. J.'s box and my cheesecake and took that opportunity—she wouldn't have to cause suspicion with an extra box of chocolates nobody'd seen before.

The more I tried to fit Gia into the equation, the more disconnected her dots became. It would've been easier for her to just leave a box of chocolates on my doorstep. I started to think I'd convinced myself of

Gia's guilt just because her car was in the lot. Maybe she was just a jealous woman not wanting to get caught stalking Duncan while he was with Hope. Or maybe Hope was the one she wanted revenge against too. A two for one!

"Is there anything else? I've had a long day," Jasmine said.

I left my frustrating thoughts, not realizing I'd been in my head too long. "I'm sorry, I was just . . ." I circled my finger near my head, indicating I'd been trying to work things out. "I was hoping to allay some of Hope's fears about her Chocolate Bliss partners. I'm sure she's going to have to deal with them contractually for a while, and not knowing if she can trust them will only make it harder for her."

Jasmine's expression suddenly turned dubious. "I'm not sure she should trust them anyway."

"Why do you say that?" My thoughts left Gia completely.

She hesitated and then shrugged. "What the heck. I'm not working with them anymore and their reputation can't get much more tarnished than it already is."

She glanced over at the other groups of seats. We were in the corner away from others, but I looked too, to make sure nobody was eavesdropping. Jasmine seemed satisfied too. I leaned forward to hear every word.

"This is not fact, this is just me . . . wondering," she began.

"Fair enough. Go on."

"You know how Pearce has his own rum now and that's the big deal about his Brenner Rum Crèmes—that they're made with Brenner Rum?"

"Right."

"So why did I see two empty rum bottles in the back of his car that weren't Brenner's?"

My mind went to Roman's mead. "If they're going to use the rum just to make the crème, maybe they don't want to spend the money to put it in the fancy bottles that they sell. That's probably the explanation."

"No, I mean, they were a high-end brand that I've seen in liquor stores."

I felt myself blinking as I computed what she was saying. "Are you saying he only *pretended* to use his own rum to make the Brenner Rum Crèmes?"

She put her hands up by her shoulders in a "Don't quote me" gesture. "Just me wondering," she repeated.

"Okay, so tell me what happened. Don't leave anything out."

"This was a couple days before the grand opening. Hope wanted to show me around the new kitchen, get me acquainted with where everything was. Riley asked Duncan if Pearce had made him come in as early as Pearce had—I guess Pearce had been there since like the crack of dawn. Duncan said no. We all knew Pearce liked to micromanage, but even more than that, he liked to be in charge. Duncan had been there for weeks doing all the planning and the legwork for Chocolate Bliss, and it seemed like Pearce was making a bunch of changes at the eleventh hour."

Jasmine played with the lid of her cup as she spoke, popping if off the cup, then clicking it back in place.

"Anyway, I got there, and Hope showed me around, got me acquainted with the layout as much as I needed to be. She was nervous because Claude had just quit, so I hung around longer than I needed to just because Pearce was so overbearing, and I felt bad for Hope. But I couldn't take much more. Pearce was berating

Duncan for ordering plain little sample bags instead of ones with their initials logo on them. I guess they don't usually even put the samples in bags, but Pearce wanted the extra grand-opening marketing to be seen around town. Hope told me Pearce and Duncan already had that argument the day before. Duncan told him he overnighted some bags with the initials and had them delivered to his parents' house in Lockwood where he's staying, so he'd be sure he got them. He said they were in the back of his car. He started to go get them, but Pearce started in on him again about the extra cost for overnighting, even though Duncan said he'd paid for it with his own money.

"I finally had enough, so I left, but I felt bad for Duncan. So I went to the car to bring the bags in for him to try to shut Pearce up, but I mistook Pearce's car for Duncan's and tried to open the back door. It was locked, so I looked in the window and that's when I saw the bag of rum bottles on the floor of the back seat. Then I noticed how expensive the interior looked and that it probably wasn't Duncan's car."

"And you're sure the bottles were empty? Not just Pearce having bought some rum for himself?"

"Oh, yeah. It's a very distinctive bottle of dark rum. The bottles were empty."

I sat back, this information weighing on me. "Does he use *dark* rum to make his crème liqueur?"

She nodded. "We had to hear the whole process of how he aged his rum in a charred oak barrel ad nauseum. He had us try it once too. I didn't think it was that great. I've definitely had better."

I considered Jasmine's bombshell. "It's not evidence of poisoning, but it means Pearce is capable of doing something secret and underhanded."

Could he have poisoned the rum before it went into the crème? Even if he wanted Duncan's shop to fail, there's no way he would've sacrificed his Brenner Rum Crèmes to do it. I was aware of his ego enough to know that. And it still wouldn't answer the question of how all the crème chocolates in the box Kevin Wallace ate were poisoned, not just the rum ones.

"Did you let the police know this?" I asked.

"Yeah. I had to tell them everything I knew. I don't think it has anything to do with the poisoning, but that's dishonest if he was using a better brand to make the chocolates and then selling them his bottles of rum for a bait and switch."

I thought about what Roman had said about his mead—that some people will get it in their head that it tastes like something just because they're told that's what it is ahead of time.

"It really shows his character," she said.

I was well acquainted with Pearce's character, but I was still shocked to think this might be true. Nix that—I was disappointed more than shocked. How he and Riley had lied to me ten years ago was still forefront in my mind when they apologized to me in my shop this morning, and yet I'd still decided to trust them over Duncan. I'd been back and forth with it after hearing from Duncan, and I questioned it again now.

"Do you think he did it just for the grand opening or that he's been doing it all along?" I wondered.

"I'm not positive, but I think it was for the grand-opening samples, because he was so adamant that the samples were what was going to catapult the new shop. He kept pushing his Brenner's Rum once people tried a rum crème sample. He seemed more interested in selling his rum than the chocolate. Higher profit margin."

"Were the batches of Brenner Rum Crèmes he made to sell different than the samples?"

"The samples were smaller than the ones they sell. I found that out the hard way when Beatrice came in to buy a box of four Brenner Rum Crèmes and they'd run out. I felt bad for her because she looked so sad about it, so I asked them if she could have some samples, but Pearce threw a fit about that, even though Beatrice offered to buy them. They told me they were smaller, and they didn't want anybody thinking that was the size they sell. It turns out, we were out of samples anyway, but he still had to give me a lecture about it."

"So Beatrice never got to take home any rum crèmes?"

"Nope. I did manage to sneak a few into Lou's box, but don't tell Pearce."

"Lou?"

"You know how Lou can be. I just wasn't in the mood to deal with his grouchiness when he wouldn't let up about not getting the famous Brenner Rum Crèmes included in his crème variety box. It was the end of the day, but I managed to find some extras while Duncan was busy flirting with Gia again. I didn't charge him. He was paying extra for the ribboned gift box, and it seemed important to him."

I wondered if Lou handed his chocolates over to the police. If he still had them, maybe there was one more chance to discover poisoned chocolates outside of A. J.'s box. This could be the break A. J. and I needed.

CHAPTER 30

I thanked Jasmine, wished her luck in her new job, and left the bookstore café in a hurry. I didn't have far to go—Lou's Market was right next door, but it was his eighteen-year-old employee, Trace, who was bringing the crates of produce displayed in front of the market inside.

"Hi, Trace. Is Lou inside?"

Trace, picking up a crate of peaches, flicked his blond bangs out of his eyes. They immediately fell back onto his lashes. "No, he said he was going next door for a minute."

"Next door? To the bookstore?"

"He went that way." Trace nodded in the direction of the alley where Carl's Hardware and my shop were located.

"To Carl's?"

Trace shrugged. "I didn't notice. Sorry. I'm sure he'll be back any minute. We're closing soon."

"Thanks, Trace."

Lou made a point of telling us how he couldn't leave his market when it was open for business, so I knew he rarely did except to bring his dad back to his assisted living community. Of all days!

I trotted across the alley and entered Carl's Hardware with a bit more intensity than I'd intended. The little silver bell on the door jangled furiously. Pudge, who'd been napping on a pile of paint-chip sample strips that were splayed on a table by the register, popped his head up.

"Sorry, Pudge."

Carl, a friendly guy with shorn red hair and a marvelous beard, came around one of the aisles. "Willa. Hi! What can I help you find?"

"Not a *what* but a *who*. I heard Lou might've come in here?"

"Not here. We're closing in a few minutes, so I was making the rounds."

I inwardly sighed. I'd have to solve the case of the missing market owner before I could get any resolve on his chocolates.

"Okay, thanks. Have a good night."

"You too," he called after me as I left, gently opening the door so as not to disturb Pudge a second time.

I walked back to my shop trying to rein in my patience. I planned to help with the closing duties since I'd played hooky all day today, then I'd find Lou afterward. He lived above his shop, so he was sure to be there sometime tonight.

When I walked into Curds & Whey, there was Lou, chatting with Mrs. Schultz.

"Lou! There you are!" I burst out.

"Willa, Lou has come up with a wonderful solution to our problem of having to find a new bakery for our sampling breads," Mrs. Schultz said.

Lou practically beamed beside Mrs. Schultz. Okay, *beamed* was probably too generous of a word, but for Lou, he looked pretty self-satisfied.

Archie walked behind the counter to empty the dust-pan in his hand.

Mrs. Schultz continued, "Lou's going to put a little bread bakery near the deli section and start making some of the bread they sell."

"And I'll give your shop a discount, of course," Lou finished.

"That's generous of you. Thank you, Lou. We'll be sure to discuss that further with you. I have a question for right now, though," I barreled on. "You remember that box of chocolates you bought from Chocolate Bliss the other day? Have you handed that over to the police yet?"

Lou's rare smile disappeared, replaced with a scowl more severe than his resting face one. "I don't know what you're talking about."

"Jasmine said you bought a nice box of chocolates from Chocolate Bliss and—"

Before I could get out more, Lou talked over me. "I don't know what you're talking about." He blew past me, saying, "Goodbye, Ruth. Talk soon!" and was out the door before I knew what had happened.

"What's going on, Willa?" Archie asked. Both he and Mrs. Schultz stared at me in confusion.

"No time to explain," I said, running out the door after Lou. "Lou! Lou!" He was walking right in front of me but wouldn't turn around.

I caught up with him in the alley at the corner of his market.

"Lou, why are you running away from me? It's a simple question."

He got as far as his sidewalk and finally turned. "I don't have any chocolates," he growled and turned again, but Trace was in the way, holding the last crate of produce. He stood in place, having overheard our shouting.

I wasn't letting up. "Yes, you do! Jasmine told me you bought them."

"You mean that white box with the red ribbon on it?" Trace interjected.

Lou gave Trace a death stare.

"So you *do* have a box! Why are you pretending you don't?" I asked. Now I was on the verge of angry.

I could see him rev down a little, with nothing to do now but tell the truth. "It's nobody's business. I didn't hand it in to the police like I was supposed to."

"Did you eat them?" I asked, concerned for him.

"No, I threw them away once the notice came out about the poisoning," he mumbled.

We heard the sound of a car approaching and I turned to see it was Baz's truck pulling into the alley to park at his apartment behind our building. He stopped, and leaned out his window.

"Hey, what's up?"

"Lou might have a box of Chocolate Bliss chocolates *with* the samples." These would be the first samples that would be tested by forensics.

Baz turned off his engine.

Lou lifted his arms and let them fall to his side in exasperation. "I just told you I threw them out."

"Where did you throw them out?" Baz asked. "In the market? In your apartment?"

"Hey, what's going on?" Archie said, appearing from the other side of Baz's truck. "Something I can help with?"

"We're trying to get Lou to tell us where the box of crème chocolates he got from Chocolate Bliss are."

"You have a box of the chocolates?" Archie asked.

"Oh, for heaven's sake, does the whole town need to know? I threw them in the dumpster!" Lou growled.

We all instinctively looked toward the market dumpster at the far end of the alley. That would've only been yesterday, and the garbage truck didn't come to collect until Monday.

"They'd still be in there," I said.

"I've got my stepladder," Baz said, hopping out to retrieve it from the bed of his truck.

"You're really going to go searching through the dumpster for it?" Lou said.

"You're right. We shouldn't. We need to call the police and let them do it," I told the others.

"You're not calling the police to come over here and make a big thing out of it," Lou said, hitching up his pants on his thin frame as if he might physically try to stop us.

"What's the big deal, Lou?" Trace asked, having little idea of the full implications of possibly finding more poisoned chocolates.

"What's going on down here?" It was Mrs. Schultz. "I locked the door, Willa. I hope it's okay."

Lou bent his head back, his face to the sky.

"Lou threw out a box of chocolates he'd bought from Chocolate Bliss and I'm about to call Heath to come and look through the dumpster for them."

"You've had a box of the chocolates all this time?" Mrs. Schultz said. The surprise in her voice was laced with disappointment.

Lou's face reddened then fell, as his anger faded. But only for a moment.

"No, I haven't had them! I told everyone three times already, I threw them out!" he shouted. I'd never heard him raise his voice to Mrs. Schultz.

I could tell she was taken aback, but not deterred from questioning him further. She used a calm tone, however. "Why didn't you hand them over to the police in the first place like they instructed everyone to do?"

He harrumphed. "Because I didn't want anyone to know I'd bought them for *you*, okay? Go ahead! Call the police! Make a big stink and let the whole town know!" he shouted.

Trace jumped out of the way as Lou stomped toward him and disappeared inside his market.

We all stood frozen in place. I didn't mean to embarrass Lou. It hadn't occurred to me he'd bought them as a gift for Mrs. Schultz. I looked over at her, hoping she wasn't embarrassed too—not by the chocolates, but by his outburst. She looked shaken up.

"I'm sorry, Mrs. Schultz. I didn't know. I didn't mean to embarrass the two of you."

Mrs. Schultz stood stiffly and sniffed. "Nothing for you to be sorry about, Willa. His behavior is unacceptable. Embarrassment is no excuse for keeping potential evidence from the police, and it's most certainly no excuse to be yelled at by him." She'd kept her composure until the last part, when her chin began to tremble.

Oh no.

"Come on, Mrs. Schultz. Let's go back to the shop," Archie suggested.

Mrs. Schultz cleared her throat. "Good idea. We've got closing duties to take care of and we still have to drop off those costumes at Beatrice's."

"I'll be there as soon as I can," I told them.

"Do what you have to do. We'll wait for you," Archie said.

Mrs. Schultz nodded in agreement, and they walked back to Curds & Whey.

My heart strings tugged for Mrs. Schultz. It seemed she'd been slowly warming up to Lou as a potential suitor, but now he'd disappointed her severely.

"You want me to take a look in the dumpster or are you gonna call Heath?" Baz asked me.

"I'm doing this one right. I'm calling Heath. I don't want anything to taint this. It could be the only piece of evidence that would clear me and A. J."

I pulled out my phone and tapped Heath's name.

CHAPTER 31

Heath didn't answer, so I called the police station directly. A police squad car pulled into the alley not long after. Baz had already moved his truck to his parking spot behind the building. Shep and his partner, Officer Melman, got out of the car. I hoped to see Heath's unmarked vehicle following, but I was disappointed. No Heath. He really was taking his decree to stay away from me seriously.

Shep ambled over to confirm what I'd said on the phone.

"Does Heath know I called?" I asked after giving him the details again.

"I informed him of the situation," Shep replied formally, but gave no further explanation as to why he hadn't come.

Melman, a squat, rotund officer about the same age as Shep, mid-thirties, clicked on the bright spotlight from their cruiser. Shep walked over to him, and they conferred. Apparently, Melman drew the short straw, because he pulled on a pair of latex gloves to start searching the dumpster. It was no surprise—Shep had earned his place as Heath's right-hand man and likely called the shots when Heath wasn't around.

Shep returned to me. "Is Lou inside the market?"

"I think so. We've been here by the dumpster, and we haven't seen him go up to his apartment," I answered. Like my setup, Lou had an outside entrance to his apartment above his shop.

Shep walked around the back of the building to the delivery door, and we heard the loud buzz of the doorbell. A few moments later, a clunk of the heavy door indicated Lou had let him inside.

Melman opened a large tarp and laid it on the ground next to the dumpster. Baz offered him his stepladder and he accepted it, grudgingly hefting himself into the smelly dumpster to begin the search.

Baz sat on the bottom step of his deck stairs to keep an eye on the progress while I went back to Curds & Whey. It should've come as no surprise that Archie and Mrs. Schultz had taken care of the closing duties.

"I'm so sorry I've been gone all day," I said.

"You were doing important things. We finally got a lead!" Archie said, excited by the prospect.

Mrs. Schultz was still quiet.

"Are you okay, Mrs. Schultz?" I asked her. I felt guilty for causing the circumstances of Lou's outburst.

"I'm okay, Willa. I'm over the shock of it. Now I'm just disappointed in him."

"Why doesn't Lou ever go to the police when he should? What's that all about?" Archie said.

Archie was right. This wasn't the first time Lou had done something like this. He believed in minding his own business, but sometimes what's right for the community is more important. Having gotten to know Lou more over these past two years—the way he'd taken Trace under his wing and how caring he'd become to Mrs. Schultz—we were seeing a new side of him. I was starting to really warm up to him, grumpiness and all. Now I was disappointed in him too.

"Let me make us some food," I insisted, walking back to the kitchen to scour the cupboards and refrigerator. Even if it wasn't too late to get something from Lou's Market, it would be out of the question.

"What are we doing about the kitchen cleaning party?" Archie asked as they followed me into the kitchenette.

"Oh my gosh, I completely forgot about that." I sighed. "I want to stay by the dumpster to make sure they get the chocolate. Maybe we can push that to tomorrow? Unless you'd rather not do it on your day off," I said to them.

"I don't have any plans," Mrs. Schultz said, still sounding a bit downtrodden.

"Tomorrow works for me," Archie agreed.

The fridge revealed the extra boiled baby potatoes left over from the raclette and potato dish we'd offered. I checked the cupboard, recalling I had a jar of marinara sauce. And of course, I had plenty of cheese. I preheated the oven and took out two of my biggest baking sheets.

"How do pizza smashed potatoes sound to you?" I asked.

"Like comfort food. Exactly what I need!" Mrs. Schultz proclaimed.

"That'll hit the spot! I'm calling June to tell her about the change in plans," Archie said, walking away with his phone to his ear.

Mrs. Schultz made cross slits in the potatoes we'd cooked yesterday, and I took it from there, pressing them with my potato masher so they were broken open and flattened. If the potatoes had been warm, it would've been an easier task, but I didn't mind using extra effort, taking out my frustrations on the potatoes. I drizzled them with olive oil and seasoned with salt, then stuck them in the oven to warm and get crispy. I started shredding mozzarella and cheddar cheeses.

"I called Beatrice as soon as we got back and told her we wouldn't be by until later to return the costumes," Mrs. Schultz said.

"The costumes! What would I do without you and Archie? You're on top of everything while I've been scatterbrained."

"Considering the circumstances, your focus is where it should be right now. It's more important for you to clear your name. We're capable of running the shop in your absence, as long as it's not permanent. Archie and I would be lost without you, Willa."

"Oh, Mrs. Schultz." I reached over and hugged her. "I'd be lost without you and Archie too. And Baz."

Mrs. Schultz took out two clean tissues from her dress pocket and we dabbed at the tears that had eked from the corners of our eyes.

"What's going on over here?" Archie asked, halting his steps as soon as the tissues alerted him that there might be crying going on.

"We're just in the middle of a friendship appreciation meeting," I said.

Archie smiled and continued forward. "Can I be a part of that club?"

"You already are. You, Mrs. Schultz, Baz, and me. Team Cheese is more than just our sleuthing group. It's the friends we trust most, the people we'll always be loyal to. There are no better friendships than that."

"I second that," Mrs. Schultz said, her good spirits returned.

"Hear! Hear!" Archie said, raising the stick of pepperoni he'd thought to grab from the cured meats section.

I took the warmed potatoes out of the oven and spooned marinara sauce over them. Then I topped them with mozzarella and cheddar. After Archie stuck slices of pepperoni atop the cheese, we returned the potatoes to the oven.

"What has Heath said to you about the case? Has he been able to make you feel better about where the investigation is headed?" Mrs. Schultz asked me while she rewrapped the cheeses.

Oh boy. I might need that tissue again.

I kept myself busy wiping the counter, trying to keep my voice light. "He suggested for appearance's sake that he and I stay out of contact until the investigation is closed, since I'm a person of interest. He was afraid Chief Jeffers might take him off the case otherwise."

"Oh, no," Mrs. Schultz uttered.

"It makes sense, but it's a bummer," Archie agreed.

"It sure is, Archie," I replied.

"I'm sorry, Willa. This must be hard to navigate without the comfort of having him here," Mrs. Schultz said.

"I thought he would've come to see about the dumpster when Shep told him I'd called it in," I said, not being able to keep the rejection I was feeling to myself.

"He's probably working double time on this case to get it solved as soon as possible so he can see you again," Mrs. Schultz said, putting a strong arm around my shoulder and giving it a squeeze. "I'm sure it has nothing to do with not *wanting* to see you."

"If *I* were the detective in charge, I'd definitely hand over the dumpster diving to my subordinates," Archie said.

Despite the fact that I felt sorry for myself, this made me laugh. "You have a point, Archie. Hey, how are things with you and June?" I was eager to take the focus off of me and Heath.

"We're good, I think. I promised I'd make it up to her for dipping out on Godzilla night. I shouldn't have done that."

"I'm glad she's so forgiving. Maybe you should take her out to the movies, just the two of you," Mrs. Schultz suggested.

"I wouldn't want her to think it's a date," he said.

Mrs. Schultz and I looked at each other eyebrows raised, which didn't go unnoticed by Archie.

"I'm just not in any rush to move out of the friendship zone. Look what happened with me and Hope. We were good friends for a long time and then we fizzled out pretty quick and now it's not the same."

"So you're afraid that'll happen with you and June?" I asked.

"Why wouldn't it? I get to hang out with her every day and sometimes we do stuff together. If things don't work out with us, that'll all be ruined," he said with a shrug, plodding over to the farm table bench and taking a seat.

Mrs. Schultz and I exchanged another glance—this time a sympathetic one.

"I had a terrible break-up with my boyfriend in college who was in the same play I was in," Mrs. Schultz told us. "We still had five shows to do together! Luckily, he was playing Hamlet where he got stabbed every day and twice on matinee Wednesdays." A wisp of a smile played on her lips. "Not long after, I met Mr. Schultz. The only way to find *the one* is to go through a heartbreak or two."

"Or ten," I said, chuckling.

"Oh boy," Archie said, laughing with me.

"Take it from me and Willa, every relationship is different. I know Hope was your first serious girlfriend, but that doesn't mean she's the blueprint for all other relationships."

"I don't think you should rush into anything, but don't keep yourself from a good thing just because you're afraid of what might or might not happen. Even friendships go through changes. Follow your heart, not your fear," I said.

"Thanks, you guys. I'll keep that in mind."

It was easy to tell Archie, but when it came to my relationship with Heath, was I following my own advice? When I was honest with myself, I wasn't comfortable in my status with Heath. I wanted a commitment, but I was too afraid to say so and rock the nice boat we were currently in . . . or had been in until the boat capsized because of this investigation.

"Is Baz coming?" Archie asked, feeling the absence of one of our Team Cheese members.

"He's on dumpster watch. Let's take our potato pizzas to go so he can eat with us. Unless you two would rather head home."

"Let's all go. I want to be there when they find the chocolates," Archie said.

"Yes, let's move this party to the dumpster," Mrs. Schultz proclaimed in an upbeat voice.

"I like your optimism. I just hope Lou's chocolates stayed in the box and they'll find it. If the chocolates fell out, it might be a lost cause," I said, unable to keep my worries to myself.

"They'll find it. I have faith," Archie said.

I checked on the pizza potatoes. The cheese was

perfectly melty on top and the skins of the potatoes crispy. We divided them onto four paper plates and began wrapping the plates in foil.

"It's either going to be a long night or a longer night," I said, thinking about the immensity of finding a small box intact in a big dumpster. "But I have to know. If any of Lou's chocolates are poisoned, it would clear me and A. J." Thinking about the case, my positive attitude quickly took a nosedive. "Still, it doesn't solve the case, does it?"

Mrs. Schultz put four bottled waters into a bag. "I wish there was something else we could do."

I turned down the lights and we walked through the stockroom and out the side door, which opened onto my narrow alley on the opposite side of the building from Lou's alley and the police's search.

"Any luck putting Gia at the scene of the crime?" Archie asked.

"When we get to Baz, I'll catch all of you up on everything Jasmine told me. Maybe you can come up with a new theory."

I had a sinking feeling we were missing something obvious.

CHAPTER 32

Rounding the back of the building, we faced the front of Baz's pickup on the opposite side of the lot, which was now parked parallel beside his deck stairs. As we got closer, we saw he was lounging in the bed of the truck surrounded by cushions, munching on a bag of snacks, with a front-row seat to the search like he was at a drive-in movie. I half expected him to be wearing Minions pajamas.

"Glad you got comfortable," I said, handing him his covered plate.

"Ooh, thanks. I figured I'd be here a while. Hop in!" He patted the cushions and pillows he'd brought from his apartment.

We got ourselves situated in the truck's bed, Mrs. Schultz and Baz farthest back, Archie leaning against the side. I was too anxious to get comfortable. I sat on the edge, keeping my legs dangled over the side.

I unwrapped my plate and picked up a potato. The skin was perfectly crisped, providing a slight crunch when I bit into it. The milkiness of the mozzarella coupled with the sharpness of cheddar provided the perfect bite to go with the zip of marinara and the salty spiciness of the pepperoni.

I was glad to see Shep was now searching the dumpster with Officer Melman. One by one, they tossed pieces of garbage onto the tarp.

Archie waved his hand in front of his nose at the odor that occasionally wafted our way without warning. "I feel bad for them. It smells ripe!"

"Maybe this wasn't the best place for dinner," I said, trying to ignore it. This was my first real meal since this morning.

Baz didn't seem bothered by the odor. He picked up one of his potato pizzas, eating it in a couple of bites, a string of mozzarella stubbornly remained like a zip line from his lips to the potato.

Mrs. Schultz provided him with a napkin and handed out the bottled waters she'd brought.

"After watching these guys for the last forty-five minutes, I'm going to put it out there—we should change the saying from "like a needle in a haystack" to "like chocolates in a dumpster," he said.

I voiced my fear. "I hope it's not all for nothing." I felt suddenly chilled and pulled one of Baz's blankets over my lap.

"They'll find it," Baz assured me.

"They have to not just find it, but the chocolates have to be poisoned. And that seems impossible because none of the others were."

"Didn't you say this box was different because it has the samples in it?" Mrs. Schultz asked.

"But it still won't explain how Kevin Wallace died," Archie echoed my thought. "Detective Heath told you that to get that much tetrahydrozoline in his system, it would've needed to be distributed to more than one or two of the chocolates."

Baz did a double take. "Tetrahy—what?"

"Tetrahydrozoline. Isn't that what you said poisoned him, Willa?"

"I did. You're just the first one besides Heath who's been able to remember how to pronounce it," I said, also impressed.

"It's not in another language like most of the cheeses I've been learning, so in comparison, it's pretty easy," Archie maintained.

Mrs. Schultz sat leaning against the cab of the truck, her legs straight out, ankles crossed. "We have to keep looking at this from every angle. One of the avenues we pursue is bound to get traction and the case will open up from there."

"What did Jasmine say, Willa? You said you'd tell us," Archie asked, working on another potato.

"She didn't have much on Gia, but what she did say was eye-opening in its own right." I continued to tell them about the empty rum bottles found in Pearce's car and the possible bait and switch he was pulling on his customers.

"If he's willing to lie about that . . ." Mrs. Schultz said.

"That's what I'm thinking. When someone tells you who they are, believe them. I should've been telling myself that from the start, but he also has the least motive. I just know he wouldn't knowingly ruin his reputation like this." Why was I still so confused?

"Okay then, what about Riley?" Baz asked.

"They're a package deal. I mean, I can tell things aren't all sunshine and butterflies between them, but I can also tell they love each other. They weren't loyal to me, but they do seem to be loyal to each other. She wants to get married and have kids. They're trying to grow their business. I can't see her doing this either."

"And Duncan?" Mrs. Schultz added, eating her potato pizzas in smaller bites.

"It is a possibility that he knew he wasn't getting the shop after all, so he planned his revenge. But when I talked to him, he seemed to believe they'd work it out and he'd get the shop. He seems really broken up about what's happened. I know that's just my opinion. He could be an excellent liar. I've been fooled before."

"A woman's intuition should never be ignored," Mrs. Schultz said.

"You don't think it's Jasmine either then?" Baz asked.

"I don't see why she would do it."

Archie crinkled his foil into a ball and tossed it in an empty bag like a basketball shot. He raised his fist in victory when it went in. "Where are we with Claude?" he asked.

"Same as Gil and Trevor—only if the chocolates were switched out. And if that's the case, the police have more to go on by suspecting me or A. J. than Claude or the candy guys." I put my plate down. Whether I'd eaten too fast, or it was the subject matter, I was no longer hungry. "This seems so dumb now. Making the police look for chocolates in a dumpster, all with the hope that one of them has the same substance in it as the ones Kevin Wallace ate, which still wouldn't prove who the killer is. This is worse than a wild-goose chase."

Just then, we heard Melman cry, "Box! Box!" His arm raised high above his head, he held a box that glowed against the harsh white spotlights like he was an Oscar-winner leaving the stage with his trophy.

I jumped off the truck, and the others were soon standing beside me.

Shep climbed out of the dumpster and Melman handed him the box carefully using two hands—from here it looked like they were handling a bomb that might detonate at any moment.

Shep kneeled on the ground and laid the box before him. I started over and he put a gloved hand up to stop me. "Willa."

I didn't go any farther. Instead, I stretched my neck like a turtle testing the surroundings outside of his shell.

Shep opened the lid and stared at the box.

Well? my inner voice shouted, though outwardly I remained silent.

He looked to Melman, who'd climbed out of the dumpster and waited on the top step of the ladder for instructions on whether to go back in or not. Shep's hand went up and he gave Melman the thumbs-up sign. Melman did a victory fist pump.

"They found them!" I turned and cried, although the others saw it just as I had. Instinctively forming a huddle, we all jumped up and down in elation, arms around one another's shoulders.

But the moment was short-lived for me. If these also came back from the lab void of any foreign substance—even the samples—it would only make the case against me or A. J. stronger.

They tapered off their celebration when they noticed I'd stopped jumping.

"What's the matter, Wil?" Baz asked.

"There's no guarantee this will help me."

"Oh, Willa, have faith," Mrs. Schultz said.

"Life is like a box of chocolates," Archie said, drawing out the words and affecting a Forrest Gump accent. "You never know what you're gonna get."

I turned back to see Shep bagging the box of chocolates for evidence. Would this get me out of this mess?

CHAPTER 33

With nothing left to be done for the case tonight, we went back to Curds & Whey to pick up the costumes to return to Beatrice. We'd decided to go together and then treat ourselves to some rich desserts at The Cellar. I texted A. J. to let him know the hopeful news.

I marveled at the costumes as we collected them from my office—I hadn't gotten a chance to see Archie and Mrs. Schultz in all of them.

"You and Beatrice are very talented in putting these together," I told Mrs. Schultz as the four of us walked up the street with the costumes draped over our arms.

"Beatrice and I make a good team. I have the ideas, she has the accessories and the skill."

We arrived at Beatrice's business, Bea's Hive of Thrifted Finds. Beatrice's apartment stairs were inside the shop, so we buzzed the doorbell to the right of the shop door. We waited, but the door didn't open.

Mrs. Schultz tried the handle and to our surprise, the door opened. It was late to have the thrift shop open, but then again, she was expecting us. We followed one another through the door to the sound of the revamped clock's cuckooing.

Unlike most of the other renovated factory buildings on our street, Bea's Hive had kept its walls in place,
which meant it was a composite of smaller rooms.
Beatrice didn't accept just anything for her shop—
she curated the best of the mid-to-late-twentieth-
century items. Much like my cheese displays, it was
an organized chaos and a feast for the eyes. Unlike my
cheese, it was overwhelming for me, even broken up
into separate rooms.

"Beatrice, it's us!" Mrs. Schultz called out.

The rope in front of her private staircase was still
in place, indicating she hadn't retired to her apartment
yet. We walked through the shop toward the back
room, which was her sewing room and where we'd
often find her.

Everything in the shop was stacked atop something
else—a cedar chest held a valise with travel stickers,
upon which sat a record player with its lid open. I peeked
at the vinyl LP on the turntable—Sonny and Cher. As
my gaze wandered, it paused at a red vinyl diner booth
situated next to a stove with signage indicating it was
a vintage 1972 harvest gold range that sported a price
tag of fifteen hundred dollars. A glass display case held
cartoon action figures of another era, labeled Looney
Tunes collector glasses that told me the characters on
them were Speedy Gonzales and Cool Cat.

I heard the meowing chirps of a cat and inspected
the Cool Cat glass more closely. I felt foolish when
Sweet Potato, Beatrice's "big-boned" orange tabby,
came scampering toward us, making her presence
known with continuous meows.

"Hey, girl!" Archie reached down to pat her, but she
ran off in the direction from which she came—an adjacent room at the back of the shop.

We continued through the thrift shop in that direction, hearing Sweet Potato's meows. The connecting room was filled with previously worn clothing, both contemporary and vintage. Mrs. Schultz couldn't help reaching out her hand to skim the display of scarves, although she owned quite a collection already.

Sweet Potato stood in the open doorway to Beatrice's sewing room and costume storage area. The light streamed through the doorway, so we knew she was inside.

"We're coming!" Baz playfully told the cat, who turned and disappeared into the room.

"Yoo-hoo! Beatrice, we're here!" Mrs. Schultz called in a singsong voice.

As we tromped into the room, I began to apologize. "I'm sorry we're running late—" My words caught in my throat as soon as the scene hit me.

"Beatrice!" Mrs. Schultz cried.

We dropped the costumes and ran over to Beatrice, motionless on the floor in front of one of her tables. Sweet Potato paced back and forth next to her, nuzzling her nose to Beatrice's face.

We dropped to the floor around her and rolled Beatrice onto her back.

Mrs. Schultz patted her on the cheek, calling her name to get her to wake up.

"Is she dead?" Archie squeaked out, his voice trembling.

I put my ear to her chest and rested my hand on her stomach and waited, willing to feel even the slightest sensation. I felt a slight rise and fall of her stomach. "She's still breathing!"

"I think I can feel a pulse. It's faint, but it's there,"

Mrs. Schultz cried as she continued to press her fingers against Beatrice's neck.

Baz was on his phone, tapping 9-1-1 and giving the emergency dispatcher the address. "I'll wait for them outside," he said to us, still on the line, as he quickly left the room.

"Hang on, Beatrice. Help is coming," I told her.

Mrs. Schultz kept hold of her hand.

Knowing she was alive and that help was coming pushed me out of my initial shock. It was enough for me to register Sweet Potato now on the desk, nudging something with her paw. She sniffed it and meowed.

I stood and saw what it was immediately—a half-eaten crème-filled chocolate. My adrenaline sped up again.

"What is that?" Archie asked.

I lifted Sweet Potato off the desk. "It's a chocolate," I absently answered.

On the desk was a small decorative pottery bowl with pins in it and a pile of paper strips, ready to be labeled and pinned to costumes. The desktop computer screen had gone black, but the green dot and low, steady hum indicated it was on. Next to the desk was a drink I recognized as Beatrice's sweet tea, which she liked to doctor with a splash of rum. Beside it was a napkin and a small white bag emblazoned with the initials C.B. in a font I recognized. My chest tightened. Chocolate Bliss.

CHAPTER 34

It seemed like far too long, but it was only a matter of minutes before the paramedics shooed us out of the way to get to Beatrice.

"What happened?" one of the paramedics, a forty-ish man, asked us.

"We're not sure. We found her this way," Mrs. Schultz answered.

"I think she may have been poisoned," I added, pointing to the chocolate on the desk.

Mrs. Schultz's intake of breath was audible.

The two paramedics glanced at each other and then got to work.

Mrs. Schultz and I huddled near the clothes racks with Archie, who'd managed to scoop up Sweet Potato. With the extra strangers in the room, the cat didn't struggle out of his arms. With our nerves in a twisted bundle, we watched as they hooked Beatrice up to monitors and fit an oxygen mask over her mouth and nose, murmuring numbers and information at each other in a controlled manner before lifting her onto a stretcher.

Baz returned to the room, and to my surprise, Shep was on his heels.

Shep surveyed the scene without comment. The male paramedic said, "Possible poisoning," and nodded to the chocolate on the desk I'd pointed out to him.

Shep immediately spoke into the radio on his shoulder, alerting the dispatcher of what they were dealing with.

"Why would she eat the chocolates now?" Mrs. Schultz groaned, shaking her head. "She knew they might've been poisoned!"

I was just as bewildered. My mind went back to our encounter earlier at the door of her shop. She'd asked me if I had inside information from Heath about the chocolates. *Oh god.* I'd told her it appeared that the box for A. J. contained the only ones poisoned! She must've taken that to heart. I had no idea she had some! A queasy feeling came over me and I grabbed onto the nearest clothes rack.

"You okay, Wil?" Baz came over, ready to keep me propped up.

The paramedics hoisted the gurney to its full height and began to wheel Beatrice out of the room.

"I'm going to the hospital with her," Mrs. Schultz declared.

"You'll have to meet us there in your own vehicle, ma'am," the paramedic announced, not breaking their stride.

Mrs. Schultz nodded and began to follow them out of the room.

"Mrs. Schultz, do you have your car?" Archie asked her.

She stopped. "Oh dear. No, just my bicycle."

"I'll take us there. Who else is coming?" Baz said.

"Me," Archie piped up.

"We're all coming," I said.

"I'll need to speak with one of you before you leave," Shep interjected.

Of course—I wasn't thinking clearly. "I'll stay back," I volunteered. I had to tell Shep what happened. "You guys go. Archie, can you put Sweet Potato upstairs first and make sure she's got food and fresh water?"

"Sure," Archie replied, carrying the cat out of the room.

"We'll catch you at the hospital, Wil," Baz said.

I nodded and gave Mrs. Schultz's arm what I hoped was a reassuring squeeze before they left the room.

Shep found another chair in the room and brought it over to me. I must've looked as bad as I felt.

"You're keeping me hopping tonight. We were still cleaning up the dumpster site," Shep said, trying for levity.

Footsteps neared the room and when I looked up, Heath strode through the door.

"Heath!" I ran to him and hugged him, sobs coming out, before realizing in an instant, I shouldn't have. I pulled away but he held onto me. Luckily, there was nobody else from the police department in the room but him and Shep.

He kept me in his arms, then led me back to the chair where I sat.

"What happened?" he asked me, stroking my hair.

I told him the scene we came upon, pointed to the chocolate I'd found on the desk, and the possibly fatal misinformation I gave to Beatrice.

"Hey. You were just having a conversation. You didn't know she'd take it as fact."

"I had no idea she had any chocolates. Jasmine even said Beatrice came in late to Chocolate Bliss looking for some, but they didn't have any of the kind she wanted."

"So you don't know how she got them?" Heath asked.

"No! I don't even know how many she ate. Why wouldn't she have turned them in?"

Heath left my side and he and Shep went over to the desk to take a closer look.

Shep pointed to the wastebasket. "Look," he said to Heath.

Heath bent down to get closer.

"What is it?" I asked.

"Does it say Mallo Cups?" Shep asked Heath.

"That's from Sweet Tooth Vintage Candy!" I said, not bothering to pretend I hadn't overheard.

They didn't respond to me but gave each other a meaningful look. Heath leaned over the table and sniffed the iced tea in her glass.

"Rum?" he said.

"She liked to spike her tea," I supplied.

"Brenner's Rum?" Shep wondered.

They looked at me for an answer, and I shrugged. "I can show you the kitchen cabinet upstairs where she keeps her rum."

"Okay, let's process this. Get the camera," Heath said to Shep, who immediately left the room to follow orders.

"I'd like to go to the hospital to be with Beatrice," I said, rising from the chair. I was feeling a bit better, now that Heath and Shep were here.

Heath came over to me and said, "That's not a good idea."

"Why? Mrs. Schultz, Baz, and Archie are there."

"You're still a person of interest in the eyes of Chief

Jeffers. You're too attached to everything. Reporters might be there. It's best if you keep a low profile right now away from anything that connects your name to more poisoned chocolates."

"But doesn't this further prove that I *didn't* poison A. J.'s chocolates? There were *more* that had been tampered with before I even took his box to the Gazette."

"Who's to say you didn't plant the box of chocolates in the dumpster? Who's to say you didn't give Beatrice those chocolates to clear your name when you saw her only hours ago?"

"What?" *Is this what Heath thinks of me?* My head started spinning again.

"I'm not saying that's what happened. I know what you've told me and Shep is the truth. I'm saying that until you're cleared, that type of speculation can be drawn by people who want to make a case against you."

My head dropped to one side, unable to hold the weight of more suspicion. Not an hour ago, I'd had the possibility of vindication and now I was worse off than ever, and Beatrice was fighting for her life.

Heath's hand slipped under my hair and wrapped around the nape of my neck. "I know this isn't easy to hear, and I'm sorry. I don't want to upset you. I know you want to be there for Beatrice but keeping you from being the easy target for Chief Jeffers is more important to me. Beatrice has people there who care about her. Please go back to your apartment. I'm sure Baz will let you know what's going on with Beatrice. If I hear anything, I'll tell you."

I nodded, knowing if I tried to speak, the lump in my throat would dislodge and make way for crying. Others would be coming soon, but he pulled me into his chest anyway and hugged me. What I wouldn't have given to stay there all night.

A herd of footsteps sounded, and I forced myself apart from him.

"You going to be okay?" he asked, just before Shep and the forensics team entered the room.

I lied and nodded again. I had to let Heath be the detective, but his continued look of concern told me I wasn't a convincing actress. I left before I changed my mind.

CHAPTER 35

The extra police presence outside, as well as the forensics van, had begun drawing a crowd. I hurried back to my building, head down and eyes on the pavement, trying to make myself invisible. *Poisoned samples. Switched rum. Switched tickets. Separate rum crème batches. A Sweet Tooth candy wrapper. A. J.'s tampered box of chocolates.*

What are you missing, Willa?

I let myself into Curds & Whey and closed the door behind me before I realized I was there. I'd meant to go to my apartment. It didn't matter. I'd be pacing no matter what.

I texted Baz for an update. He told me Beatrice hadn't awoken yet, but her vitals were good—a positive sign. He asked where I was, and I relayed what Heath said in as few words as possible.

The positive news about Beatrice was a blanket of comfort, but it could easily be ripped off me if the culprit wasn't caught and I ended up being Chief Jeffers' number one suspect.

If only I hadn't offered to take the chocolates to A. J. "If only I hadn't written that stupid note!" I yelled aloud. I plunked myself on the farm table bench, replaying that moment in slow motion in my mind. I paused at the part where I placed the note—*You're in trouble! W.*—atop the gleaming identical chocolates.

My racing thoughts came to a halt. I saw the chocolates. It wasn't for long, but I remembered what they looked like. They'd all been identical.

I hastily ran to the kitchenette and opened the two drawers, one of which had what I was looking for. It was the brochure Duncan had given me of all their chocolates, the names beside each photo. Their top crème chocolates were displayed side by side in pairs on one page. I scanned the page, my finger stopping at each one. Each chocolate was a different shape. Some were milk chocolate, some were dark, and there were white chocolates as well. Some were textured on top, some smooth. No two looked alike.

The chocolates I brought to A. J. were from Chocolate Bliss's kitchen. It hadn't occurred to me that they weren't supposed to be identical. If only the rum crème samples were poisoned, those were the ones inside A. J.'s box—eight of them, looking exactly alike. I'd taken Pearce's, Riley's, and Duncan's word for it that it contained four crème varieties. Thinking about it now, I believe the three of them packed that box with four pairs of different crème chocolates, but one of them went back and replaced them. Kevin Wallace ate all eight samples of Brenner Rum Crèmes made with the poisoned rum that Pearce later hid in his car. Does that mean it was Pearce who did it? Did Riley and Duncan know? If all of them knew Pearce used the other rum for the samples, any of them could've poisoned those bottles, but if Pearce was doing it all in secret, then he was the culprit. For the other customers, eating only one sample—as they'd handed out—wouldn't kill anyone. Plus, there'd be no evidence after the fact. It was the perfect batch to poison. But why did they want to kill A. J.? Or was it me someone wanted revenge on all along?

I jumped at the knock at the door. Were my friends back with news of Beatrice?

I hurried to the door but stopped in my tracks when I saw who stood under the glow of the lamplight. It was Pearce and Riley.

CHAPTER 36

I stood in my shop, frozen in place, only a glass-paneled door between me and Pearce and Riley. I could see them. They could see me.

"Willa!" Pearce called with another rap on the door.

Before I could decide what to do, the door handle turned, and the door opened. In my haze, I'd forgotten to lock it behind me!

Pearce entered without asking and Riley followed. To my great relief, Hope was behind them.

"Hope!" I said, praying I didn't sound as unnerved as I felt.

"Willa, we saw you leaving the thrift shop with all the police there and forensics. What happened?"

"Please don't tell me it's another poisoning," Riley begged.

They were fully inside my shop now and had closed the door behind them. With Hope here, I didn't think they'd try to hurt me. They obviously wanted some information, so I'd have to use this time to get some of my own out of them. If Pearce did this, I had to have proof.

"Somehow Beatrice still had some of the poisoned chocolates and she ate them tonight," I informed them.

"Oh no." Riley sunk to the ground and Pearce lifted her up.

"You're going to be fine, Ri. Come on, sit down." He brought her to the café area and led her to a chair, with Hope following. I reluctantly joined them.

"Poor Beatrice. Is she . . . dead?" Hope said, her eyes squinted against oncoming tears.

"No, she's at the hospital. They think she's going to pull through." Would they be worried if she was alive and able to talk to the police about what had happened?

"Thank goodness," Riley said. "What a nightmare this is."

Pearce was thoughtful for a moment. "Beatrice. She's the one who looks like she stepped out of the nineteen seventies, right?"

I nodded at the assessment.

"I remember her. We had a nice talk about my rum," he said.

"Did she buy some?"

"No. She sticks with one kind, but she knows her rum. She was disappointed we were out of the Brenner Rum Crèmes. She's a rum lady, that one."

I wished I'd gone up to Beatrice's apartment after all to see if he was lying and her liquor cabinet held a newly opened bottle of Brenner's Rum.

"She didn't buy any chocolates from you that day?" I asked him.

"No," he said, looking to Riley for confirmation. She shook her head too.

Hope got a confused look on her face. "But Pearce, I could've sworn I saw you at the register with her when she was paying."

"Yeah, I was. She preordered a box of four Brenner Rum Crèmes for the next day, which obviously never materialized." He took a second glance at Hope, whose momentary fear that Pearce was lying still echoed on her face. "I swear! She didn't have any chocolates when she left that day. Our chocolates weren't poisoned!"

"What did the police find at Beatrice's?" Riley asked.

"Your monogrammed sample bag," I told them.

"There it is then! It's a setup! You think we'd leave a calling card? Really?" Pearce yelled.

Angry, he stood up quickly, snorting like a cornered bull in the ring. I took several hasty steps backward.

As soon as he saw my fearful reaction, he backed off and tamped down his anger. "I'm sorry. I didn't mean to scare you." He linked his hands atop his head and paced, taking several deep breaths. He sat back down next to Riley, who rested her hand on his forearm. "I shouldn't have yelled. You're just trying to help. Oh man, we just wanted to go home and leave all this behind."

I kept my distance. "You said you were out of the rum crèmes, but did you give her some samples?"

"I'm sure Duncan gave her one like everyone else," Pearce replied.

"Would he have given her any extras, because she liked rum?"

"I made it clear to only give out one per customer. We wanted as many people as possible to try a sample, so they'd buy the chocolates or my rum, or both, preferably."

That tracked with what Jasmine had said about him.

"Riley, how about you? Do you remember giving her samples?"

"Duncan was in charge of the samples. Pearce and I took care of the sales."

"By the time she came in, Duncan was handing out

the last of the samples anyway," Pearce said. "It was one apiece."

"I have samples," Hope said in almost a whisper.

"What?" I asked.

Pearce and Riley stared at her as intently as I did.

"Duncan gave me a little bag of them. I completely forgot about it until now. I was saving them for when I could enjoy them. I thought maybe we'd eat them together after we finished the day, so I stuck them somewhere." She stopped to think. "I don't remember where. But then we were pretty much done for the day and Gia came in wanting to take Duncan out to celebrate when he was finished closing. So, I left with Pearce and Riley to celebrate on our own. Do you think the poison could be in the samples?" Hope asked me, her voice rising in concern.

"Wouldn't the police have taken them in their initial search?" Pearce asked.

"They couldn't have," I said. Heath told me they didn't have any of the samples. "You need to find where you stashed them and get them to the police so they can test them."

"It can't be the samples. The box for the editor didn't have any of the samples," Riley said.

I wished I'd had more time to think about what I'd say, but I had to keep them talking in hopes that they'd spill some information that might incriminate them.

"Are you sure about that?" I asked.

"Of course, I'm sure. I was right there when Pearce packed them. So was Duncan," she said with conviction.

"Eight of your finest crème chocolates. Each one unique, right?"

"Yes," Riley answered slowly, looking at me skeptically now.

"What are you getting at, Willa?" Pearce asked. His eyes squinted, almost as if he was trying to peer into my mind.

"I looked at the chocolates when I put them on A. J.'s desk. They all looked the same. Completely identical," I said.

"What does that mean? That they were switched?" Riley asked, looking at me and Pearce for answers.

"That proves it then!" Pearce slapped his hand on the table. "Why didn't you tell that to the police in the first place? They were switched out, just like I said. I knew it was those guys at that candy shop. Didn't I tell you, Hope? It was those Sweet Tooth guys who tried to make a stink before we opened. They made new chocolate and poisoned it and waited for the right time to frame us." Pearce sat back, his mouth pulling back in a Jokerish grin. "We got 'em. We finally got 'em."

"I saw the chocolates, Pearce, which means they had to have been switched sometime on the day of your grand opening after you packed them, but before I picked them up." I paused to look at each of them, trying to glean someone's guilt and work up my nerve. "It couldn't have been the candy guys. It had to be someone in your kitchen."

Pearce's blank expression turned stony. Riley buried her face in her hands. Hope looked sickly.

Uncovering her face, Riley said, "Then it has to be Duncan. He was the one in charge of the samples. He would've had them to make the switch."

"But he gave some to me," Hope said. "He wouldn't hurt *me*!"

I felt for Hope, but what Riley said made sense.

"Hope, you need to get those to the police to see if they're poisoned too," I said.

Pearce was angry, clenching his fist in and out like he was squeezing an invisible stress ball.

"It's not Duncan. It can't be. I don't believe that's true. Why would he do that? We were going to run our shop together!" Hope looked from one to the other of us, her eyes pleading for us to give her another name.

"He must've given up on getting the shop," Riley finally said.

"No! He hadn't!" Hope insisted.

She turned to address Hope. "Maybe you don't know this, but he wouldn't sign Pearce's contract."

"I don't think Pearce was going to change the terms of the contract." I looked to Pearce for confirmation.

"No, I wasn't," he said.

"Why would you do that to Duncan?!" Hope shouted, surprising me. Pearce and Riley looked shocked too. "He's been nothing but good to you. Without him, that Ashland shop would've never opened. He told me so. If he did anything wrong, it's your fault! You bait and switch people all the time! With your rum! With your false-promise handshakes and your contracts! You did this! You caused this!" She got up and ran to the front door.

"Hope! Wait!" I yelled after her, but she ran out the door, slamming it behind her.

I was left alone with Pearce and Riley in the silence that followed.

"We don't want it to be Duncan either," Riley said softly, her voice cracking. Pearce reached for her hand and squeezed.

I felt awful for Hope, and even for Pearce and Riley,

but I'd been waiting for all the dots to connect, and they finally had. They finally led to one person, and Hope had the evidence to prove it. Or almost prove it. It was enough for Heath to interrogate him with confidence. I was betting Duncan would fold.

I let out a long breath. This would finally be over.

CHAPTER 37

I tried to convince Pearce and Riley to go back to their room at the inn and wait for the police to contact them, but they insisted they were going to the police station themselves. When I thought about it, I realized the information would be better coming from them than from me. If Chief Jeffers was already eyeing me as a suspect, how would it look to him if I was the one who told the police I knew the samples were poisoned and I knew where more were? He'd eventually have to consider my testimony about the identical chocolates, but I thought he might give the rest of the information more consideration if it came from the source.

"Thanks for everything, Willa," Riley said at the door to Curds & Whey. "I know we don't deserve your help, but we appreciate it." She grabbed me in a hug before I even saw it coming.

Stiff at the embrace, I patted her back, so she'd let me go. I took a step backward so Pearce wouldn't try the same. He didn't.

"Thank you, Willa. And don't worry, after this you won't ever see us in Yarrow Glen again. Trust me!"

We exchanged an awkward smile, and they left my shop. I was glad to close the door behind them. Trust him? He may not be a killer, but I'd never trust him again.

This time I locked the door and checked it twice. I also checked my phone and saw a missed text from Baz: *Beatrice is awake! Shep is in with her now. They said we can see her soon.*

I closed my eyes, allowing relief to flood in. I texted back *Great news!* with celebration emojis. *I've got some of my own too. I'm coming to the hospital.*

I turned down the lights and took the shortcut through the side-door alley to my apartment. Once inside, I immediately went to Loretta.

"I'm sorry, Loretta. Mama had a murder to solve," I said, sprinkling her dinner into her fishbowl.

I started to laugh, but as it kept coming, I didn't feel a joyousness, only a release of all the built-up tension of the last three days. I went to my bedroom to change before visiting Beatrice. Along with my work clothes, I shed the heaviness of the last few hours. I felt lighter. I'd figured out the killer, and Beatrice was going to be all right. By the time I'd arrive at the hospital, she would have told Shep exactly what she'd eaten, and hopefully Duncan would have been picked up by the police already. Soon after that, Yarrow Glen's newest chocolate shop would be a memory best not remembered.

I was looking forward to a true celebration with my friends when I slipped on my Keds, said goodbye to Loretta, and headed out my door. There was an odor of garbage that still lingered, and I found out why when I had to steer my car carefully around the pile that remained on the tarp. I guess the police had a bigger mess to clean up now.

At the end of the alley, I checked both ways before pulling out, although there were no cars on the street.

This side of downtown was always subdued after dark. All the action this time of night was up by The Cellar, Apricot Grille, and the taco truck. To the left, I still saw a little activity down the block in front of Bea's Hive of Thrifted Finds, but from here it looked like people must've gotten bored and the spectacle had waned. To the right, all was quiet. I thought of Hope. She was really upset about Duncan. Surely, it wouldn't keep her from bringing the samples to the police station. Would it?

I had a sickening memory of another time two years ago when I stupidly trusted someone to go to the police and it never happened. I pulled out to the right and drove the half a block to Hope's Cakery. I parked in front and hopped out. My freedom was on the line, and I wasn't about to let Hope's crush on Duncan ruin this.

CHAPTER 38

I knocked hard on the door to Hope's Cakery. No answer.

I went to the recessed door to her apartment and rang the bell, peering in one of the darkened windows while I waited impatiently. No answer. I tried the knob, but it was locked. Was she hiding from me so she wouldn't have to incriminate Duncan?

I went around back, not realizing I was holding my breath until I didn't see a phantom car in the lot like last time. That had only been Gia, but now I knew Duncan was the culprit. I buzzed insistently at the back door and waited. Nobody answered.

Maybe she was already at the police station, and I was letting that one horrible incident from two years ago cloud my judgment of Hope. That niggling memory wouldn't let go, however. I walked back around to the front and cupped my hands to the window of the front door of the cakery. Inside, the display case lights glowed, revealing empty shelves.

"Willa?"

I jumped at the sound of Riley, who was walking down the sidewalk toward me.

"I thought you and Pearce were going to the police station."

"We did but Hope wasn't there, so we decided not to give our statements without the chocolates as proof. I texted Hope and she said she didn't want to be the one to turn in evidence that would incriminate Duncan, she wanted us to. Since she was so angry at Pearce, I came by myself."

"So where's Hope?"

"Good question. Let me text her again." Riley quickly tapped a text and sent it. We waited. "Maybe I should call Pearce, and we can look for her," Riley suggested.

"Forget Pearce. What if she's changed her mind and taken the samples?"

Riley unsnapped the small purse at her hip and took out a ring of keys. "Let's go in. We can look for them ourselves." She unlocked the door of the cakery, and we went inside.

"Hope?" I called out. I really hoped I'd find her in the kitchen with the bag of chocolate samples and maybe all she'd need was a shoulder to cry on and a little coaxing to do the right thing.

Riley and I continued into the kitchen, glancing around for Hope. The stainless steel baking tables cutting across the middle of the room were sparkling clean. Utensils, bowls, cake pans, and baskets of ingredients were stacked neatly on open shelves above the counters on both walls. The place was spotless.

"Why would she ask you to come down here and then hide them from you?" I asked. None of this made sense.

"I don't know, Willa, but these chocolates are the

only evidence the police might have. And I intend to find them." She began to search the bakeware and supplies on the shelves that ran the length of the walls and stopped at the walk-in freezer on one side and the ovens on the other. I was anxious to find the samples too, so I joined the search. As I checked inside bowls and lifted pans, the path that led me here played back in my mind.

"Pearce pointed the finger at Duncan almost right away, but you seemed to never quite be on board with that until tonight," I said.

"I like Duncan. He's been great for Chocolate Bliss, and I wish it had worked out for him here. I never would've thought he'd do this, but I'm not going to let him get away with ruining us," she said without pausing her search.

"It seems like it could've worked out if Pearce hadn't changed the terms they agreed upon."

Now she did stop and put a hand on her hip in annoyance. "Is that what Duncan told you? Or is this because Hope freaked out?"

"It's kind of what *you* told me too, isn't it?"

She returned to lifting items off the shelves. "I'm softer than Pearce is when it comes to business decisions. I liked Duncan so I wanted him to have a shop of his own because it's what he always wanted. But at the end of the day, Pearce isn't about to give someone a Chocolate Bliss franchise without getting proper compensation in return. You have your shop, Willa. You know it's just business."

I thought about what I'd do if Archie ever wanted his own shop, and I knew for a fact I'd give up a percentage of my profits to see his dream come true.

"His loyalty didn't count for anything?" I couldn't help it.

"Those people who work in your shop? They're your *employees*, Willa. They're not your friends or your family. They'll leave you in a heartbeat for something better. Pearce has always said that, and he's right. He said Duncan's loyalty runs as far as his paycheck."

I couldn't disagree more, and I could feel myself getting irritated. "He was loyal enough to keep your secret about using a better rum for the samples to boost your rum sales."

Riley stopped and deliberately turned her attention to me.

"How do you know about that? Duncan?"

So she did *know.*

"No, it wasn't Duncan."

"Who then? That boyfriend detective of yours talked to you about our case?"

I wasn't about to rat out Jasmine. "You're lying to your customers."

She crossed her arms, seeming to forget about the search. "Hey, we're not charging for the samples, and it costs us more to use someone else's rum, so who are we hurting? Pearce had to keep reminding Duncan of that. If Duncan wasn't fine with it, he should've spoken up years ago. Suddenly he had the big idea he'd be able to fight Pearce on doing it here because this was *his* chocolate shop." She scoffed. "Pearce didn't consider that loyal at all. Duncan was only the manager—it's not like he knew what it took to make Chocolate Bliss what it's become. Pearce says there are things you have to do that you might not want to do to stay in the black, and Duncan suddenly thought he knew more than

Pearce and could do it better. Now that I think of it, I probably shouldn't have defended him so much."

Duncan and Pearce seemed to be bumping heads about this shop. That gave Duncan motive for the poisoning, but what about Pearce?

"When Pearce switched the terms of their agreement, did Duncan threaten to tell people the lie about the rum?" I asked.

"You're acting like we're lying about our rum. Brenner's Rum is completely legit. Do you know how much time and money Pearce spent developing that rum? It's all ours. We tried to make the crème with our rum—it just didn't give it the right flavor. The chocolates had gotten popular using the other rum and people didn't like that they tasted different. People don't like change, that's all it is."

Was she dodging the question or just super defensive about their rum?

"That's not what I asked. Was Duncan threatening to blackmail you and Pearce unless you changed the contract back to what they'd agreed upon?"

"No! Of course not."

"Do you know that for sure, Riley? Pearce was the one who tried to convince you that A. J.'s box should contain only the Brenner Rum Crèmes, not Duncan."

"We were all there when Pearce assembled that box. Hope and Jasmine might've even been there too."

"Sure, he put the box together like the rest of you wanted, but what if behind everyone's back, he switched them out to all the sample rum crèmes? As an added bonus for Pearce, it would be a dig to Duncan, putting in the ones you pass off as having Brenner's Rum in them. Those were the ones Pearce poisoned."

Riley's green eyes widened. "Pearce? No. You're wrong, Willa! Pearce wouldn't poison those chocolates. You don't know him," she said, shaking her head.

"I think I do. He's a walking red flag of *not to be trusted*. He wanted to pin this on Duncan from the start, and he wanted to manipulate me to do it. That's why he asked for my help. And I think he's manipulating you too."

She pressed her curly hair behind her ears and started biting her lip. Her curls immediately came loose again. "He hasn't and you don't know what you're talking about."

"How can you be so certain? Was it you, then?" I blurted out, just so she'd stop defending Pearce.

"No, it wasn't me! Willa, can you please stop this nonsense? It was Duncan, not me or Pearce. Come on, you know us!"

I stopped to think. "You're right. I do know you."

"Thank you. Now can we get back to looking for the evidence that'll clear our names?"

She started her search again, but we'd come to the end of the counter where two convection ovens and a stove stood. Beyond that was the pantry, Riley's next destination.

I was convinced I was right about Pearce. The only question was whether Riley knew. If she was willing to keep his secret about the rum, maybe she was keeping this secret too.

"It's admirable in a way that you're fiercely loyal to him," I said.

She stopped walking and turned, sighing heavily. "Pearce is my soulmate, Willa. Maybe you'll find yours someday and understand."

"You'd do anything for him, wouldn't you? Even keep his secret about poisoning those chocolates," I said.

"Why are you stuck on this? Pearce would never kill anybody. Neither of us would."

"Which explains why he poisoned only the samples. Because a little of it only makes people sick. And a bunch of people who felt ill after eating a new chocolate aren't likely to want to come back."

"Willa—"

"You wanted this to work out with Duncan running it. You said all you wanted was a house and a family and a picket fence, but Pearce wanted to keep growing the business with chocolate shops everywhere and then with his rum. When Duncan knew it would get taken away from him, just like the Ashland shop, he threatened blackmail. So Pearce decided he'd get his revenge. The editor of the *Glen Gazette* getting sick on chocolates too and writing a bad review would've been the final blow for Duncan, wouldn't it have? Pearce switched the box to contain all samples to ensure the poisoned rum crème samples would be what A. J. ate."

"It can't be Pearce. It just can't be!" Riley lowered her chin, her face hidden by her mane of curly hair, and when she looked up again, she was crying. "Oh, Willa, do you really think he did this?"

"I'm sorry, but I do."

"I don't want to believe it," she said, her voice shaky. "You must have it wrong."

"Riley, you can't protect him. What he did was wrong. And now he's ready to incriminate an innocent man. We have to make this right."

"Pearce wouldn't kill anyone!" she yelled. "Who eats

eight premium chocolates in one sitting?" She wiped a fat tear that slid down her cheek.

"I'm sure he didn't mean for anyone to die. That'll help his case." I needed her to believe turning him in would be okay.

"It's so hard to break away from a man like that. He's so controlling," she said quietly. She wouldn't look me in the eye.

"I'll help you. I know it's hard, but you don't have to protect him anymore. Let's just go to the police station. They can come and look for the poisoned chocolate samples."

Head still down, she nodded, wiping more tears.

I put a hand on her back, wanting to lead her out of the cakery, when I saw a sticky note on one of the middle tables. I lifted it off. It read SURPRISE!

"Surprise? What does that mean?" I asked.

"I don't know."

Note in hand, I read it again when I noticed the floor in front of me. "Is that . . . ?"

"Blood?" she said, noticing it too.

I crouched to get a closer look. A larger blob of crimson trickled into a path of smaller red dots.

"Did something happen to Hope? I was with Pearce, it couldn't be him. You don't think she called Duncan too, do you, and he showed up first?" Riley said, her face mirroring my alarm.

Had I gotten it all wrong like Riley had been saying?

We followed the trail of blood that led to the walk-in freezer. With each step, a sickening certainty grew that something had happened to Hope.

I opened the freezer door, afraid of what we might see.

Hope was in the back corner, crumpled on the floor.

"Hope!" I cried.

Riley and I raced in. I kneeled beside her and shook her by the shoulders.

She was cold to the touch and didn't move, but I thought I saw her eyes flutter. A frozen trickle of blood extended from her temple to her cheek.

"I'll get help!" Riley declared before I could even get my bearings.

She raced out of the freezer, then suddenly turned around in the doorway. "I'm sorry, Willa." She slammed the door shut, locking me and Hope within.

CHAPTER 39

"Riley!" I yelled. I pushed myself off my knees and raced to the door. I pulled on the door handle, but it didn't budge the door open. I pounded on the door. "Riley! What are you doing?" Each whack of my palm on the cold door shot a pain through my hand. The light flicked off. I was in complete darkness.

I felt my pockets and my tightened chest eased just a bit when my hand felt my phone. I pulled it out. The glow of its blue light when it came to life felt like a lighthouse beacon. But when I tapped the emergency number, nothing happened. There were no bars. I tapped again and again. I shook the phone, as if that would do something. It wouldn't work. The phone was no use.

"Okay, okay." I tried to calm myself down. I felt around the door for an emergency latch, the skin of my hands dragging on the icy metal. "Come on, Willa!" I kicked myself for my stupidity, as I reached for my phone again to swipe on its flashlight. My hands were wet and quickly stiffening from the cold and the phone seemed to jump out of my hands. I heard it hit the hard floor. I fell to my knees and felt around for it with both icy hands splayed.

I found it. This time I gripped it hard while I swiped and tapped the button for the flashlight to come on. I traced the door with the light beam but saw nothing. Was this freezer too old for an emergency handle? Had Riley pushed something heavy against the door anyway and it wouldn't matter?

I returned to Hope and kneeled beside her, tapping her cheeks firmly. "Hope! Hope! Wake up!" I trained the light on her face, praying to see another sign that she was alive and would regain consciousness, but the shadows played tricks. Her skin was cold and scabbing with ice.

The whirring noise of the fans filled my ears, the cold breeze seeming to settle beneath my skin. I had to disable the fan.

I focused my beam on the walls of this twelve-by-eight frozen coffin that seemed to be closing in on me by the second. With effort, I stood and scanned the shelves with the light, feeling with my free hand for anything my eyes may have missed. I searched for anything with a pole or a handle to ram into the fan and stop the turning blades. It was all jars and tubs and bags. I went to the floor by the far wall where I'd just been pounding on the door and moved large tub-like containers away from the wall in case some kind of broomstick was hidden behind them. There was a button on the wall by the floor. The emergency latch to open the door!

I was about to punch it, when I panicked again about Riley. What if she was waiting for me? I had to be able to get Hope out and still get away from Riley.

I went back to Hope. Using both hands, I carefully put my phone in my pocket, from where its flashlight still glowed. I crouched beside her and forced my arms under her armpits to drag her to the door. She felt stiff and cold.

"You can make it, Hope. We're getting out of here," I told her.

In the dark, I dragged her across the freezer floor. My foot slipped out from under me and sent me down on my butt, my twisted leg beneath me breaking the fall. Luckily for Hope, her head fell on my lap and not the floor. I carefully stood and continued pulling her. Two more tugs and Hope and I were there. I could feel where the door was, so I propped her up in a seated position so she'd fall backward when the door opened and land on the doormat just outside it.

I rubbed my palms together to attempt to unstiffen my fingers and carefully pulled my phone out. I flashed the beam of light on the wall to find the emergency button again. I stood in front of it. I could hit it with my foot and then take two sidesteps to the right and I'd be able to push my way through the door. As long as Riley hadn't blocked it with something too heavy.

I shook my head of the thought. I'd use all my might to barrel through that door.

"Here we go," I said to myself, working up my courage to face whatever was out there.

I pushed the button with my foot.

At the click of the latch, I sidestepped and threw myself against the door with everything in me. The door opened, and with my body propelled forward my foot caught on the rubber mat, catapulting me farther and slamming me onto the floor. A pain shot through my kneecap as it hit the hard tile.

I pushed myself off the floor, biting back the pain, my eyes darting everywhere for any sign of Riley. She wasn't here. Hope lay on the floor, the door pinning her half in and half out of the freezer. I hobbled over to her and pulled her all the way out.

I patted my pockets. *Oh no. My phone!* It must've flown out of my hand, but a quick scan of the floor didn't locate it.

I sat over Hope and squeezed her hands in mine, rubbing them to try to get some warmth into them. I glimpsed a flutter of her eyelashes.

"Hope?"

Nothing more. Maybe it was wishful thinking.

"I'm going for help," I told her.

With effort, I stood, favoring one leg. The back door was close—I could make it. I took two steps toward it when Riley appeared from the pantry.

She lunged at me, and I juked to the left, straining the same bruised knee that had connected hard with the floor. I held onto the stainless steel table to keep my footing, but I had to keep moving. Riley still came for me. I grabbed anything my hands found and threw them at her. Wooden bowls, plastic containers, metal pie pans. They hit her outstretched arms and clanked to the floor. My fingers gripped a heavy bag, and I swung it at her. It hit her shoulder and burst open, coating us in a powder of white flour.

My eyes immediately stung, clouded, then watered. My throat constricted, trying to expunge what I'd inhaled. I could hear Riley's coughing and sensed she was still coming for me. I kept moving. The path to the back door was now behind me and wasn't an option any longer—Riley was blocking it. I'd have to make it out of the kitchen to reach the front door of the cakery.

My arm swiped the counter and upper shelves, sending glass jars and cake plates crashing to the floor behind me as I hobbled toward the swinging door.

Through watery eyes, I kept the blue door in sight as it got closer. Almost there, I pushed through the pain now radiating up my leg into my hip, and sprinted. Two more strides and I'd be through it, but it suddenly swung inward, and I body-slammed the figure in the doorway.

My whole body reverberated as he faltered backward, holding onto me. My knee gave out and I clung to him in return, but it was no use. I slid to the floor.

I wiped my eyes with my shirt sleeve and looked up. It was Pearce who stood over me. Two against one. My odds weren't good.

CHAPTER 40

❧

"Pearce, thank God you're here!" Riley said. "Don't let her go! She tried to kill me and Hope!"

"What?" I cried.

Pearce straightened his glasses. I watched his face contort from confusion to anger.

"No, I didn't. Pearce, I didn't! Riley locked me and Hope in the freezer!" *Would he believe me? Was he in on this?*

Pearce stood there, massaging his sore shoulder from where I'd rammed him, his skeptical glance bouncing between me and Riley. "Ri, what are you talking about?"

"Willa doesn't want me to find the chocolate samples. She poisoned them to ruin us."

"That's not true!" I screeched. I pushed myself backward away from Pearce and tried to stand, but the effort seared my knee with pain.

"She's been holding this grudge all these years and now she's taking her revenge. She came after me!" Riley began to cry, tears making tracks in the fine layer of flour on her face.

I was beginning to think Riley was able to cry on command.

"Pearce, you know I wouldn't do that." I steadied my voice to reason with him. "Who was chasing who?"

He looked back at Riley, and I thought I'd gotten through.

"I wasn't going to let her get away after she tried to kill me and poor Hope."

"If you don't believe me, then call the police right now," I said. "Hope needs help! Call them, Pearce!"

"You mean, call your *boyfriend*? Pearce, she'll twist this to frame me. She'll succeed in ruining us," Riley insisted.

Pearce ran a hand through his hair. "Why would you do this, Willa? Did we hurt you that much?"

"I didn't! I swear, I didn't! Listen, Riley put those vials of eyedrops in the rum so your samples would be poisoned." Now I appealed to Riley. "I know you didn't mean to kill anybody. You didn't want to run another franchise when it became clear Pearce wouldn't hand this one over to Duncan. Pearce, haven't you paid any attention to what she's been saying? She wants a family, not an empire. She poisoned the samples to make people feel nauseous so they wouldn't come back to Chocolate Bliss." Again I turned to Riley. "I don't believe you expected A. J. to eat all eight rum crème samples you put in that box, not knowing that amount would kill the guy who *did* eat them."

"That's not the way it went," Pearce said in a robotic voice that no longer sounded like his own. "I'm the one who secretly switched A. J.'s chocolates. I'm the one who killed that journalist."

The pit that opened in my stomach swallowed me with dread. "Why would you poison your own chocolates?"

"I didn't know they were poisoned. I just wanted

to make sure he reviewed my rum crèmes. I wanted him to rave about them. Why would you do this to me, Willa?"

"I didn't! Use logic! How would I have poisoned them before you swapped them?"

"She's just trying to confuse you. We have to do something," Riley said, looking around the kitchen.

"Like what? What can we do?" Pearce asked her.

"This is her town. I don't think we stand a chance if it's her word against ours."

"What are you saying?" Pearce asked. He was growing pale, and tiny beads of sweat had formed beneath his hairline.

"I-I don't know," she said.

She looked around the kitchen, now returned to its messy state with almost everything from the shelves on the floor and flour dusting the tabletops and tiles. Her gaze alighted on a magnetic knife rack on the wall. Why hadn't I seen that when I needed it? She walked toward it and pulled off the biggest knife.

"Oh, come on, Riley! Pearce?" I heard the pleading in my voice that couldn't be helped. "Doesn't this prove what she's capable of?" I searched his face for some realization that this confirmed she was a killer.

"Ri, I-I don't think . . ." he began.

"It's the only way," she said, tightly gripping the handle of the long blade so her fingers reddened.

I tried to stand again when I heard another voice.

"What's happening?" From the corner, Hope appeared, her skin and hair damp with melted ice. She stood across the room, hunched over, leaning on the table closest to her.

"Hope! Thank goodness. Hope, tell him!" I urged.

"Willa, what's happening? Riley, why did you knock me out?" she said through chattering teeth.

I wanted to weep but fear still gripped me. Would the truth matter to Pearce? It hadn't for as long as I'd known him.

"She doesn't know what she's saying. Willa hit her in the head with a cast iron skillet," Riley told him.

"It wasn't Willa." Hope teetered toward the back door but didn't get far. "I'm going to be sick," she mumbled, doubling over.

"Pearce you have to call for help," I begged him. "She's hurt."

He reached in his pocket for his phone.

Riley's eyes bubbled again with tears. "It'll be over, Pearce. Everything you've worked for will be wiped out. Her boyfriend won't go against her. Her town won't go against her. She was trying to say *you* poisoned the rum. She thought it was you!"

"Ri, we have to, or we'll be as bad as she is. I'm already responsible for killing that poor journalist."

"It wasn't your fault. You didn't know they were poisoned! I knew you swapped them. I should've changed them back or thrown out the box, but I only hid it with Willa's cheesecake."

"You wanted to kill me," I said, no longer surprised.

"No. I knew you wouldn't eat chocolates made by us. I knew you still thought we were horrible people."

"If you didn't poison them, why did you try to hide them?" Pearce asked Riley. Finally, logic was kicking in.

"Well, I-I . . ." She shook her head. "I'm confused."

Peace's hands went to his temples and his head slowly swung back and forth, wanting to reject the truth of what he was hearing. "After we found out that journalist died, and I confessed to you that I'd put all the samples in the box, you told me not to tell the police. That's why, isn't it? Did you do this? Riley?"

At first Riley shook her head in denial, but once her chin dropped and she looked up again, she seemed to be resolved to telling the truth.

Pearce saw it on her face and his own turned a sickly pale. "Oh no. Why?"

"Oh, Pearce. How does Willa know me better than you do? You've put our life on hold since you and I fell in love. First it was Willa keeping us from getting married, and then the shop, and then the rum, and more shops . . . I wanted our life together to start. You couldn't bring yourself to hand this shop over to Duncan, just like you ended up doing with the Ashland shop. And the money and time you poured into making that mediocre rum! We had a dream together, but over the years, it turned into *your* dream and my nightmare." She stiffened and said in a stronger voice, "Willa couldn't wait to tell everyone you swapped the rum and then she was going to tell them you poisoned it, you know."

I looked past Riley, willing Hope to get to the back door, but she'd slid to the floor, her head in her hands. *Hang on, Hope!*

"I'll do it, Pearce." Riley's grip on the knife tightened again. "I know it's my fault, but I'll save us."

I didn't want to take my eye off Riley and that knife, but I had to know what Pearce was thinking.

He left my side to go to Riley. "No. I won't let you sacrifice yourself. Give it to me."

Oh no.

She handed it over to him.

I started to push myself backward toward the swinging door using my good leg and both arms. There was no way I'd make it in time, but I had to try.

Pearce didn't come toward me, however. He walked to the wall rack and put the knife back.

"Pearce," Riley's voice trembled.

He returned to her side. "We're calling the police. We'll be okay, Ri. I won't let anything happen to you. Trust me, okay?"

Riley began to cry. Nodding, she wrapped her arms around Pearce. He held her and reached for his phone.

The door behind me swung open, sending me scrambling sideways. It was Gil, Trevor, Claude, and Jasmine. Their wide smiles turned to looks of horror at the scene before them.

"What happened?" Claude demanded. "We just had this place spotless!"

The dispatcher's voice sounded through Pearce's phone. "Nine-one-one, what's your emergency?"

I let the tears of relief flow.

EPILOGUE

The following morning, I sat propped against the arm-rest of my love seat with my leg elevated on the opposite armrest. Heath made sure I had an icepack at the ready to ice my knee regularly. Luckily, it was only a sprained ligament and was expected to heal on its own in a week or so. This morning, however, I was still popping ibuprofen. Heath handed me an omelet he'd just whipped up in my kitchen.

"You don't have much in the fridge, so sorry. There's nothing but cheese in it," he said.

"You're sorry there's only cheese? Have you met me?" I replied.

He chuckled and kissed me on the forehead.

"Thanks for taking care of me." I took a bite of my fluffy omelet—he was an omelet pro, so I knew it would be good, especially with melty Baby Swiss.

He checked his watch. "I can't stay much longer. I hate to leave you."

"I'll be fine," I said, wolfing down the omelet. "My friends already texted to see when they can come over. Besides, I can get around. I've got crutches. How did it go with the interrogations last night?"

Heath sighed. "Pearce tried to take the blame for Riley, but she'd already confessed."

"Even when she ruined their business? He really loves her. It's so sad that it took this for him to show her how much. Was that her plan all along? To ruin Chocolate Bliss?"

"Not according to her. She didn't want the Yarrow Glen franchise to get a foothold once Pearce made it clear he wasn't selling it to Duncan. It would be one more shop to worry about, and one more thing taking Pearce away from moving forward with their lives. Riley had come across information about tetrahydrozoline, that it would give you an upset stomach if it's ingested, so her intention was to make everyone who had a sample feel sick. She maintains she had no idea how much to put in the rum and that she didn't know it could be fatal."

"That's really dangerous."

"No kidding. The box for A. J. didn't have any of the sample rum crèmes and she wanted to make sure he ate one and gave them a bad review, so she took the box in secret to switch one out for a poisoned one. That's when she saw they were all swapped and knew Pearce had done it, not knowing they were poisoned. He only wanted A. J. to review his rum crèmes, and he was determined to get his way. Riley had the box over by Hope's cake orders so as not to get caught, but Duncan came by so she hid the box behind your cheese-cake. She was nervous about eight of them being in the box and wanted to switch some back, but the variety of chocolates that had originally been in there had already been ditched by Pearce. Before she had a chance to get it back, Jasmine had already given it to you."

I sighed, taking it all in. "I feel bad for them, but even

if it was unintentional, she killed someone and put this whole town through the wringer."

"Including you, which was very intentional."

"She and I went into the cakery together. It didn't occur to me she'd already been inside."

"She went to Hope's almost as soon as she left your shop. They got in an argument about Duncan, and Hope told her she'd tell the police and everyone else about them switching the rum. Hope accused Pearce of poisoning the chocolates, and that's when Riley hit her with the cast iron pan. She started looking for the samples when she heard you at the door. She was afraid you'd manage your way in and discover Hope before she was able to find the poisoned samples. When she heard you buzzing at the back door, she dragged Hope into the freezer to hide her and left out the front door. She hid in the alley until you came back to pretend like she was coming from up the street all along."

I stopped eating my omelet, having suddenly lost my appetite. "I had no idea she was capable of such a thing. She was ready to let me and Hope freeze to death." I shook my head.

You just *had* to get involved in the investigation, even though I told you not to."

"I know, but—"

"But it's lucky you didn't listen to me."

My fork slipped from my grip in surprise. I put my almost empty plate on the coffee table next to Loretta—Heath had moved her bowl to be closer to me.

His hand reached around to the back of my neck and began gently massaging it. "You saved Hope's life. I absolutely hate you putting your own life in danger, make no mistake about that."

"I didn't know I was," I rushed to explain. "I thought

I was making sure Hope was going to the police. I didn't realize it was Riley until it was too late."

"I know. But next time—"

"Next time I'll listen."

"Next time you'll be just as stubborn."

We laughed together and he kissed me. I didn't bother to deny it.

"I'm glad it's over. Now we don't have to stay apart, and we can go back to the way things were," he said.

"Yeah," I agreed, a slight sadness creeping in. We'd been dating for months without anything official tethering us together and I had to face the fact that I wasn't happy about it. It was time I took the advice I'd given to Archie and apply it to myself. I began mustering up the courage but didn't get the chance.

Heath continued, "Except I don't want things to be the way they were."

"What?" Was he breaking it off with me?

"The thought of almost losing you made me realize how important you are in my life. It wasn't like I was seeing other people anyway or even considering it. I think I was just too afraid to make this exclusive. So at the risk of sounding like a sixteen-year-old, Willa, you want to make this official and be my girlfriend?"

If I could've jumped off the love seat into his arms, I would have. Instead, I almost fell off it reaching to hug him. He caught me just in time and we hugged.

When we loosened our embrace, I said, "Yes! That's what I want too."

We kissed, which was interrupted by a knock on the door. Heath reluctantly pulled away to answer it.

To mask the huge goofy grin I was sure I had, I reached for my latte. I heard Heath snort in laughter when he opened the door.

Baz walked through with a paper nurse's cap on his head. "Here for my shift!"

I burst out laughing, almost spilling my drink.

"It looks like you're in good hands," Heath said, fist-bumping Baz. He came over to me for one last kiss before leaving. "I'll come by when I break for lunch. Call me if you need me."

"I will," I said, my heart feeling so full it might burst.

He passed Baz with a shake of his head and more laughter. They exchanged a wave, and he turned back to me one last time and winked before he left, sending my already fluttering insides into overdrive.

Baz inspected the scene. "Breakfast and a latte with Loretta. This might not have been a good tradeoff for you. I'm not much of a cook."

I smiled at Baz and his old-fashioned nurse's cap. "I'm full now, so you're off the hook."

Baz walked behind my armrest and began pulling and fluffing my pillows, jostling me with each smack and shake.

"Um, okay, Baz?"

Luckily, another knock on the door took him away.

Mrs. Schultz and Archie came in with a casserole and a vase of flowers.

"How's our patient?" Mrs. Schultz said.

Archie was too busy laughing at Baz to say anything. Baz pulled off his homemade nurse's cap and tried sticking it on Archie's head, where it slid off.

"Thanks for coming," I said.

They put the casserole in the refrigerator and the flowers on the butcher-block island before coming over for hugs. Archie grabbed a stool and brought it into the living room. Mrs. Schultz sat where Heath had been, and Baz took a seat in the chair by my dangling foot.

"How's Beatrice?" I asked. I'd popped in on her last night before leaving the hospital, and she looked surprisingly well.

"She's home already," Mrs. Schultz said.

"We went over to feed Sweet Potato, and she was there with a friend," Archie said.

"Oh, good. Did you get a chance to talk to her about the Chocolate Bliss samples she ate? I was too out of it with the pain meds last night to ask her."

"She'd collected a few samples from friends who know her love of rum, including Gil's and Trevor's samples," Mrs. Schultz explained. "Gil and Trevor accepted them when they went in to snoop around the shop at the grand opening, but they refused to eat them on principle. Beatrice went to Sweet Tooth for a little gossip session after the grand opening, knowing Gil and Trevor wouldn't be too happy about their candy competitor. They know she loves her rum, so they gave her their samples. She wanted to savor them, so she said she was going to eat them the next day once she was done with all the sewing, and then she heard they might be poisoned. She planned to take them to the police, but by the time she was going to, she'd heard there weren't any other chocolates that were poisoned, so she didn't want them to go to waste. She ended up eating three and a half chocolate crèmes."

I cringed. "That was my fault. I told her it looked like it was just A. J.'s box that was poisoned. I feel horrible for steering her wrong. I wish I had known she had some!"

"I don't think it was because of you. She told us she read it in the *Gazette*," Archie said.

"Really?" That eased my guilt a little.

"I was going to call Hope later this morning. Have you heard from her, Archie?" I asked. We'd also checked on her at the hospital last night, making sure she was okay. They were keeping her overnight to monitor her concussion and hypothermia, but she was expected to make a full recovery.

"I called her first thing to see about visiting hours, but she said she was getting discharged. Duncan was there. He was taking her home," Archie replied.

"Sorry, Arch," Baz said.

"They were business partners, so it's normal that they would become good friends," I said, trying to ease the blow.

"It's okay. I'm ready to get off the roller coaster. She's still got a lot of stuff to deal with."

"Does she plan to reopen the cakery?" I asked.

He shrugged. "It sounds like Duncan's planning to stay in Lockwood, so maybe he and Hope will find a way to rebuild the shop together. I hope so, anyway," Archie said.

It sounded like Archie really was moving on. I hoped he was right, and Hope would have the support to reopen her cakery.

"So no more Chocolate Bliss?" Baz asked.

"Here in Yarrow Glen? No way. I don't think Pearce is going to be able to save any of the shops, not with Riley confessing to poisoning the chocolates. But if I know Pearce, he'll find a way to rise up doing something else." I surprised myself by how sad I felt for them.

I'm glad Hope's okay, thanks to you, Willa," Mrs. Schultz said.

"Thank goodness. You're a real hero," Archie said, coming over to give me another quick hug.

* * *

"I'm thankful it all worked out," I said. They'd already given me enough praise last night at the hospital. "I'm sending a cleaning service to Hope's Cakery to clean up her kitchen once and for all."

"I was shocked when you told us Claude, Gil, Trevor, and Jasmine cleaned her kitchen," Baz said.

"I think that one took us all by surprise. Happily so," Mrs. Schultz agreed.

"Claude and the candy guys realized they'd been too harsh on Hope, and Jasmine felt bad that Hope would have to deal with everything by herself. Even when we didn't show up to clean, they decided to do it themselves to surprise Hope. They came back to see what Hope thought of it—you should've seen their faces when they saw it was a mess again!" I shook my head and chuckled. It was absurdly funny now that it was all behind us.

"They were the ones who wrote that note that said *Surprise*," Archie deduced.

"Yup. Cryptic notes have not worked out in my favor," I said, also thinking of the one I'd left in A. J.'s box of chocolates that had gotten me into so much trouble in the first place.

"Did anyone ever find the chocolate samples that Hope stashed somewhere?" Baz asked.

"The police were able to figure that out last night when everyone was at the hospital with her. The samples Hope thought were still in her kitchen were actually the ones that Jasmine had taken and given to Lou. She'd seen Hope stash them on a shelf, but when they were still there after Hope left for the day, she let Lou have them."

"So Riley ended up going back there for no reason," Baz said, shaking his head.

"Except for what Hope and I had to go through, it was a good thing she did or we might never have figured out it was Riley," I said. "Oh, and Heath got a text this morning from forensics—the tetra . . ."

"Tetrahydrozoline," Archie supplied.

"Right. Tetrahydrozoline was found in Lou's samples."

"Woo-hoo!" Archie cheered with a fist pump.

Baz joined in, clapping in celebration. "I bet Shep and Officer Melman are happy to hear that their dumpster diving wasn't for nothing."

A quick rap on the door sent Baz to answer it. When he stepped aside, I saw A. J. holding a bouquet of daisies.

"Flowers?" I blurted out, not able to hide my surprise—A. J. was not known for his sentimentality.

"You don't like daisies?" he asked.

"Actually, they're my favorite," I answered, smiling.

"Oh. Well, good. Where do you want 'em?"

"I'll put them in water," Mrs. Schultz said, rising from her seat.

He passed them off to her with everyone exchanging hellos. He stood uncomfortably, his hands stuffed in his Salvation Army jacket pockets.

"Thanks, A. J. You can get a stool and join us," I said.

"Nah. I just came by to see how the knee's doing."

"Well, thanks. It still doesn't feel so great now, but it's supposed to heal on its own in a week or so."

"Good. Good. I took care of lunch today. You'll be getting a delivery from Let's Talk Tacos, but this time it'll be for you."

"Wow. That's really nice of you." It *was* really nice, but I couldn't help but ask myself what he wanted.

"Yeah, well, I . . ." He looked around at the others.

"I didn't expect an audience for this, but uh, ya know, you saved my hide. So I just wanted to, ya know, thank you." He cleared his throat. I was sure those words weren't used to coming out of it.

"It was for purely selfish reasons," I said, wanting to ease his discomfort. We were both used to our transactional friendship.

"Yeah, I know. But still," he replied.

I couldn't help but laugh inwardly. A. J. would always be A. J.

"Did you ever figure out the car thing?" he asked.

"Roman confirmed that when I talked to him on the phone this morning. He'll be by later, by the way," I told the others. "He said Gia admitted it was her. She didn't believe Duncan when he said he had a meeting with Hope about the shop. She was waiting for Hope's apartment lights to come on to find out if Duncan was with her afterward."

"Nothing like a little Saturday night stalking," Baz quipped.

"So you weren't *too* crazy thinking someone was waiting in the parking lot for a reason, it just wasn't the reason you thought," A. J. said to me.

"My instincts don't usually steer me wrong, they just don't have the most accurate GPS," I admitted.

Mrs. Schultz returned with the daisies in a glass canister and set them beside Loretta's fishbowl on the coffee table. "They're very pretty," she said.

"They are!" I agreed, smiling. "Daisies are such happy flowers."

"Well, I've got interviews to do and articles to write. I'm going to need the A-to-Z of last night from you, so I'll be in touch."

"Thanks for coming by and for the flowers." I felt a

little teary thinking again about A. J.'s uncharacteristic sentimental gesture.

Everyone said goodbye to him and he went out the door. Someone else was on the deck when he left, and he kept the door open for them to enter. An even bigger surprise than A. J.—Lou!

"Lou!" Mrs. Schultz exclaimed.

"Hi, Lou," I said, as he stood on the threshold, not quite coming in.

"I heard what happened. You okay there?" he asked me, staying where he was.

"I'll be okay by next week. It's a minor knee injury," I said. "Do you want to come in?"

"No, thanks. I saw Archie and Mrs. Schultz turn down the alley so I figured she was here. Can I speak with you privately, Ruth?"

Mrs. Schultz approached the door, but said, "Anything you have to say to me can be said in front of my friends." She stood before him, rigid, chin up.

He hesitated, then finally stepped inside and closed the door behind him. "Okay. I suppose I owe everyone an apology anyway. I'm sorry I shouted at all of you about the chocolates, especially you, Ruth." He hitched up his pants. He didn't have his market apron on, but he still wore his baggy khakis and white short-sleeved buttoned shirt. "The reason I threw them out and the reason I got so mad when Willa insisted that they had to be tested was because . . ." he paused. His lips puckered, tightly clenched, and his jaw pulsed, as if fighting against him to speak. "It was because I was mortified that I could've killed you." He looked at Mrs. Schultz, his bushy brows furrowed and his eyes haunted.

Mrs. Schultz's stiff posture eased.

"It made me sick to my stomach to think I could've hurt you. Or worse! I threw them out because I couldn't bear to think about it. I'm sorry I couldn't say that last night."

Mrs. Schultz's mouth opened and closed a couple of times, but words didn't come out. I'd never seen Mrs. Schultz at a loss for words. Finally, they came to her, and she spoke gently. "It wouldn't have been your fault, Lou. You couldn't have known. It was a sweet gesture to buy them for me."

Lou's mouth twitched in a fleeting smile, and he looked down at his feet.

"Thank you for explaining," she said.

He nodded. When he saw her toothy smile on full display, he grinned too, this time not so briefly.

"I just had to tell you that. I have to get back to the market," he said, now with a flush to his cheeks.

"Thank you, Lou," Mrs. Schultz said before he turned to leave.

"Lou, I'd still like to talk sometime about your plans for baking fresh bread at your market," I called to him.

His grin stuck around. "Sure. Anytime. I was thinking of hiring Claude, but I heard he's working for you now?"

"Oh, I bet he'd prefer to go back to baking bread. Don't worry about us."

He nodded. "I'll see you around then?" He was speaking to all of us, but his gaze landed on Mrs. Schultz.

"We'll be doing a Gouda-themed cheeseboard at the café this week. Your favorite," Mrs. Schultz said to him.

Baz and I glanced at each other, hiding our smiles. Archie was focused on his phone.

"I'll be sure to stop by!" Lou said enthusiastically. With a wave to us and one last smile for Mrs. Schultz, he left with a spring in his step.

"Well," Mrs. Schultz declared with a sniff and a satisfied expression. "Do you need another ice pack, Willa?" She walked to the kitchen without waiting for an answer.

I'd set my ice pack aside quite a while ago, but I let her fetch me another, understanding she might not be comfortable talking about her feelings about Lou right now in front of all of us. She gently placed the fresh ice pack on my knee and returned the other to the freezer.

"Something about the case, Arch?" Baz asked him, also noticing he had barely stopped texting in the last few minutes.

"Huh?" Archie looked up from texting. Oh, no. Just texting with June. She says she's glad you and Hope are okay."

"Tell her thanks and to come on over this afternoon. We've got tacos coming," I said.

Archie's grin widened and his thumbs flew over his phone's keypad.

The four of us spent the rest of the morning chatting about everything but Lou until it was lunchtime. Roman came with food from Let's Talk Tacos for all of us and a couple bottles of his mead. June joined us and Heath stopped by too, intercepting the delivery A. J. had ordered, which added to the taco smorgasbord. Loretta wiggled happily in her fishbowl at all the activity.

The throbbing ache in my knee no longer mattered. My life was back to normal and everyone I cared about was still here.

RECIPES

No-Bake Chocolate Cheesecake Jars

I can't make a cheesecake as good as Hope's, but these chocolate cheesecake jars are an easy and delicious substitute . . . if you like chocolate!

Start to Finish Time: 15 minutes + 1 hour chill time
Serves: 12 (using 6 oz. glass Mason jars)

Ingredients for Crust
- 20 Oreos
- 2½ tablespoons melted butter

Instructions
1. Crush Oreos into crumbs. Stir in melted butter. Spoon about 1½ tablespoons of mixture into each jar, pushing slightly down to form a crust. Once all twelve jars have equal amounts of crust, set them aside.

Ingredients for Cheesecake
- ½ cup semi-sweet chocolate chips
- ¾ cup heavy cream, divided
- 12 oz. softened cream cheese
- ¼ cup sugar
- ¼ teaspoon vanilla extract
- Piping or ziplock bag

Instructions
1. Melt the chocolate chips in *only* ½ cup of heavy cream until they are melted just enough to stir smoothly. Set aside to cool for a bit.

2. In a separate bowl, beat the cream cheese until it is completely smooth. Scrape the sides of the bowl and make sure there are no lumps.

3. Add the sugar and vanilla extract, mixing to combine.

4. Add the melted chocolate. Keep the mixer running low while adding the chocolate so it doesn't harden too fast.

5. Slowly add the remaining ¼ cup of heavy cream, mixing as you pour. Then turn the mixer up to medium and beat until smooth.

6. Add the chocolate cheesecake mixture to a piping bag or a gallon size ziplock plastic bag, and pipe the mixture over the crust in the jars.

Ingredients for Whipped Cream
- 2oz. softened cream cheese
- 1 tablespoon sugar
- ½ teaspoon vanilla extract
- ½ cup heavy cream
- Extra crushed Oreos or semi-sweet chocolate chips

Instructions
1. Beat softened cream cheese until smooth.
2. Add sugar and vanilla, mixed together.
3. Slowly pour the heavy cream, as you go, turn up speed and beat until mixture is fluffy and holds a peak.
4. Pipe whipped topping over chocolate cheesecake mixture.
5. Top with extra crushed Oreo cookie or semi-sweet chocolate chips.

Chill for 45 minutes to an hour and enjoy!

*Recipe from Jennifer "Mama Jen" Brunetti-Irizarry

Swiss or Miss Dip

This creamy dip Mrs. Schultz made was a hit with me and my Curds & Whey crew.

Start to Finish Time: 15 minutes + 2 hours sitting time
Serves: 8

Ingredients
- 2½ cups freshly grated Swiss cheese
- ¾ cup mayonnaise
- 3 tablespoons red onion, diced
- 2 tablespoons milk
- 2 tablespoons chopped fresh parsley
- 1 tablespoon fresh lemon juice
- pinch of salt
- 1 tablespoon chopped fresh chives for topping (optional)

Instructions
1. Mix all the ingredients (except the chives) together until combined.
2. Cover and let sit in the fridge for a couple of hours to let the flavors meld.
3. When ready to serve, sprinkle with chives. Serve with crackers or pretzels. Enjoy!

Pizza Smashed Potatoes

Team Cheese and I enjoyed this mashup of pizza and potatoes. These are filling enough for a meal but great finger foods for a gathering.

Start to Finish Time: 1 hour
Makes: 15 mini pizzas

Ingredients
- 15 baby potatoes, scrubbed
- 1 tablespoon salt
- 1–2 tablespoons olive oil or spray bottle
- ⅓ cup marinara sauce
- 1 teaspoon dried Italian seasoning
- 1½ cups mozzarella cheese
- 1 cup cheddar cheese
- 2–3 oz. sliced pepperoni or mini pepperonis
- Red pepper flakes (optional)

Parchment paper will be needed.

Instructions
1. Preheat oven to 425°F.
2. Put the potatoes in a large pot and just cover with water. Boil potatoes with salt for about 12 minutes until fork tender. (Don't overcook.) Drain.
3. Cover two baking sheets with parchment paper. Put the potatoes on the parchment and score them with a sharp knife about halfway down in a crisscross pattern. Flatten them carefully by pressing down on each potato with a potato masher or use the bottom of a glass with parchment or wax paper between the glass and the potato (to keep them from sticking). Drizzle or

spray with olive oil and season with salt. Bake in oven for 20 to 25 minutes or until they start to turn golden brown on their edges.

4. Remove the potatoes from the oven. Cover each potato with about 1 teaspoon of marinara sauce and Italian seasoning. Top with mozzarella and cheddar. Top that with pepperoni. Put the potatoes back in the oven until the cheeses are melted and golden. Add red pepper flakes if desired.